"This superbly gripping novel about dreams coming true is itself a dream come true. Lewis and Tolkien come alive as real-life characters, playing their sagacious parts to realistic perfection as the protagonists follow their Arthurian quest pursued by deadly enemies. For lovers of Arthurian romance and for admirers of Tolkien and Lewis, this is indeed a dream come true!"

—**JOSEPH PEARCE**, author, *Tolkien: Man and Myth*

"A highly engaging historical mystery adventure that brings C. S. Lewis and his friends and ideas to life. Fans of Lewis and Tolkien will love it. I couldn't put it down!"

—**PETER J. SCHAKEL**, author, *The Way into Narnia* and *Imagination and the Arts in C.S. Lewis*

"The subtitle of this book is 'An Inklings Novel.' That claim might seem presumptuous at first. But lo—it is an Inklings novel. My own guess is that Lewis, Tolkien, and Williams would all be mightily pleased with it. All three of them, as it happens, figure as characters in the story, which is Arthurian, but set in the contemporary world—very much in the vein of *That Hideous Strength* and *War in Heaven*. The Inklings themselves are flawlessly depicted, as are the two protagonists, a very appealing young man and woman. All Inklings lovers will be highly delighted."

—**THOMAS HOWARD**, author, *Narnia and Beyond*

"Steeped in Arthurian lore, the mystery of the grail legends, and World War II intrigue, this engaging tale of a young man's search for a hidden relic ultimately uncovers treasure of a far different kind. David Downing's homage to C. S. Lewis, J. R. R. Tolkien and Charles Williams succeeds masterfully in bringing these historical figures to life in the midst of an unfolding spiritual thriller. This is a beguiling and enjoyable read—laced throughout with romance, wry humor and questions of eternal consequence."

—**MARJORIE LAMP MEAD**,
Associate Director, The Marion E. Wade Center,
Wheaton College

"Downing sets out to echo the Inklings, and this he has done to perfection. Lewis said that in order to judge something, whether it be 'a corkscrew or a cathedral' you had to judge what it was intended to accomplish. Downing accomplishes exactly what he set out to do. It was a lark, a sheer pleasure. If I had any criticism it's that I was sorry that it came to an end."

—**JAMES PROTHERO**,
President of the Southern California C.S. Lewis Society

# LOOKING FOR THE KING

### DAVID C. DOWNING

AN INKLINGS NOVEL

PARACLETE
FICTION

PARACLETE PRESS
BREWSTER, MASSACHUSETTS

2020 First Printing

*Looking for the King: An Inklings Novel*

Copyright © 2020 by David Claude Downing

ISBN 978-1-64060-349-3

Paraclete Fiction is an imprint of Paraclete Press, Inc.; the Paraclete Fiction
name and logo (wing) are trademarks of Paraclete Press, Inc.

Library of Congress Cataloging-in-Publication Data

Names: Downing, David C., author.
Title: Looking for the king : an Inklings novel / David C. Downing.
Description: Brewster, Massachusetts : Paraclete Press, [2020] | Summary:
  "A novel set in 1940s England, two researchers set out in quest of the
  Spear of Destiny, aided by the Inklings"—Provided by publisher.
Identifiers: LCCN 2019048835 (print) | LCCN 2019048836 (ebook) | ISBN
  9781640603493 (trade paperback) | ISBN 9781640603509 (mobi) | ISBN
  9781640603516 (epub) | ISBN 9781640603561 (pdf)
Subjects: GSAFD: Historical fiction.
Classification: LCC PS3554.O93423 L66 2020  (print) | LCC PS3554.O93423
  (ebook) | DDC 813/.54--dc23
LC record available at https://lccn.loc.gov/2019048835

LC ebook record available at https://lccn.loc.gov/2019048836


10 9 8 7 6 5 4 3 2 1

Published by Paraclete Press
Brewster, Massachusetts
www.paracletepress.com


Printed in the United States of America

# Contents

## Looking for the King

← 1 →

Here lies buried the renowned King Arthur with his wife Guinevere." Tom McCord studied the marker in front of a coffin-sized rectangle in the grass, outlined in stone.

Or maybe it's the marker that lies, thought Tom. He knew the story: There had been a great fire in Glastonbury in the twelfth century, destroying most of the abbey and its relics. Pilgrims had started going elsewhere—Tintagel, Malmesbury—until the town's soothsayer located the supposed graves of Arthur and Guinevere, right there on abbey property. The pilgrims returned—gladdening the hearts of the monks and fattening the purses of local innkeepers and tradesmen.

"If Arthur did not exist," Tom muttered to himself, "it might be necessary to invent him." He shifted the pack on his shoulders and took a step back to survey the ruins of Glastonbury Abbey. Between the blue sky and green lawn were scattered acres of fallen stones—crumbling yellow walls, staircases to nowhere, dog-toothed blocks jutting out of the earth. Straight ahead were two halves of a broken arch, reaching up to the sky like supplicating hands. This had been a magnificent edifice once, a city in itself, a fortress of faith. But all that remained were walls without a roof, foundations with nothing to support. It was a splendid ruin, but forlorn too. Like religion itself, thought Tom.

Walking past the broken arch, Tom spotted a stone building in the corner of the grounds that looked like an abbey in miniature, with sturdy buttresses, arched windows and a funnel-shaped ceiling. This was the abbot's kitchen, all that remained of what once had been a grand palace. Tom strode toward the building and peeked in through its single arched doorway. Inside he saw a dim room where motes of dust swirled and danced in the slanting light. Stepping in, he found one great room under a dome-like ceiling, with cavernous fireplaces, taller than he was, built into every corner. What feasts must have been prepared here! There was plenty of room for a score of workers and dozens of cupboards and tables. He could almost see a great boar roasting on a spit in one corner, a giant stewpot simmering in another, delicate cakes coming out of an oven nearby. Clearly, the abbot did not live by bread alone. The room was nearly empty now, except for a long wooden bench in front of the fireplace nearest the door.

Tom sat down on the bench and set his pack on the ground. He took out three metal rods and screwed them together, making a pole about as long as a broomstick. Then he attached a metal disk to one end and a handle to the other. Clamping a black box onto the handle, he strung two wires from the box down to the disc. Finally, he took out a set of headphones, plugged them into the black box, and put them over his ears. Rising to his feet, Tom held the disc a few inches above the loose flagstones on the floor, and took a few steps ahead, moving the device in a slow sweeping motion, like a scythe. Tick! he heard suddenly. He took another step forward. Tick! Tick! Tick! Tom snatched off the earphones, set down the device, and got down on all fours for a closer look. His rubbed his finger in the dirt between two flagstones and felt some kind of metal object. His pulse quickened as he dug in with his fingernails to undercover whatever it might be—an ancient coin perhaps or a gold bracelet fallen between the cracks. Scratching at the dirt until his fingers were almost raw, Tom finally exposed the metal object: a rusty hairpin.

Well, at least the Metallascope works, Tom sighed. He was just reaching for the earphones again when he was startled by a voice behind him: "Lose something?"

Tom scrambled to his feet and looked around. At first all he could make out in the dim light was a silhouette, a tall man wearing a broad-shouldered suit and a fedora. "Excuse me?" said Tom, not really in the mood for conversation.

Stepping forward in a shaft of light, the man doffed his hat, revealing a square jaw, graying temples, and sad eyes. "I asked if you lost something," he said. Glancing at the headphones on the floor, he added, "I suppose you didn't hear me come in."

"I guess not," said Tom absently. He held up the hairpin. "I didn't lose anything. But this is what I found."

The man reached out for the hairpin, inspected it carefully, and handed it back "Someone's lost treasure," he said without smiling. "You found it with that gadget there, I suppose?" he asked.

"That's right," said Tom. He picked up the device and demonstrated how to hold it. "It's called a Metallascope. It detects metal objects on the ground or just under the surface."

"I thought so," said the sad-eyed man. "They've got those in the army now, for detecting mines." Holding his hat in front of him, the man gave Tom a long looking over. "You don't look like a military man," he said.

Tom unconsciously brushed his sandy blond hair out of his eyes. He didn't really feel like having a chat, but this fellow seemed to insist on a conversation. So Tom decided he could keep it up for a least a few minutes, out of politeness.

"No, I'm not," he said. "I've over here from America. Doing some research for a book."

"Good to meet you, son," the man said, reaching out his hand. "My name is Huffman, Joseph Huffman. One doesn't meet too many Yanks over here, with the war on."

"Tom McCord," said Tom, shaking hands. "I came over several months ago," said Tom. "When I crossed the sea, it didn't look like there was going to be much of a war. After Poland fell last autumn, nothing much happened. 'The Phony War,' we called it in the States."

"That's what the papers called over here too," said Huffman. "But now that the Huns have gone up to Denmark and Norway, it's starting to look like the real thing."

"I guess Hitler has overreached himself this time," said Tom. "It's one thing to overrun Poles and Danes. But I don't suppose the little corporal and his Wehrmacht will be any match for the French and the British."

"We'll see about that," said Huffman solemnly. "That's what they said back in 1914. They told us we'd be home by Christmas." Huffman mused to himself a moment, then turned back to Tom. "So, tell me about this book you're writing," he said.

Tom had been trying to wind up this conversation, but suddenly he grew more animated. "It's a guidebook to all the Arthurian sites in Britain," he said. "I've already been to Tintagel, where legends say Arthur was born. And down to Bodmin Moor, where Arthur got his sword from the Lady of the Lake. And, of course, I've been spending a lot of time in dank, dusty archives."

Huffman gave Tom another long looking-over and pointed to the Metallascope. "Surely, you don't need that thing to locate books," he said with a wan smile.

Tom was feeling that this little chat was turning into an interrogation, and he wasn't sure how much more he wanted to say. "It's not all book research," he explained. "I've studied archaeology too. I'm over here looking for Celtic artifacts. I'd like to prove once and for all that there really was an actual king named Arthur."

"And how do you propose to do that?" asked Huffman. Perhaps realizing that this question sounded too aggressive, Huffman added in a softer tone: "I fancy myself a student of archaeology too. They've been trying to settle that question for about a thousand years now, haven't they?"

Tom noted the British habit of ending a statement as if it were a question, and he wasn't sure if he was expected to answer. But he tried to explain: "There's a recent theory by Professor Collingwood at Oxford, backed up by a colleague of his named Tolkien. They've shed a lot of new light on who the historical Arthur might have been. As the Empire fell apart, the Romans pulled out of Britain in the fifth century, leaving the Celts on their own. The Britons fought among themselves for a few generations, until they realized the true threat was coming from the east, from waves and waves of Teutons arriving from across the Channel."

"Same thing we're worried about now," said Huffman.

"Something like that," answered Tom, warming to his topic. "Collingwood argues that a Celtic leader named Arthur could see that the only way to stem the pagan tide was to do as the Romans had done—to organize troops of cavalry. The Angles and Saxons were strictly foot soldiers, lightly armed with shields and spears. So Arthur must have trained companies of horsemen, adopting hit-and-run tactics. He seems to have harried the Saxons up and down the land, keeping them out of the western kingdoms for half a century."

"That's all very interesting," said Huffman, sounding not very interested. "But you still haven't explained this," he said in a surprisingly direct tone. "How is hunting up hairpins in Glastonbury going to help you find King Arthur? And how did you get hold of your own military equipment?"

Tom didn't like Huffman's tone, and he decided it was time to go. "I told you, I'm writing a guidebook to all the Arthurian sites. And while I'm here, I'm looking for artifacts." Tom picked up his knapsack and slung it over his shoulder, as he added a few words of explanation. "I rented the metal detector from a specialty shop in London. It's a simplified civilian model. I was testing it out in here, to see if I might find an old hinge, a metal latch, something to suggest a buried entrance."

◁ • ▷

Feeling that he'd said enough, or more than enough, Tom strode toward the doorway. Huffman gave a slight whistle and suddenly there appeared in the entrance a burly man with a red face. He stood right in the narrow exit with his arms folded across his chest, wearing a wrinkled shirt and a baggy tweed jacket.

Tom had played fullback in high school, and his first instinct was to bowl the man over and not look back. But he didn't like the odds, and he wasn't sure who else might be outside. He turned back to Huffman. "You're not letting me leave?" he asked.

"I wouldn't put it that way," said Huffman with unconvincing friendliness. "It's just that we were having such a lovely chat. This is my associate, Mr. Durham. He has some interests similar to yours and mine." Durham nodded his head without unfolding his arms.

"Mr. Durham," continued Huffman, "allow me to introduce Mr. Tom McCord from America. He's over here looking for King Arthur."

"Last I heard, the bloke was dead," said Durham gruffly.

"Perhaps not dead," said Huffman cheerfully. "The legends say he was brought right here, to the Isle of Avalon, to recover from his wounds. He's supposed to return in times of trouble, like the ones we're having now."

"I wouldn't hold my breath," answered Durham. "I'd rather see a few armored divisions from America."

Durham stared directly at Tom, as if he were supposed to answer for all his countrymen. Tom decided the better part of discretion lay in evasion. "Not speaking for myself," he said, "but a lot of Americans can't figure out what we were doing over here in the last war. They're quoting George Washington about avoiding entangling alliances."

Durham took a step forward, as if he'd heard fighting words.

"Halt!" said Huffman to Durham in a tone of command, holding his hand straight out. Then he added in a soothing tone. "Come, come, Mr. Durham. We're all friends here. Mr. McCord isn't a diplomat or a soldier. He's over here writing a book."

Durham stepped back into the doorway. Gesturing toward the Metallascope, he said, "That don't look like a typewriter to me. More a wireless transmitter."

"It's a metal detector," explained Huffman casually. "Mr. McCord thinks it might help him locate an underground chamber at one of the Arthurian sites he's visiting."

Durham's eyes widened. "Oh, he does, does he? And what gave him that idea?" Huffman and Durham both looked at Tom, as if he'd have to answer that one for himself.

"It's an open secret," said Tom. "There's supposed to be a crypt below Cadbury Castle, that old hill-fort not far from here. Some people think that's the real Camelot. And everywhere I go, there's some old fellow in a pub telling me about a buried tunnel or a cache of Celtic weapons and jewelry."

"Is that what you've been doing?" asked Huffman. "Questioning the locals?"

Raising himself to his full six feet in height, Tom dropped his pack to the ground and gripped his Metallascope with both hands. "No more questions," he said. "I'm not looking for any trouble here," he said. "But I can take care of myself if I have to."

Huffman made a downward sweep of the hand, as if trying to calm everyone down. "No need for that kind of talk," he said calmly. Durham just grinned and patted something underneath his jacket.

"Let me say this one last time," said Tom with his jaw clenched. "My name is Tom McCord. I'm an American citizen over here researching a book. I have the papers back in my room to prove it. So if this gentleman would just let me by—" Tom took a step toward the door, and Durham glanced at Huffman, as if seeking instructions. Instead of looking at either of them directly, Huffman took out a pack of cigarettes and offered one to Tom. Tom shook his head, and Huffman took out a lighter, lit up, and blew out a gray puff of smoke into the dusty air. "Well, that's an admirable quest, Mr. McCord," he said casually. "Sailing clear across the Atlantic—dodging U-boats all the way, I shouldn't wonder—looking for the king. That's a fine cover."

"Cover for what?" said Tom. "I don't understand."

Huffman threw his cigarette down and ground it under his shoe. "Oh come now, Mr. McCord, let's drop the charade. As long as we're in this quiet little chapel, don't you think it would be a fine place for confession?"

Tom backed toward the wall and gripped the metal detector like a baseball bat. "It's not a chapel, it's the abbot's kitchen," he explained between clinched teeth. "The peaked roof is to let smoke out. Any student of archeology would know that."

Durham took a step toward Tom, but Huffman signaled for him to stand still.

"I stand corrected," he said. "But we know who you are and we know what you're looking for. And I think you know who we are."

"I already told you who I am," said Tom. "And I have no idea who you are. Though I've ruled out the tourist board." A little grin flickered across Huffman's face. But then he said slowly and sternly, "This isn't a game, son."

Let's find out who he really is," said Durham, stepping out of the doorway and reaching for the pack at Tom's feet. Tom pointed the metal detector straight ahead, like a lance, and turned up the dial on the box until it made a distinct hum. "Keep your distance," said Tom. "That is, if you ever hope to have children!" Durham froze and then took several steps back, pulling his jacket down tight in front of him. Huffman laughed out loud, the sounds reverberating throughout the small enclosure. "He's bluffing, you idiot!" said Huffman.

Tom scooped up his pack and ran toward the entrance. Durham made a quick lunge at him, grabbing hold of Tom's jacket. Not having a free hand, Tom tried to stomp on Durham's foot but missed.

"Let him go, Durham, let him go," Tom heard over his shoulder. Breathing heavily, Durham thrust his face about an inch away from Tom's, glared at him eyeball to eyeball, then let go of his jacket and walked back to Huffman's side. Tom clutched the pack and the metal detector to his chest, and caught the welcome sight of green grass and blue sky just over his shoulder. He backed out of the room, seeing the forms of the two men still standing near the doorway.

"Just one more word?" said Huffman, with the same forced politeness he had used when the conversation began. Tom knew it would be wiser to just keep walking, but he wanted to show them, and maybe himself, that he was no coward. So he stood in the doorway, his back to the sun, and glared at the two figures standing in the dim light.

"Maybe you really are who you say you are," said Huffman.

"And maybe you're as thick as you seem to be," added Durham.

Even in the dusky light, Tom could see Huffman cast a withering glance at his stocky partner—or minion. "One last piece of advice," said Huffman. "Even if you find what you're looking for, you may discover it's not worth the price."

Tom thought this over this a moment and then replied, "That's true of most things in life, isn't it?" Huffman grinned and nodded his head, then, made a wave of his hand, as if to say, Be off with you.

"Auf wiedersehen," Tom heard behind him. "We'll see you again." He walked hastily away from the stone kitchen, toward a guard booth he'd seen when he entered the grounds a few hours before. His heart was thumping in his chest, partly for the sheer joy of being outside in the open air, safe and free and surrounded by ordinary people just enjoying the day. But there was also anger and fear in that beating heart. Who were these men and what did they want? How dare they treat him that way? And how dare he let them? Tom had visions of taking on both of them, and leaving them on the ground writhing in pain. But that sort of thing seemed to work better in movies than in real life. Tom glanced over his shoulder to make sure no one had followed him. His stride had almost become a run, and he forced himself to slow down to a brisk walk.

When he got to the entrance to the abbey grounds, there was no one in the guard booth, but there were plenty of people coming and going, so he felt safe enough. What a relief and a pleasure it was just to see a little red-cheeked girl reaching up with stubby fingers to grab onto her mother's hand. Or to watch a white-haired man and his frail wife standing close together to admire the pink wildflowers growing on top of a stone wall.

Tom sat on the lawn and laid down his pack and his Metallascope. He started to disconnect the wires, but it took a few tries because his hands were still trembling. Taking a deep breath, he steadied himself and carefully unhooked the wires, coiled them up and put them into the pack. Then he removed the disk at the end and unscrewed the sections of pipe. It was good to have something to do with his hands, something he didn't have to think about.

The more he relaxed, the more the whole incident seemed almost farcical to him. Here he was trying to write a book about King Arthur, and those thugs acted like he held the fate of the world in his hands. What was it they thought he was after? If Huffman's intent was to quench Tom's curiosity, then he had mistaken his man. An hour ago, Tom would have been thrilled to find a Roman coin or a centuries-old shoe buckle. But now the question that blazed in his brain was, *What* should *he be looking for?*

## ← 2 →

*Oxford*
*Late April*

T om surveyed the labyrinthine aisles of books, stacked floor
to ceiling, with neatly hand-lettered signs pointing to more
books by the thousands on the floor above. He could have
stopped to ask one of the clerks in Blackwells, Oxford's most
well-stocked bookstore, where to find studies of medieval
literature. But he preferred to wander the maze on his own,
making a passing acquaintance with Greek philosophers,
Persian poets, and British military historians until he sensed
he was somewhere in the right neighborhood. He spotted
Bunyan's *Pilgrim's Progress* on a high shelf, so he figured his
own pilgrimage must be progressing satisfactorily. Knowing
he had to travel back another four centuries or so, and then
find the commentators, he eventually located the book he
had been searching for, *The Allegory of Love* by C. S. Lewis.
Though the book had only been published a few years earlier,
it had already become required reading for graduate students
in America.

Tom reached out for the book, and almost bumped elbows
with someone else trying to take a book off the same shelf.
"Pardon me," he said reflexively, turning to see a young woman
with searching eyes and dark curly hair. "I didn't see you there."
She offered a polite smile, revealing dimples that offset those

serious eyes. "Sorry, I didn't see you either," she said, her accent revealing that she was another American. They both extended their arms again, but this time their hands touched. They were reaching for the same book. The young woman laughed a bit nervously. "I guess we're after the same item," she said.

"I saw it first!" Tom said, only half-jokingly. He really wanted to have a look at this book.

"I can tell already you're an American," the young woman said. "No manners. Haven't you ever heard the principle, 'Ladies first'?" Her tone was also light, but Tom was no great reader of women, and he wasn't sure how serious she was being. He made a mock chivalric bow, and replied, "Ordinarily, that is my life's creed. But I do have a special reason for wanting to look at this book right now. I'm meeting its author for lunch in half an hour." Tom was afraid this sounded too much like boasting, but he wasn't it making up. He really was going to meet the Magdalen don for lunch at the Turf Tavern at one o'clock. That's why he wanted to peruse the book. For one thing, he was hoping to find out what "C. S." stood for prior to meeting the man behind the initials.

"Well, aren't I impressed!" the young woman answered. "Any other books here by friends of yours?"

"No, really!" Tom insisted. "When I was working on my master's thesis, I wrote Professor Lewis about some of his references to Camelot. He wrote me back and invited me to meet him for lunch if I were ever in Oxford. So I called him up as soon as I arrived here last week, and arranged to meet him for lunch today at the Turf." Tom realized he was explaining more than he needed to, recalling as well his tendency to babble when flustered.

The young woman took the book off the shelf and handed it to Tom. Then she made a sweeping curtsey, every bit as courtly as Tom's sweeping bow a moment before. "I yield to the greater claim," she said. "I was merely seeking knowledge."

Tom really did want to review the book before heading over to the Turf, but he wasn't exactly in a hurry to end this conversation. "I don't claim to be an expert," he said. "But if you have a particular question, maybe there is something I could help you with."

At this, the young lady turned slightly pink and she interlaced her fingers. "It's actually something personal. Just something I'm trying to figure out."

"That's all right, I understand," answered Tom, even though he didn't. She was looking for personal answers in a book on medieval allegory? The silence hung heavy in the air between them, so Tom continued. "Thanks for allowing me to peruse the book. I'm not going to carry it off. You can have it back in a few minutes." She looked up and nodded, and he decided to forge ahead. "By the way, my name's Tom. Tom McCord. From California." He reached out his hand, and she shook it, exactly one shake. She had soft fingers.

"Laura," she said. "Laura Hartman. From Pennsylvania." They both smiled, and Tom added limply, "Pleased to meet you."

"Listen," said Laura, "if you are going to do some last-minute cramming before meeting the author, you'd better get to it." She tapped on the book for emphasis and turned to go. As she stepped away, she called over her shoulder, with a hint of mischief in her voice, "You should probably know: your pen pal has written an allegory of his own, not to mention a science fiction novel." Tom raised his hand, as if wanting to ask a question in class, but she kept on walking till she turned a corner and went out of sight.

Tom looked down at the book in his hands. He still wanted to give it a quick review, but what he looked at just now was the exact spot where she had tapped its cover. He glanced back at the vacant aisle, then turned to the book and began reviewing its pages. After a few minutes, he checked his watch, put the book back in its place, and headed toward the entrance of the bookstore. Near the front, he stopped at the clerk's desk, but the bespectacled young man sitting on a stool there seemed entirely absorbed in his copy of *The Future of an Illusion*.

Tom stood at the counter for as long as his patience would allow and then said, "Excuse me."

"Just one moment," answered the clerk without glancing up from the page. Finally, he turned a page, dog-eared its corner, and looked up. "Yes, what is it?" he asked brusquely, as if he'd just been interrupted in the middle of a meal.

"I'm wondering what books by C. S. Lewis you have in stock," said Tom.

"I'd have to go check," answered the young man.

"Could you please?"

"The young man sighed, put down his book, and turned to look at a small card catalog.

"*From Feathers to Iron*," he intoned. "*A Time to Dance and other Poems*."

"What about *The Allegory of Love*?" asked Tom.

"*Allegory of Love*?" said the young man quizzically. That's by that other Lewis, the Christian, not the Communist."

"Yes, C. S. Lewis," explained Tom, trying to keep the exasperation out of his voice.

"I thought you said, 'C. Day Lewis,'" explained the young man curtly. "I haven't quite developed an ear for the American drawl." He flipped back a few cards and then found what he was looking for. "Yes, here it is. C. S. Lewis. *Allegory of Love*. Literary criticism. That's near the back on the left, aisle seven, I believe."

"Yes, it is," said Tom. "I was just back there looking at it. I wanted to know about *other* titles by C. S. Lewis."

The young man gave a little shrug, as if to say there was no pleasing certain customers. Then he read off several more titles. "*Dymer*. A narrative poem. *Out of the Silent Planet*. Fantasy. *The Personal Heresy*. Literary criticism. *The Pilgrim's Regress*. Christian allegory. *Rehabilitations . . .*"

"That's fine," said Tom. "I get the idea. The man sounds positively prolific. I wonder if he has any time left over for teaching."

"You're not a student here, I assume?" asked the young clerk.

"No, just visiting from America. Why do you ask?"

"Actually, C. S. Lewis is more well-known around here as a lecturer than as an author. Quite possibly the most popular speaker in Oxford. Even when he lectures on a Saturday morning, about some seventeenth-century poet no one has ever heard of, the hall will be packed, with people perched on windowsills."

"Maybe they come to hear the man who's written all those books?" Tom wondered aloud.

"Not likely," sniffed the young clerk. "He's earned his place among the literary critics. But science fiction novels? Christian allegory? A popularizer *and* a proselytizer. It's such wretched bad taste. How could one of the most promising scholars of his generation turn out to be a bullyragging Bible-thumper?"

"Good question," said Tom. "I'm having lunch with Professor Lewis right now, and I'll ask him." With that, Tom turned on his heels and headed for the front door. He didn't look back to take in the clerk's expression. He preferred his own mental picture, a young man with mouth agape and eyes wide behind those spectacles, his face a mixture of surprise, wonder, and probably envy.

◁ • ▷

Tom pushed open the door and went out onto Broad Street, enjoying not only his well-staged exit, but also the crystalline April sky above and classic elegance of the Sheldonian Theater, just across the street. Stepping briskly through traffic of bicycles and black sedans, Tom crossed over to the Clarendon Building, originally the home of Oxford University Press. He looked up momentarily as he walked by. There were nine gigantic lead statues posted around the rim of its roof, each representing one of the muses. Rumor had it that some of them were coming loose from their base, so passersby had developed a habit of glancing up, just in case one of the immortal sisters chose that moment to come crashing to earth like a Luftwaffe bomb.

Tom continued east down Broad Street, crossed Catte Street, "street of the mouse catchers," and continued on to Holywell. Taking a right at Bath Place, which seemed hardly more than an alley, Tom wondered if he made a wrong turn when the lane ended abruptly after half a block. But then he saw a low door there, framed in black timbers, and the words "Turf Tavern" half hidden behind a burst of blossoms from hanging flowerboxes. Tom stepped inside and found a low-ceilinged room with rough-hewn rock walls and a scuffed wooden floor. He had no trouble believing that this was the oldest pub in Oxford, going back to Chaucer's time. It was full of young people, though, mostly fashionably dressed men with pomaded hair.

Tom scanned the crowded room until he saw a slender, silver-haired gentleman sitting alone at a table, reading a leather-bound book. He made his way over to the table and asked diffidently, "Excuse me. Professor Lewis?" The older man looked up with momentary bewilderment, then pointed without a word to a back corner of the room. Tom looked over and saw another man sitting alone, a portly, ruddy-cheeked man with thinning hair, wrinkled baggy pants and an ill-fitting coat. He looked more like a country farmer who'd stopped in for a ploughman's lunch than a celebrated man of letters. Tom glanced down again at the distinguished-looking gentleman to see if there was some mistake, but the other man just offered a thin-lipped smile and nodded his head in confirmation.

Tom worked his way past several more tables and approached the second man, who was holding a book called *Diary of an Old Soul* in one hand and a pint of cider in the other. "Excuse me. Professor Lewis?" he tried again. "Yes, yes," said the other genially, rising to shake hands. "And you must be McCord," he added in a deep resonant voice, gesturing at the empty chair across the table. Tom took a seat, stared across the table at that round, friendly face, the broad forehead and the big, liquid eyes. Suddenly Tom discovered that he had completely forgotten how to make words come out of his mouth.

"So, you've come over from America, I understand?" said Lewis.

All the words in the English language suddenly vied for Tom's tongue, and he wanted to say, "California" and "research grant" and "Arthurian romance" and "great admirer of your work" all at once. Finally, he mustered all his verbal powers and answered, "Yes, that's right." He paused for several seconds, until subjects and verbs started finding each other in his brain, and then he continued: "I'm over here working on a book. I don't know if you recall my letter, but I did my master's thesis on Arthurian literature and now I'm doing some follow-up research."

"Yes," answered Lewis, "I recall the letter. Reality and romance. From history to legend to literature. That sort of thing. I think I recommended Collingwood? And perhaps Tolkien's essay on Beowulf?

"Yes, sir. Both very helpful. I'm over here visiting the traditional Arthur sites. I'm looking for evidence of actual historical figure, a Romanized Celt who kept the Saxons out of the west country."

The two men ordered lunch, a plate of fish and chips for each, with a pint of bitter for Tom and another cider for Lewis. Lewis briefly bowed his head before taking a bite, then returned to their topic: "So you've been studying King Arthur at university, have you?"

"Yes, sir. I just finished my master's at UCLA."

Lewis had a puzzled look, so Tom went on: "That's the University of California. In Los Angeles."

"Ah," said Lewis, with a sudden look of recognition. "California. Where they have all the sunshine."

Tom nodded.

"I'm more of a polar bear myself. I prefer a fine winter's day to the blaze of summer."

"In the States, people move clear across the country for our balmy skies," said Tom.

Lewis pondered this a moment. "I wouldn't think of moving somewhere just for the climate," he said. "Unless I were a vegetable. Before I moved house to a new city, I'd want to know about the sort of people I'd meet there. And the beauty of the landscape."

"You'd get conflicting opinions on both those topics about California," said Tom. "I grew up in a little town called Ventura. I just went to UCLA because it was fairly close to home."

"And what subjects did you choose for your examinations?" asked Lewis.

"Well," explained Tom, "we don't do things the same way over in the States as you do here. Instead of tutoring and comprehensive exams, we sign up for several classes every semester. Each time you earn a passing grade in a course, you are awarded credits. Then once you've accumulated enough credits, you earn a bachelor's degree."

"Oh, yes, that's right," said Lewis, nibbling on piece of fried haddock. "I believe I've had that explained to me before. I don't think it's a system that would suit me. It sounds like someone judging a horse not by its speed or strength, but by how many oats you've tried to feed it."

Tom grinned at the analogy. "Yes, that's about how it feels from the horse's point of view as well."

"And what about the master's degree?" asked Lewis. "More provender?"

"Well, more coursework. But I did write a master's thesis. I called it 'Arthur through the Ages.' Nothing terribly original. Just an overview of what you might call the many layers of Arthurian legend."

Lewis kept eating and kept listening, so Tom assumed he wanted to hear more: "At the bottom layer, a Celtic commander who kept the Saxons at bay. Then the Welsh bards and chroniclers, turning Arthur into a world conqueror and adding the wizard Merlin to his retinue. Then the French romancers, less interested in the knights as warriors than as lovers. Lancelot moves to center stage, his adventures involving less armor and more *amour*, you might say."

Tom paused, hoping to detect an appreciative smile on Lewis's face. But the older man just kept eating, so Tom continued: "Finally, the Grail quest stories and the newest character, Galahad the Good."

"Yes, it's true," said Lewis, finishing off a chip and licking his fingers, again reminding Tom more of a country farmer than an Oxford don. "Even in a fairly late version like Malory's, you can see Christian characters like Arthur and Galahad, mixing with the almost druidical Merlin. It looks like Britain in that twilight era between the Romans and Saxons. For me, Arthurian tradition is less like layers, and more like a cathedral—the work of many hands over many generations."

Not waiting for the inevitable question, Tom decided to explain: "I'm over here working on a book, a guide for visitors who want to visit the most famous Arthurian sites for themselves." Lewis looked up quizzically, and Tom thought he saw another inevitable question coming. "I suppose you must think I'm nuts—uh, daft, I guess you would say—for coming over here to research a book when there's a war on."

"On the contrary," said Lewis, "I quite understand. And I approve. War does not create fundamentally new conditions. It simply underscores the permanent human condition. There is really no such thing as 'normal life.' If you'd actually lived in past eras that we think of as settled and peaceful, I'm sure you would find, upon a closer look, that they were full of crises, alarms, conflicts, and tribulations. Civilization has always existed on the edge of a precipice."

Lewis took a sip of cider and continued: "Besides, it's just human nature. War, terrible as it is, is not an infinite thing. It cannot absorb the full attention of the human soul. Soldiers read novels in the trenches. Old men propound new mathematical theories in besieged cities. Just a few months ago, I saw a student of mine right here in Oxford with a brightly colored hawk tethered to his wrist. Here is a young man who could be called into the army any day now. And yet his whole mind is focused on reviving the ancient art of falconry. I say, Blessings upon his head!"

"I wish you'd been there when I was trying to explain this trip to my father!" exclaimed Tom. "But a moment ago," he continued, "when I brought up my research over here, I thought I saw a skeptical look on your face."

"Oh, that wasn't about the war," answered Lewis. "I just wondered if you'd found what you were looking for. For me, the enchantment of the old romances lies in the literary artistry, not the local geography."

"I'm not sure I understand," said Tom.

"When I was about your age, I took a trip down to Tintagel—magical name!—where the old books say Arthur was born. The fierce waves tumbling against the rocky coast and the crumbling castle on the edge of a cliff were worthy of Layamon or Malory. But the old tin mines that scarred the landscape. The derelict farms with broken walls and gates off their hinges. Worst of all, right there by 'Merlin's Cave,' as they call it, some blackguard, cursed by all the muses, has built a monstrosity called the King Arthur Hotel! It has cement walls, stamped to look like stonework, covered with an absurd miscellany of armor—a Highland shield next to a faux medieval breastplate, jostled by a helmet from Cromwell's time. And right there in the main lounge you will find THE Round Table, of course, complete with all the knights' names embossed in their proper places!"

"Yes, I have seen some of that," answered Tom. "I suppose it is inevitable wherever there's a dollar—or a quid—to be made. But it can work the other way too. When I was down at Cadbury—really, it's just a tall green mound ringed with ancient earthworks. But in my mind's eye, I could see a stout timber palisade on the hilltop, a great gate swinging open, two hundred horsemen, with leather helmets and crosses on their shields, galloping out to fall upon a Saxon host. For me, the actual site didn't betray my imagination. Rather the place was transfigured by it."

"Yes, yes," I know exactly what you mean," said Lewis, speaking for the first time with unfeigned enthusiasm. "When I was growing up, my family went on holiday to the Wicklow Mountains in the south of Ireland. As my brother and I were cycling around, the whole landscape seemed to me like something right out of Wagner. The entire time we were there, I kept expecting to see the fair Sieglinde just around the hill. Or I'd peer down into a crevice and wonder if I might see Fafnir the dragon guarding his horde. I loved nature for what it reminded me of before I learned to love it for itself."

Tom nodded in agreement. In that moment, they were not a distinguished, middle-aged professor and an eager young American sharing lunch in a pub. They were two men who knew exactly what the other was talking about. Tom leaned in a little and said, "Can I tell you something? When I was down in Cornwall, I also went to Bodmin Moor, to Dozmary Pool."

"Ah," said Lewis, "the Lady of the Lake. Where Arthur received Excalibur."

"And where Sir Bedivere returned it, on Arthur's strictest orders, as the king lay dying. Well, Dozmary is just a round pond on a flat heath, surrounded by reeds. You could almost throw a stone across it. I'm sure there are twenty lovelier scenes within an hour's hike of the pool. But there is something eerie about the place, knowing what they say about it. I stood there on the edge, looking at slate-gray water under a leaden sky. And I just couldn't help myself. I found a dead branch, about three feet long, and I heaved it into the pool, just to see what would happen. I couldn't help but think of those lines:

"So flash'd and fell the brand Excalibur;
But ere he dipped the surface, rose an arm
Clothed in white samite, mystic, wonderful . . ."

To Tom's surprise, Lewis took up the verse, in his deep, booming voice:

"And caught him by the hilt and brandish'd him
Three times, and drew him under in the mere."

The two men looked at each other in a shock of mutual recognition. "You know Tennyson!" said Tom. "*Idylls of the King.* I'm afraid he's fallen badly out of fashion."

"Oh, I have a pathological aversion to what is fashionable," explained Lewis. "I think the poetry they publish nowadays will be known to literary historians as the 'Whining and Mumbling Period.'"

"And yet," said Tom, looking down at his plate, "I suppose it would be a kind of compliment if later generations took any notice of you at all."

Lewis cocked his head slightly and kept listening, so Tom tried to explain: "I was in Blackwells this morning, all those rows and rows of books—including several of yours. I have to wonder what it would feel like to visit there again someday and see a handsome book on the shelf with *my* name on the spine."

Lewis smiled and nodded that he understood. "Oh, yes, *that,*" he said, "'The House of Fame.' When I was your age, I positively ached to take my place on Parnassus. I spent most of my twenties working on a book-length poem that I hoped would put me in the company of Wordsworth, Tennyson, and Yeats."

"What happened?" asked Tom, leaning forward.

"The worst possible fate!" answered Lewis, laughing to himself. "The poem was finally published, and no one took any notice!"

"I would think that would just fuel your ambitions," said Tom. "To try and write another book in hopes that, like Byron, you might wake up one day to find yourself famous."

Lewis laughed again with his great hearty laugh. "I suppose that was my first response," he confessed. "But when I became a Christian a few years later, all that seemed to change. I ceased to want to be original, and just to do the best work I could. As for getting published, I think you'll be surprised when your book comes out, as I have no doubt it will."

Tom wasn't sure he understood, so he just kept listening.

"There's an itch to see your name in print," continued Lewis. "You can hardly think of anything else. But once the book is published, you've scratched that itch and you find that nothing much has changed. The simple absence of an itch is not usually ranked among life's great pleasures."

Tom thought about this as he sampled a bite of mushy peas, and quickly washed them down with a swallow of beer. "I'll have to take your word for it," he said, "until I see my book in print—if that day ever comes." He paused a moment and then added. "Professor Lewis, can you think of any reason some Englishmen might resent this project of mine?"

"I'm not sure what you mean," said Lewis. "Perhaps they think Americans should be over here helping us fight the Nazis, not writing books."

"Yes, that topic did come up," said Tom with a nod. "But there was something more. I was accosted by two louts down in Somerset. They seemed convinced that I was up to no good, that I had something more in mind than just looking for the historical Arthur."

"I wouldn't know about that," answered Lewis. He looked straight into Tom's eyes, then leaned in and spoke barely above a whisper: "I do believe, though, that beyond our history, in the usual sense of the word, is another kind of history. A sort of 'haunting,' you might call it."

Tom leaned in, as if willing to hear more of the secret, and Lewis continued: "Behind the Arthurian story may be some true history, but not the kind you have in mind. Throughout the English past, there seems to be something else trying to break through—as it almost did in Arthur's time. Something called 'Britain' seems forever haunted by something you might call 'Logres.'"

"Logres?" asked Tom. "The Welsh word for England?"

"Well, yes, that," said Lewis, "but also more than that. Look it up in Christian poets like Spenser or Milton and see if it doesn't mean something more. Or better yet, have a look at Charles Williams's new book of poems, *Taliessen through Logres.* I think you'll see what I mean."

"Actually, I did pick up that book once," said Tom. "To be honest, I couldn't make heads or tails of it."

Lewis nodded ruefully. "Yes, poor Charles. He's a friend of mine. He's always been plagued by the problem of obscurity." Lewis looked like he was about to launch into an extended explication, but then he had a better thought. "Say, you're in luck—or 'holy luck,' as Charles would call it. He's right here in Oxford lecturing this term. You should go hear him speak and ask him yourself what he means by his books."

"Is he a colleague of yours at Magdalen?" asked Tom.

Lewis leaned back slightly. "Here in Oxford, we pronounce it 'Maudlin,'" he explained. "And, no, he's not at any of the colleges. He's an editor at Oxford University Press. Their London office relocated here when the war started last September. He's a brilliant man, an autodidact—writes poetry, plays, novels, biographies, histories, even theology." Lewis paused, then added a surprisingly soulful note: "He's a great man. I'm proud to call him my friend."

"I will most certainly make a point to read his books and attend his lectures while I'm in Oxford," said Tom. "If for nothing else, to find out the secret of Logres."

Lewis grinned and asked, "And how long to you plan to be here?"

"I'm not sure. A few months, I expect. I'll be using Oxford as my home base, making forays out to some Arthurian sites."

"Say, I have another idea," said Lewis. "Williams, Tolkien and I have a little band of brothers that meets here in Oxford, Tuesday mornings at the Eagle and Child, just for talk. Would you like me to ask the others if you might join us?"

"I'm honored that you would ask," said Tom. "I had hoped to meet Professor Tolkien while I was here." But then he added, rather diffidently, "But I'm not sure. I'm just an untutored colonial. I wonder how well I would fit in with a clique of Oxford dons, sipping sherry and discussing 'The Meaning of Meaning.'"

Lewis burst out laughing, in a deep, hearty guffaw. "Now I *know* you ought to come!" he said. "It's not like that at all. We gather in the back parlor of the 'Bird and Baby,' as we call it, for some frothy ale and frothier talk. It's quite a lively group, lots of laughter. People in the front room think we must be talking ribaldry, when we're really arguing theology! And we love to skewer those linguistic birds who write books like *The Meaning of Meaning!*"

Tom smiled and agreed that he would like to come, if the others consented. They continued to talk for more than an hour, more like old friends than two men who had only met that day. Throughout the conversation, Tom had an odd sensation: instead of feeling smaller in the presence of this brilliant man, he somehow felt himself more intellectually keen than usual. It was odd how Lewis's enthusiasm and learned repartee didn't make Tom feel overshadowed. Rather he felt he shined all the brighter himself.

As the time came for them to leave, the two men stood and walked toward the door of the tavern. At their parting, Tom began feeling more formal again. "Well, Professor Lewis, may I say what a privilege it has been talking to you. I don't know if I got my questions answered, but I'm sure this lunch will be one of the highlights of my trip to England."

"You don't need to call me professor," said Lewis. As they shook hands, he added, "And don't worry too much about those unanswered questions. Perhaps our lunch of fish and chips today was part of that other kind of history I was talking about before."

As Lewis smiled and turned to leave, Tom pondered that last remark. He realized he'd just acquired one more question.

## ← 3 →

*Oxford*
*The first of May*

Tom's pulse quickened as he turned down Catte Street, heading for what C. S. Lewis had called "the most beautiful room in all England." It was the first of May, and Tom was going to hear Lewis's friend Charles Williams speak on "The Meaning of the Grail" at the Bodleian Library. Tom decided to arrive early for the mid-afternoon lecture, to get a good look at the Divinity School room, and to get a good seat for the lecture.

Walking down the narrow street under a lowering sky, Tom arrived at the east entrance to the Bodleian and turned in at the gate. His first response to the Schools Quadrangle, the courtyard east of the main building, was disappointment. Having seen so many velvet lawns and spectacular flower gardens in the college quads, he was surprised to find a large enclosure with nothing but slippery flagstones. The eastern façade of the Bodleian made no better impression, a soot-stained slab with little ornamentation except for long vertical lines, almost like jail bars. How odd, Tom thought, that one of the most famous and venerated libraries in the world should look like an old prison.

Tom crossed the quad, following others through a large wooden door and into a narrow passageway that led to the

Divinity School. Emerging from the dark corridor into the lecture hall, Tom instantly changed his mind about the Bodleian. Entering the Divinity School room was like moving from darkness to light, from confinement to liberation, from all that weighs down the spirit to all that makes it soar. The whole room was suffused with an amber glow, the afternoon sun warming the cream-colored walls, which seemed to radiate a light all their own.

The whole interior commanded Tom to look up. The floor was unadorned flagstone covered with rows of wooden chairs. But the lofty arched windows with delicate tracery carried his eyes upward toward the ceiling, where he saw rows of ornately carved pendants, hanging like lanterns, each one radiating fan-shaped curves, like shafts of light chiseled in stone. The plain stone floor and the portable chairs, crouching humbly under that magnificent vaulted ceiling, seemed to suggest that all the richness and gladness of life comes not from the plane on which we live and walk, but from higher planes of intellect, imagination, learning, and faith.

The chairs in the lecture hall began filling quickly, even as Tom was admiring the room. He had wondered what sort of audience a publisher's editor would attract, and he soon had his answer. He found a seat near the center, about five rows back, before every seat was taken as the clock neared three. There were a few men who looked like dons scattered around the room, but most of the listeners were about Tom's age, with more women in the crowd than he had seen in any one place since arriving at Oxford.

Precisely at three o'clock, Mr. Charles Williams stepped briskly stepped to the lectern. He was a tall man in his fifties with wavy hair, wearing a black gown and gold-rimmed spectacles. Tom was not accustomed to lecturers wearing academic gowns, so his first sight of Williams made him think of a priest or wizard. Williams briefly surveyed his listeners and smiled. The furrows on his cheeks ran all the way down to his jaw, giving the impression that someone had placed his mouth in parentheses. Tom heard someone in the row behind him whisper the word "ugly," but that was not quite accurate. There was a look of energetic intelligence in Williams's face, the owlish eyes and simian jaw giving a sense of endearing homeliness, not mere coarseness.

Williams set down his notes and hardly glanced at them again for the next hour. "Did any of you buy a newspaper this morning?" he began. There was a hint of Cockney in his voice, an accent that certainly wouldn't impress the person who had whispered the word "ugly." Abandoning the lectern, Williams paced back and forth in front of the room, looking into individual faces for the answer to his question. Several nodded that they had, and Williams smiled to see his hypothesis confirmed. "You offered a coin and received a newspaper in return. A mutually satisfactory transaction. That is the life of the city. Exchange." Williams paced briskly back toward the lectern and continued: "And thus you took one step closer to the Holy Grail." Pausing to let this comment have its effect, Williams came out toward his listeners again and asked, "Did any of you hold a door open for someone today? Did you help someone who'd dropped an armful of books?" Seeing a few nods in the audience, Williams smiled again and continued. "Giving your effort, your labor, for someone else, perhaps a stranger. Courtesy, yes. But also substitution. Another step in your quest for the Grail."

"What is this Holy Grail we hear so much about?" asked Williams, pacing back and forth so rapidly that Tom could hear keys or coins clinking in his pocket. "Is the Grail the holy chalice used by Jesus on the night of the Last Supper? Is it a cup in which Joseph of Arimathea caught drops of Christ's blood as he was stretched out on the cross?" Again, Williams peered into individual faces, speaking to over a hundred people, but giving each one the impression he was talking just to him or her. "Or perhaps you favor the Loomis school: the Grail is a bit of 'faded mythology,' a Celtic cauldron of plenty that somehow got lugged into Arthurian lore?"

Williams paced back and forth some more, throwing his hands into the air, as if to say, Who can answer all these imponderable questions? Then he plunged in again: "There is no shortage of texts on the subject. Let's start with Chrétien de Troyes: 'Percival, or the Story of the Grail,' written sometime in the 1180s. This is the first known account of the Grail. The young knight Percival sits at banquet at the castle Carbonek and sees an eerie procession—a young man carrying a bleeding lance, two boys with gold candelabras, then finally a fair maid with a jeweled grail, a platter bearing the wafer of the Holy Mass. Percival doesn't ask what it all means and thereby brings a curse upon himself and on the land." Williams surveyed the crowd again, as if waiting for someone to stand and explain all this to him. The room was silent as a church at midnight, so Williams went on, listing all the famous medieval texts and their retellings of the Grail legend, noting how their dates clustered around the late twelfth and early thirteenth centuries.

"So much for the literary versions," he continued. "But what is this Grail *really*? What lies behind the texts? Some describe it as a cup or bowl, some as a stone, some as a platter. The word Grail, by the way, comes from Latin *gradalis,* more like a shallow dish, or paten, than a chalice." After another strategic pause, Williams exclaimed, almost in a shout, "How extraordinary! Here we have what some would call the holiest relic in Christendom and no one seems to know what it looks like."

Pacing some more, as if trying to work off an excess of agitation and intellectual energy, Williams went back to the lectern and leaned on it heavily, dangling a graceful, eloquent pair of hands over the edge. "And here's another problem: why this sudden fascination with the Grail in the twelfth century when no one in Christendom seemed to give it a thought for the previous millennium? We hear a lot about relics in the first thousand years of the Church. Handkerchiefs from St. Paul with healing powers. Constantine's mother in the fourth century going to Jerusalem and finding what she considered to be the true cross. Cities fighting over the cloak of St. Martin, patron saint of France. But where was the Grail all those years? And why was no one looking for it?"

Williams pulled a handkerchief out of his coat sleeve, removed his gold-rimmed glasses and wiped them, and put them back on, as if to suggest he needed the clearest possible vision to try and answer these questions. Then he strode back out into the audience. "Ladies and gentlemen, I submit to you that there was no *real* Grail, no relic from the life of Christ, and *certainly* no Celtic cauldron of plenty lying behind the medieval texts. The Grail exists only in the texts themselves. It is an imaginative response, not to Bible archaeology or Welsh mythology, but to Church theology."

Williams returned to the lectern, smoothed back his wavy hair that was becoming unruly, and surveyed the audience, as if expecting a rebuttal. Hearing none, he continued, speaking rapidly but never slurring his words. "What did I mean earlier when I talked about buying a newspaper or holding open a door? Exchange. Substitution. That is the way of community, the lifeblood of the city. But, more than that, in a Christian understanding, it is a part of the *imago Dei* within us, the image of God. It is Co-inherence."

"Co-inherence," said Williams again, repeating a word Tom had certainly never heard before. "Christians believe it is built into the very fabric of the universe, a reflection of the Trinity: Father, Son, and Holy Spirit, three persons in one being, eternally expressing their natures in relation to the others. At the very foundation of being is a fellowship."

Tom wasn't sure he followed, and he looked around the room to see if others looked as puzzled as he was. But those around him seem almost mesmerized by what they heard, so Tom turned to listen again. "Co-inherence leads to substitution," Williams was explaining, "Christ's dying for all humanity in order that they might be lifted up. The redeemed of the Lord co-inhere in their Maker, living in the Spirit, as he lives in them, joining in the Company of Co-inherence."

Tom was beginning to feel that he had indeed wandered into church and was listening to a priest, albeit an obscure one. He was wondering how all this fit into the Grail stories. As if hearing Tom's thoughts, Williams continued: "At the same time all the great Grail stories were being written, there was a great stirring in the Western Church, a quest for clarity about the great sacrament of co-inherence—the Eucharist, 'the great Thanksgiving,' Holy Communion, 'The With-oneness.' In that sacrament lay all the mysteries and miracles of Co-inherence—the Arch-natural in the Natural, a symbol that is more than a symbol, Christ giving himself to the Church as the Church gives itself to Christ. As St. Augustine explained the sacrament, 'If you have received well, you are that which you have received.'"

Williams went on with his lecture, the audience rapt with attention, interweaving two terms, Logos and Logres. Logos was the Word made flesh. Logres was Arthur's kingdom, the attempt by humans to embody the City of God in the city of men. Williams did not see the Grail as any kind of physical object or person. Rather it is symbol of the soul's progress toward God. A carnal seeker like Lancelot was "the old self in the old way," never progressing too far beyond worldly quests for bliss, such as the bed of Guinevere. Percival did a little better, "the old self in the new way," someone who sought after the "Limitless Light," but who only attempted self-improvement, not self-transformation. Only Galahad found the object of his quest, "the new self in the new way," one whose quest had changed the very nature of who he was.

Williams concluded that the Grail romancers were not unusually devout men. They were simply good story-tellers who recognized the imaginative power of the theological questions of their day, the miracle of the loaf and the wine as the Bread of Life and the Cup of Heaven. Williams concluded that all attempts, in literature and in life, to fully embody the ideals we most deeply believe, are ultimately doomed to failure.

As he neared the end of his lecture, Williams returned to the podium and leaned on it heavily. He asked the audience to indulge him for quoting a few lines from his own book of poems, *Taliessen through Logres*. Then closing his eyes and lowering his head, as in both weariness and prayer, he quoted from a scene in which Merlin the wizard looks on at Arthur's coronation, seeing in the glorious founding of Camelot "the glory of Logres, patterns of Logos in the depth of the sun." Williams ended by noting that, even at that glad moment, Merlin knew in advance that it would all end in chaos and ruin:

"At the door of the gloom sparks die and revive;
the spark of Logres fades, glows, fades."

Williams's voice sounded husky as he ended his lecture, perhaps because he had been speaking continuously for nearly an hour. But Tom sensed in those last few words not only Williams's sadness at the fall of Camelot, but some greater sorrow, perhaps some unspoken grief of his own. Perhaps there was something too in that broken voice about this new war, perhaps the whole "turbid ebb and flow of human misery."

When Williams had finished speaking, no one moved for several seconds. The man up front in golden spectacles almost seemed unaware that there was anyone else in the room. He seemed to gaze above and behind the sea of faces, as if the very stone walls of the Divinity School were a transparent screen through which he could see something else. Gradually, though, people began stirring and gathering up their things. Most filed quietly toward the exits, but at least a dozen listeners made their way to the front to meet Mr. Williams and ask questions. Tom himself had some questions to ask, so he too walked toward the lectern. He stood a few paces back from those who pressed close to Williams, noticing that most of them were young women. Several were carrying notebooks, with pencils out to scribble a few more notes. But Tom couldn't help but think of a Broadway star walking out a stage door to be greeted by a mob of autograph seekers.

Tom waited patiently, as individuals asked questions, nodding their heads or taking notes, then leaving one by one. One young woman in a fuzzy sweater and a feathered hat wanted to know why Williams dismissed the "Celtic school" so lightly. Williams answered simply that there was no evidence that the Continental writers knew any Welsh folktales, but he was certain they knew about the debates raging in the Church on the meaning of the Eucharist. He also found the idea of noble knights leaving all behind, risking life itself, in quest of a self-refilling stewpot simply foolish. As the group of questioners thinned out, Tom noticed that Laura Hartman was among those waiting to get a word with Mr. Williams. She was wearing her hair curled in front, long in back, so that it cascaded over the fur collar of her beige coat. Tom surprised himself, as he didn't remember names too well and he didn't usually pay much attention to what people wore. But in this case, he didn't seem quite his usual self.

Williams looked at Laura, as if awaiting her question, but she said, "My question is a little more involved. I can wait for the others." Tom felt the same way, so he too hung back from the knot of inquirers. Finally, when there only Tom, Laura, and two others still gathered around the lectern, Williams said, "The Kings Arms is just up the street. I wonder if we should seek some refreshment as we continue this discussion?" The other two listeners both declined the invitation. One was a middle-aged man who wanted to challenge Williams on a question of pronunciation. The other a young woman who simply wanted Williams's signature on a copy of his new book, *Descent of the Dove*. But Tom was glad for a chance to join Mr. Williams at the Kings Arms and glad too that Laura wanted to come along.

◁ • ▷

It was drizzling outside when Tom, Laura, and Mr. Williams left the Bodleian and walked up the street toward the King's Arms. Williams had removed his academic gown, and was wearing a navy blue suit, gray silk tie, and flawlessly polished shoes. He and Laura brought out their umbrellas, but Tom just pulled up the collar on his jacket and followed closely behind. When they reached the Kings Arms on Holywell Street, they went inside, found a cozy table near the fireplace, and ordered drinks. Taking off his misty spectacles and wiping them with a handkerchief, Williams looked at the two young people across the table from him as if he were just seeing them for the first time.

"So, you are both Americans, yes?"

"That's right," answered Tom. "But I'm from the left margin of the continent, California, and she's from the right margin, Pennsylvania."

"And did you come over together?" Williams asked.

"No, we did not," said Laura quickly. "We just met tonight after your lecture." Tom thought her answer was more emphatic than it needed to be, and he wondered if Laura didn't remember him as the one she had talked to in Blackwells the previous week. But he decided to let it pass.

"We're getting ready to send evacuees to North America, in case the war takes a bad turn," said Williams. "I wonder what brings you two expatriates in the other direction?" Even in asking this simple question, Williams's hands did half the talking. When he mentioned evacuees, his arms reached out, as if pushing a rowboat away from shore. But when he used the word *expatriates*, he pulled his hands back in toward his chest with fluttering fingers.

Tom looked at Laura, remembering the Ladies First policy she had proclaimed at Blackwells. Laura looked back at him, as if she preferred to waive her rights in this instance, but Tom just kept waiting politely. Finally, she looked back at Mr. Williams. "Actually, it's the war that brought me in this direction," she explained. "My Aunt Vivian lives here in Oxford. She came over in the Great War as a volunteer nurse and married an Englishman. But he was called up for war work in Scotland, and there are no children, so she's been alone all winter. My parents thought it would be good if I came over to keep Aunt Viv company, at least until her husband can get reassigned closer to home."

"That's a lovely thing to do," said Williams.

"Oh, I really don't mind," said Laura. "I finished college last year, and I've been living at home, working part-time at a library. So I was ready for an adventure." Laura paused a moment, as if deciding whether she'd said enough or not, then continued: "And I also have some personal things I'm looking into. Somehow I feel the answers are over here somewhere."

Both Williams and Tom kept looking at Laura and listening, as if they were expecting to hear more. "But we can talk about that later," she said, taking a sip of coffee. "Tom, why don't you tell Mr. Williams what you're doing over here?"

Tom was gratified that Laura remembered his name, so he acknowledged her cue and took his turn: "Well, I did my master's thesis on Arthurian romance. I came over to research a book on the historical sites associated with King Arthur. I'm putting together a guidebook." Tom usually liked to talk about himself and his projects, but he recognized what Laura had been feeling a moment ago. There was something slightly unnerving about Mr. Williams's earnest gaze, the big eyes behind those shiny glasses that seemed to peer into your soul. Tom thought about volleying the conversation back in Laura's direction, but then he remembered the question he wanted to ask. "I asked Professor Lewis a question last week and he referred me to you. I was wondering why somebody over here might take exception to my poking around Arthurian sites."

"Is that what happened?" asked Williams.

"Yes it did. I ran into a couple of ruffians down in Somerset who tried to scare me off. They seemed worried about my finding an underground chamber somewhere."

"Professional jealousy perhaps," said Williams. "They may think any important new finds should be reserved for Englishmen. There's still a lot out there, you know. A few years ago, they were digging around in Cornwall and found the ancient tomb of 'Drustanus,' most likely the famous Tristran, lover of Isolt in Arthurian legends. And just last summer, before this Nazi rudeness, they uncovered a buried ship at Sutton Hoo, complete with silver and gold, helmet and shield, everything fit for a great Saxon lord."

Tom nodded his head and smiled, clearly aware of both discoveries. "And in your novel, *War in Heaven,* you have the Holy Grail itself turn up in Hertfordshire, of all places! Who would have looked for it just north of London?"

Williams chuckled to himself, as if enjoying his own literary audacity. Then he explained: "If you've followed recent theories, the Grail has been turning up everywhere—in Wales and Scotland, even in Eastern Europe. So why shouldn't humble Hertfordshire put in its claim?" Williams took a sip of his rum and hot water, then continued: "I grew up in Hertfordshire and found the county brimming with Grail legends. Not from Celtic sources, but from the Crusades. In the twelfth century, Hertfordshire was an important hub for the Knights Templar. They had castles and lands in Royston, St. Albans, Baldock, and a half dozen other places within a day's ride of London. They claimed to have brought back all manner of sacred treasures from Jerusalem—splinters from Christ's cross, fragments from the crown of thorns, and, of course, the Grail itself."

"They would have benefited from your lecture," said Tom. "You seem to say that the Grail is just a literary device, a religious symbol, not an actual relic one might go questing after."

"I wouldn't put it quite that way," replied Williams. "I would say that Grail is all the more sacred, all the more worth questing after, because it means so much more than any relic ever could."

Tom took in these words for a while and then replied. "And yet your novel suggests that the Grail has some sort of stored-up power or supernatural energy, so that it could be used as a vessel of great evil as well as great good."

"Keep in mind it *is* a novel," said Williams, "not one of my books on doctrine. And yet, surely you know, such a notion is not original with me. The whole premise of the Dark Arts—baptisms of blood, the Black Mass, crucifixes turned upside down—is that holy vessels can be put to other uses, that power meant for good can be turned to evil by cunning and depraved minds."

"I can't say I'm a believer," said Tom. "It all seems like wish-fulfillment and hocus-pocus to me."

Laura winced, but Williams didn't seem to mind the comment at all. "Fair enough," he said. "It is only the arrogant or the insecure who claim to *know* about such things, unless perhaps you are a genuine mystic. For the rest of us, all we can do is choose what to believe.

This sort of topic made Tom uncomfortable, so he quickly returned to their earlier discussion: "The Knights Templar and their relics—I wonder if that is something I should include in my book?"

"I would think so," answered Williams. "The Templars certainly saw themselves as a company of Galahads, chivalric knights sent out to protect pilgrims and liberate Jerusalem."

Tom took out a little notebook and jotted down a few words. "Hertfordshire isn't too far from here. Maybe I'll go over and have a look around."

"Yes, it might be worth your while," said Williams, "if only for the Knights Templar sites. Such treasures they claim to have brought back to England! Be sure to visit their hideaway at Royston Cave and see if you can decipher the writing on its walls."

Laura had been listening intently and almost motionlessly as the two men talked. But she leaned forward and almost spilled her cup of coffee at the mention of Royston Cave. "A secret cave?" she asked. "With writing on the walls? Is that what you said?"

Williams and Tom were both somewhat taken aback by her sudden outburst. Tom smiled, but Williams looked at her sympathetically. "Yes, that's correct, Miss Hartman. Royston Cave. It's right beneath the streets of town. And the walls are covered with arcane symbols that seem to have been etched there by some Templars in hiding."

"Has anyone ever deciphered the hieroglyphs?" Laura asked.

"There are a number of theories," said Williams. "Are you a student of the Knights?"

"No, nothing like that," said Laura, retreating into her habitual reserve. "But that is what I was hoping to talk to you about."

Williams kept listening, so Laura continued: "I want to ask you about another of your novels, *Descent into Hell*. You show a young woman in the here and now who has visions of the distant past. She sees one of her ancestors in the sixteenth century being martyred for his faith. And when she prays for this man, who has been dead for five hundred years, he is strengthened in his time of suffering, and goes bravely to his death proclaiming, 'I have seen the salvation of my God.'"

"Yes, I recall that part of the novel," said Williams, blinking his eyes several times.

"Do you believe in that sort of thing?" asked Laura, tilting her head to one side.

"Believe in which sort of thing?"

"The part of about someone having visions of the past."

"Well, again, please remember you are quoting from a novel," answered Williams. "But I would say I certainly believe in the principles behind that novel. For one thing, I don't think God experiences time the same way we do. We are like characters in a play who must act out our scenes in their proper order, not knowing what comes next. But God is like the author, who can see all the pages at once."

"You said principles—plural," noted Laura.

"So I did," replied Williams. "I also wanted to make it clear we are sometimes called to bear one another's burdens—quite literally.

"Do you mean moral support, financial help, that sort of thing?" asked Tom, knowing even as he spoke that Williams had something more in mind.

"That much, at least," said Williams. "But also the principle I discussed in my lecture—Co-inherence."

Tom groaned inwardly when he heard that strange word, and he wanted to find his way to some more common ground. Rather than following Mr. Williams back into those mystical mists, he broke in and asked Laura, "Does that answer your question? Is that what you wanted to know about *Descent into Hell*?"

Laura gave Tom a little frown, as if she knew exactly what he was up to, but she went ahead and answered. "Actually, my question was simpler than that. I just wanted to ask about the possibility of people having visions of the past—not memories from their own lives, or imagined re-creations from things they'd read in books. Direct viewings of long-past events."

Laura picked up a spoon and stirred her coffee as she said this, even though the cup was almost empty by now.

"Do you feel this has been happening to you?" asked Williams gently.

"Something has been happening. I don't know what it means. That is part of why I wanted to come to England. It seems to me somehow the answers must be over here."

Tom was feeling uncomfortable again and was wondering if they could go back to the topic of Co-inherence. He touched Laura lightly on the arm and asked, "Would this be a good time for me to excuse myself?"

Laura thought a moment and then said, "No, that's all right. You can stay if you want to. You have more right to be here than I do. You're writing a book. I'm just having dreams."

"Could you tell me something about these dreams?" asked Williams. He studied Laura's face intently as he spoke, as if all his learning and wisdom were entirely hers for the asking. Laura paused to collect her thoughts and then explained: "There are certain dreams I've been having since I was a little girl. I have the usual dreams, the kind you forget two minutes after you wake up. But other dreams of mine come over and over, and they don't even feel like dreams. They feel more like visions."

"Can you describe what makes them feel that way?" asked Williams in the same quiet, earnest tone.

"It's hard to say," said Laura. She thought some more and then gave it a try: "I'm not much for movies, but perhaps this might help. When I watch a film, I'm looking at pictures on a screen. I'm always aware that I'm in the real world looking at something make-believe. But in my vision dreams, it is as if they are what is real and it's me that's make-believe."

"And you remember the dreams?" asked Williams.

"Every single detail," said Laura, "as far as I can make them out. They're always just the same. A sleeping king with a lion at his feet. Some sort of crypt with strange writing on the wall. A Celtic cross as tall as a lamppost. An old village church with animals going in and out."

"Do you have lots of these dreams?" asked Williams.

"No," said Laura, "there are exactly five. Always the same ones. Some still, like a picture, others moving, like a film or a play. That's why I wanted to come over here. It seems to me the answers are here somewhere." Without waiting for what seemed to be the obvious next question, Laura continued: "The sleeping king with a lion at his feet. He never moves. Is he dead? Lying in state? But the crown and the flowing robes. I can't imagine such a thing in America. And the village church. It's not like anything from home."

"But why cross the sea?" asked Williams. "Do you find the dreams disturbing? What do you hope to find?"

"I don't find them disturbing—except for one," answered Laura. "But they seem like parts of a puzzle that demands to be solved. Do these images say something about me? About my past? My own ancestors are from England, Quakers who were driven out by the Puritans. I hope this doesn't sound too grandiose, but maybe what I hope to find here is a part of myself."

"I get it," said Tom, not quite getting it. "So when you read that passage in *Descent into Hell* about the young woman, it made you think of yourself."

"More than you know!" answered Laura, pressing her hands together. "There's one other dream I haven't mentioned yet. But it's something like the one in the novel." Laura paused for several seconds and stared into the nearby fire as if waiting for the scene to appear before her eyes. Then she began speaking, softly and slowly in low even tones: "There has been a great battle. The dead and wounded are still lying on the trampled earth. Armed men on horseback are gathering up shaggy-headed warriors who have thrown down their weapons. One of the prisoners, a man with braided hair and beard, is dragged before the victorious general, who's wearing a golden wreath and a silk tunic. The prisoner clasps his hands and pleads for mercy, but the general orders one of his captains to strike the prisoner down, right then and there. The captain steps forward and unsheathes his sword, but then sadly shakes his head. The leader raises his fist and screams out another order, but the officer refuses him again, taking off his own helmet and kneeling beside the shaggy-haired man. He sets his spear on the ground, crossing it with his sword. The two men bow their heads together, side by side, as the general shouts out one more time. The other soldiers close in on the two kneeling men and raise their swords for slaughter. . . ."

Laura closed her eyes as if she couldn't bear to watch and held them closed a long time. Then she opened her eyes, blinked, and looked around the room, as if awaking from a trance. Tom felt mesmerized himself and had nothing to say. But Williams was nodding his head, as if he had seen the vision too. Can you describe the surrounding terrain?" he asked.

"It's in the mountains," answered Laura. "Rugged country, with tall dark trees and patches of snow."

"And the captain who disobeys?" asked Williams. "I wonder if he has darker skin than most of the other soldiers?"

"Yes, he does!" said Laura, her eyes widening. "How would you know that?"

"The whole scene sounds like the martyrdom of St. Maurice in the third century," explained Williams. "He was a Roman general from north Africa, but also a Christian. He was executed by the Emperor Maximian because he refused to kill some Gaulish rebels who were fellow Christians. Some say his whole command, the Theban Legion, was martyred by the hundreds, or even thousands, because they wouldn't bow to Roman gods or execute fellow Christians."

"And where did all this supposedly take place?" asked Tom.

"In present-day Switzerland," explained Williams. "The town of St. Moritz is named in honor of Maurice."

Laura's eyes glowed, and she had a look of profound relief on her face. "I always had the feeling I was seeing something real," she said, "not just my imagination. Maybe I'm not crazy after all."

"Or maybe you read about it in a book," said Tom, "and it just stuck in your unconscious."

Laura tilted her head and considered this. "I suppose that's possible," she said. "But I would think I'd remember. I've read plenty of books in my time, and I've never had dreams about them like my vision-dreams." Then her look of relief disappeared, as some new problem came into her mind. "But even if it all really happened once, why would I keep dreaming about it?"

Laura addressed this question directly to Charles Williams, almost as if she had forgotten Tom were there. Williams pondered the question, tapping his fingers on the table. "I wouldn't know," he said finally. "I wonder if you're meant to pray for him, to help carry his burden?"

Tom had been perplexed at Williams's lecture, but now he was simply astounded. He thought he simply must interject some sardonic remark, but the look on both Williams's and Laura's faces bade him keep silent.

There was a long pause in which no one seemed to have anything more to say. Finally, Williams glanced at his watch and stood up from his chair. "I'm sorry," he said, "I've lost track of the time. I actually have a dinner engagement this evening with one of our authors at the University Press." Turning to shake Tom's hand, he said, "It was splendid meeting you. If I can be of any service in your research, don't hesitate to call." Tom nodded and offered his thanks. Laura lifted up her hand and, for a moment, Tom thought Mr. Williams was going to kiss it. But he simply gave her a firm shake and thanked her for coming to hear his lecture. "The privilege was all mine," answered Laura enthusiastically. "And thank you for coming to talk with us. I simply can't tell you how much this time has meant to me!" As Laura looked up at Mr. Williams, there was a softness in her eyes and a warmth in her smile that gave Tom a twinge inside, something akin to jealousy. Mr. Williams made a slight bow with his head, grabbed his overcoat from a nearby rack, and walked briskly out of the pub.

Laura began to rise as well. "I should be going too," she said. "I'm glad we got to talk some more," she added with a politeness that seemed perfunctory. "My Aunt Viv is going to wonder what's become of me."

"Could you stay just a minute?" asked Tom. Laura sat back down, on the edge of the chair, not really settling back into it.

"Listen, I realize we just met," said Tom. "But I've decided to go over to Hertfordshire next week and have a look around."

Laura gave a little nod, waiting to see where this was going.

"I get the impression you might want to come too. Have a look at Royston Cave perhaps."

Laura nodded again noncommittally, but her nostrils flared involuntarily at the mention of that secret crypt.

"Listen, I'm going to be in Oxford for a few months," explained Tom. "I'm also going to make some excursions out to some places I want to cover in my book. I could really use a research assistant." Tom half expected a long string of excuses why Laura couldn't do this, but she sat back further in the chair and thought about it.

"I might be interested," she said. "I'd have to talk to Aunt Viv," she added.

"I suppose she needs you around to look after her?" Tom asked.

Laura relaxed a little and shook her head. "That's just the thing," she explained. "Vivian is my mother's younger sister. She's barely over forty. And she's got plenty to do here in Oxford, especially with the war on. She's a trained nurse, so she already has a part-time job. And she has her Victory Garden, and her friends, and she's very involved in her little church over here. My parents sent me over here to look over my 'poor Aunt Viv,' but poor Aunt Viv seems to think it's her job to look after me!"

Laura laughed a little, and Tom laughed to see Laura laugh. "Do think about my offer," he said. "I could really use the help. There are a lot more sites to explore than I expected. You could come with me if you wanted, travel around and see more of the country."

Laura leaned forward, not quite fully in her seat again. "That's a possibility," she answered. "I really would like to see more over here than just Oxfordshire. And I know it sounds silly to you, but I do want to find out some more about these dreams of mine. You simply don't know how much it means to me to find out that someone could make some sense of them!"

Tom nodded, though he still had no idea what to make of that earlier conversation.

But just so we understand each other," added Laura, lowering her voice. "I'd be happy to help with you with your research and maybe even do some traveling. But this is strictly a business arrangement."

"Of course, I understand that," said Tom, feeling both slightly disappointed and slightly insulted. "I really do need some help with my research. But if you wouldn't feel comfortable. . . ."

"Oh, I'd be comfortable, as long as everything is clear." Laura hesitated a moment, then decided to add, "I have someone waiting for me back in the States." She picked up her spoon again and started stirring it in her empty coffee cup.

"I'm glad to hear you're not an orphan," said Tom, trying to keep the conversation light.

Laura gave a quick smile and went on. "I have a *young man* waiting for me. Timothy Higgins. He's in seminary."

"I notice you don't have an engagement ring," said Tom matter of factly. Laura glanced at her left hand, as if checking to confirm Tom's observation. "No, we're not quite that far along. But we have an 'understanding.' We grew up in the same church back home in Pennsylvania. His parents have known my parents since before we both were born."

"So, you're saying it is an arranged marriage? Something to bring peace to warring factions perhaps?'

Laura laughed out loud and covered her mouth with her hand. "No, nothing like that. Nothing's been arranged. Not a marriage. Not even an engagement. Just an understanding. I'm waiting for Timothy to finish seminary at Princeton. And he's waiting for me to come back from England. Then we'll see where things go from there."

"Well, if I were Tim—"

"You are definitely not Tim!" Laura exclaimed. "And he goes by Timothy, not Tim."

"Timothy. More biblical I suppose," said Tom. After a pause, he added, "Now you made me forget what I was going to say."

"Sorry for interrupting," said Laura. "I don't usually do that."

"Oh, that's all right," said Tom. "My friends back home tell me I am eminently interruptible."

"In any case," said Laura, "I'll talk to my Aunt Viv about your offer. I might even drop in on Mr. Williams and get his advice too."

"Really?" said Tom. "He's very stimulating to listen to. But I wouldn't count on him for any practical advice. He seems a bit airy to me."

Laura's lips tightened. "That wasn't my impression at all. I can't remember the last time I met someone who sees so deeply into things," she said.

"Did you gather all that in?" said Tom. "Co-inherence or in-coherence or whatever that was?"

"Now you're simply being unkind," said Laura coolly.

Tom wished his mouth didn't so often run ahead of his brain, and he tried to backtrack a few steps. "I don't mean to offend," he explained. "That was very nice of him to come share a drink with us. But I've just never met anyone like him before. All those weird notions of his. I don't mean to judge, I guess I just don't quite understand. Didn't he seem the least bit odd to you? So wound up, so herky-jerky when he lectured, like a man-sized marionette."

"I found him charming," said Laura firmly. "Singular in his mannerisms, I agree. But I take him seriously if for no other reason than for the rare privilege of seeing that he takes me seriously."

Tom nodded in silent acknowledgment, congratulating himself inwardly that for once his brain was one step ahead of his mouth.

## ← 4 →

Tom was feeling carsick—or rather coach-sick. He and Laura were on a cream-colored bus lumbering along a rutted country road, with farms and woodlands on both sides. Leaning his head against the window, Tom gazed vacantly at pasture after pasture after pasture, sheep then cows then sheep then cows then sheep then cows then sheep.

"I wonder if we are first to set out on a grail quest by riding a bus," Tom said, still looking out the window.

Laura was sitting in the seat across the aisle with a lapful of maps and guidebooks. In her white cotton blouse and pleated, navy blue skirt, she looked like a college student studying for her exams. "I didn't realize we were hoping to find the grail on an overnight field trip," said Laura, without looking up from her reading.

"Well, if we're going to spend half a day lurching to Royston today, and half a day lurching back to Oxford tomorrow, I hope we find something worthwhile. If not the grail, then at least some Crusader's decoder ring."

Still not looking up, Laura replied, "My research indicates that they didn't have decoder rings back then. Nor Cracker Jacks neither."

"Is that so?" said Tom, with mock surprise. "Dark Ages indeed." He continued gazing out the window, and started counting all the colors of wildflowers he could see along the roadside—white, yellow, red, orange, violet—then a shade of blue so intense it almost glowed like neon.

A long silence was broken by Laura's voice from across the aisle: "So Mr. Williams' lecture last week didn't shake your faith in the grail?"

"There wasn't any faith there to get shaken," said Tom, turning away from the window and looking at Laura. "None of the candidates for the *actual* Grail are very impressive. There was a cup in France called the Emerald Chalice, but it turned out to be green-tinted glass. And there was a wooden bowl in Wales called the Nanteos Cup, but it shattered into pieces. Recent grail hunters haven't fared any better than Arthur's knights. No one seems to be as fortunate as Galahad."

"Maybe they lack purity of heart," said Laura, turning to look at Tom. "But I thought the grail was supposed to be hidden away in a secret vault somewhere."

"So the story goes. There's the Chalice Well in Glastonbury, where they say the grail is buried underground. But no one has ever claimed to have seen the actual grail there. Then there's a theory that the grail is hidden at Rosslyn Chapel in Scotland. But that notion didn't even arise until suspiciously late—the eighteenth century—so it doesn't have much appeal, except to the gullible."

"What about the old idea," suggested Laura, "that Sangreal, 'holy grail,' is a mistake for Sang Real, 'royal blood'? That the Grail is not an object at all, but some other kind of holy vessel—a person perhaps?"

"That doesn't really work," said Tom. "In the earliest stories it is simply in Old French 'un graal,' a serving dish. The idea of *the* Grail, much less the *Holy* Grail, comes later, as does the term Sangreal. I'm beginning to think Mr. Williams was right after all: people are wasting their time looking for an actual, physical grail."

"Mr. Williams was right about all the Templar sites in Hertfordshire too," Laura said, organizing her notes in front on her lap. "Shall I report?"

Tom nodded, so Laura continued. "As you know, the Knights Templar were an order of fighting monks sent out to protect pilgrims in the Holy Land. They built their headquarters on the Temple Mount in Jerusalem, which is where they got their name—Order of the Temple or Templars. Since they were right there on the site of Solomon's temple, there were soon a lot of stories about all the fabulous relics they found."

"So how did they end up hiding in places like Royston Cave?" asked Tom.

"Patience, kind sir," said Laura, rearranging the papers in her lap. "After the last of the crusades failed," she continued, "the Templars began to fall out of favor. They still had castles and lands all over Europe, though. The King of France, especially, who owed them a lot of money, decided it was time to get rid of the Templars, and he began accusing them of heresy and cultic rites. He even arrested some of their leaders and had them tortured and burned at the stake."

"There seems to be a lot of blood and fire in Church history," commented Tom wryly. "Isn't there something in the Bible along the lines of showing you are Christians by your love?"

"Yes, there is," said Laura, looking up from her notes. "And it also says you can't serve two masters, God and Mammon. Would you care to editorialize a bit more, or should I continue?"

Tom waved for her to go ahead.

"Anyway, the Templars were eventually banned, so all the kings of Europe made a grab for their wealth and property. That's when they began hiding out in spots like Royston Cave. They still had their money and their relics, but they had to start looking for safe places to stash them. To this day, there are still rumors of fabulous treasures buried under old Templar castles and manor houses."

"So," said Tom, "Do you think Royston might be the crypt you've been seeing in your dreams?"

"Only one way to find out," said Laura. "But, to be honest, I think everybody's been over Royston with a fine-toothed comb. There's somewhere else, not far ahead, where we might make a stop. It's Temple Despy, south of Hitchin. Three Knights Templar from there were imprisoned at Hertford Castle by the king because they wouldn't reveal where their treasures were hidden. They all three took their secrets to the grave. So you have to wonder what you might find at the site of their old manor-house."

Tom sat up in his seat. "That does sound interesting," he said. "I wonder if we could arrange to make a visit on our way back to Oxford tomorrow?"

Laura cleared her throat and shuffled the papers in her lap. "I thought you might feel that way," she said. "So I went ahead and made a few phone calls from Oxford. I found out we can get off the bus at Hitchin and store our luggage in some lockers at the station. Then we can take a taxi down to the site of Temple Despy. I spoke to a fellow there named Lionel Mirden, who said his employer wouldn't mind if we stopped in for a visit tomorrow afternoon."

"Who's his employer? A guy in a white mantle riding a horse?" said Tom.

"No, his name William De Lott. Some sort of antiquarian and collector. I think he might have the impression that you are a gullible American relic-hunter. Maybe that you'll pay top dollar for some Roman baubles."

"Oh, is that right?" said Tom. "I guess he doesn't know how we feel about Mammon, does he?"

Laura grabbed the seat in front of her as the bus bounced over a pothole in the road. "It was just an inquiry," she said, still looking ahead. "I didn't promise we'd come. I hope you don't mind."

"No, no, just the opposite," said Tom. "I like your initiative." He wanted to reach across the aisle and pat Laura on the shoulder, but he thought that might seem a little too familiar. "But that's tomorrow," Tom added, "I guess we should figure out what we're going to do today."

"We can't be too far away from Royston," said Laura. "By the way, I didn't make any reservations. I want to see the rooms first."

"We don't need to worry about that," said Tom. "I'm sure there will be rooms over one of the local pubs. There always seems to be a Red Lion or a Royal Oak in these little burgs where you can get a room for the night."

"I'd prefer to stay away from pub rooms," said Laura. "Too much noise downstairs or in the street. I think I'll look for a little Bed and Breakfast. Some quaint little cottage run by a talkative lady with two cats."

"So you're saying I should drop you off at one place and find my own room at another?"

"I think that would be the way to go," said Laura. "It would be better for propriety's sake."

"Really?" said Tom. "You're thinking about propriety? We're just two anonymous Americans traveling around on our own. Who cares what anybody thinks?"

"I do, for starters," said Laura, grabbing the seat in front of her again. "Besides, Americans don't have the best reputation over here. Everyone seems to think we live like the people they see in Hollywood movies."

"Is that so?" asked Tom. "And yet I notice the local Bijou is packed every time one of those movies comes to town."

Laura just shrugged, so Tom continued: "Besides I hear the Brits aren't as 'old-school' as they used to be. There's a war on, you know. Bombs could start dropping out of the sky any day now. Who knows how much time anybody has got? I think the new mood over here these days is *Carpe diem*."

"Oh sure," said Laura, with a hint of weariness in her voice. "'Seize the day.' I heard that one a lot in college. Drink deeply of life, live for the moment, that sort of thing."

"And what's so wrong with that?" asked Tom.

"I think it would be all right if people really thought through what they were saying," explained Laura. "But when I hear a guy shout, 'Seize the day!' what he usually has in mind is to seize the nearest bottle or the nearest wench."

Tom grinned, as he had to agree that *Carpe diem* was the unofficial motto of just about every college fraternity he knew. "Ok, then, Miss Killjoy-was-Here, do you have a better motto in mind?"

"Oh, I don't know," mused Laura. "How about 'Seize tomorrow'?"

"Which means?"

"I guess it means, 'Live today so that you don't have any regrets tomorrow.'"

"Nobody likes to get into trouble," said Tom. "But I don't know if just being careful adds up to a philosophy of life."

Laura mused a moment and then replied: "Okay, then, how about 'Seize Eternity'?"

"Now you've really lost me. I know how to seize the day—"

"Yes, I believe most young men do," Laura interjected.

"—But what would it mean to seize eternity?" Tom asked.

"I'm not sure what it means," admitted Laura. "I'm just thinking out loud here."

"Give it a try."

"Actually, I do have an idea, but I don't feel like explaining. You'll just make fun." Laura looked at Tom with those serious eyes of hers, and he made an X gesture over his chest. "Cross my heart," he said. "If you'll tell me what you mean, I'll bite my tongue."

Laura folded her hands in her lap and closed her eyes for several moments as she spoke: "I don't suppose you can actually seize eternity. It's more of a gift. But I would like to live my life knowing that one day I will stand in a place of unspeakable radiance. And I would like to hear a loving voice say, 'Well done, my good and faithful servant.'"

Laura need not have worried about a quip from Tom. He looked at her with a baffled expression and had not a word to say. He had never met anyone like her. There was a depth there, a spirit like an ocean, one that made him feel like a pond.

"Oh look!" said Laura, "we're coming into Royston now!" Tom looked out the window and saw the bus station up ahead. Once they had come to a full stop, with a piercing screech of the brakes, Tom and Laura grabbed their luggage, climbed off the bus, and stretched their legs. They agreed to separate and find their own lodgings, then rendezvous after lunch at the entrance to Royston Cave. Tom watched Laura walk up Priory Lane, where there were sure to be plenty of small B & Bs, then he took a room at the first public house he came to, The Bull, right on the main street of town.

◁ • ▷

After a quick lunch of fish and chips, Tom consulted his map and began walking up the High Street toward Royston Cave. He had expected the cave entrance to be on the edge of town, in a wooded valley perhaps or cut out of the side of a bluff.

But the signs pointed him to one of the busiest intersections in the city. As he approached, he saw Laura already standing there, studying a guidebook. "Welcome, pilgrim," she said, looking up, "we're standing over the cave right now. Follow me."

She turned and walked down a gravel walkway between two buildings on the main road, which led to a handsome little out-building of timber and whitewashed plaster.

"This looks more like Royston Garage," said Tom.

Laura pointed to an image on the wall of the shed, a woman with a crown holding a spoked wheel like a ship's helm. "This is called Katherine's Barn," she explained. "The entrance to the cave is in there."

"You would think the Templars would be more subtle about their secret hide-out," said Tom.

"Oh, they were," explained Laura. "This entrance was dug out much later. Some workmen found the cave by accident in the eighteenth century when they were refurbishing the town market."

"Some people have all the luck," said Tom. "And I suppose they discovered a jar full of gold coins down there?"

"They hoped to," said Laura. "They let down a small boy on a rope, carrying a torch. He said there was a big cavern under there, mostly filled with rubble. So the whole town got involved digging it out to see what they could find."

"Which was?" asked Tom.

"Mostly just dirt and rocks. But they did find a skull. And a brass seal with a *fleur de lis* on it. But the most interesting part was all the pictures on the walls," Laura added with excitement.

"Pictures of what?" asked Tom.

"Let's go and see!" said Laura. She went over and pulled open a door at the side of Katherine's Barn. Tom held the door and insisted that Laura go in first, then followed her in to find a young woman wearing too much lipstick sitting at a small table. Tom paid for two tickets and a guidebook of his own, then turned to see a stone staircase leading down through a tunnel carved out of the white chalky ground underneath the building. The staircase had naked light bulbs mounted on the ceiling casting eerie shadows on the walls. "This reminds me of spelunking," Tom said. "We used to visit my cousins out in Colorado, and they would take us to these natural caverns in the mountains—"

Tom looked over his shoulder, finding that he was alone on the stairs, talking to nothing but the echoing air. He went back up and found Laura standing at the top, still studying her guidebook. "Shall we go and see, as you suggested?" asked Tom. Laura looked up at him, seeming more anxious than excited. "Oh, there you are," she said. "Are you ready to go down?"

"Ready?" said Tom. "I was already halfway down when I discovered you weren't there."

"Ok, let's have a look," said Laura, taking a little gulp of air as if she were getting ready to dive underwater. Tom went back down the stairs, which turned right, then right again, taking them back in the direction of the street. The tunnel was well-lit the whole way, but the air felt heavy and stale. When they got to the bottom, they found themselves in a bell-shaped cavern dug out of the chalky ground, about 20 feet across and 25 feet high. Looking up, Tom could see cloudy sky through a ventilation grate, with people's shoes walking by on the street above them. All the way around the cave, just at eye level, there were intricate carvings in the cream-colored walls, a crowded montage of people, horses, swords, hands, and hearts. It looked like a cross between a Hieronymus Bosch painting and graffiti he had seen in those caves back in Colorado.

Tom turned to Laura, who seemed both disappointed and apprehensive. "Anything here look familiar?" he asked. Laura glanced over her shoulder, up the staircase from which they had just come, then back at Tom. "No," she said flatly. "The crypt I see in my head has stonework and timber. And there's writing there, not all pictures." She looked at the walls around the cave and back down at her guidebook. Tom opened his guidebook too and began taking a closer look around the cave. There were just a few other people there. There was a gray-haired couple to his right, both leaning on walking sticks, taking a close look at one of the figures in front of them. The man said something that made the woman laugh, and she pulled his head close and kissed him on the cheek. On his other side, Tom saw an apple-faced woman in a nun's habit speaking to half a dozen children. The little boys wore blue blazers and the little girls blue-plaid skirts. The woman asked a question in a soft voice, and one of the boys yelled out, "I bet they were hiding from dinosaurs!" The nun patted the air with her hand, indicating that the boy should speak more quietly. Then she called on one of the girls, who turned to the boy and said confidently, "Dinosaurs died out in the Cretaceous period, long before humans. The people down here were Knights Templar, hiding from a greedy king." The nun smiled, and so did Tom. Why was it, he wondered, that every other British child he met seemed such a prodigy? Maybe they spent more time indoors reading, during all those rainy days, he decided.

Tom began making his way around the walls, looking at the figures etched into the chalk. There was St. Christopher, carrying the child Christ on his shoulder. Then came a crucifixion scene, with little hearts floating in the sky all around the cross. He turned to comment to Laura on the odd combination, that solemn Passion scene surrounded by valentine hearts. But there was Laura, still standing by the entrance, glancing at her guidebook, then back up at the scenes on the wall. Tom went over to her and asked, "Don't you want a closer look?" he asked. "You can't see much detail from here." Laura went to the center of the circular cave and surveyed the walls, only gazing briefly at any one image. Then she looked down at her guidebook again. "Oh, I see," she said. "The woman with the wheel is St. Katherine. And the knight with the sword must be St. George."

"It's not an eye test," said Tom. "You can go up and take a closer look if you want to."

Laura looked back towards the staircase. "I think I've seen enough," she said. "It's interesting, though. You can stay down here as long as you want to. I might just go back up for some fresh air."

Tom pointed to the grate directly above their heads. "There's fresh air right up there," he said. "I'm sure the ventilation here is fine."

As they were both looking up, Tom saw a camera appear in the grate, with a pair of stubby fingers holding it. There was a blue flash and he blinked his eyes a second, waiting for the momentary blindness to subside. "I wonder if that guy is too cheap to pay for a ticket," Tom said. But turning to look, he discovered that Laura had disappeared again. No one else was in the cave but the older couple and the teacher with her pupils. He headed back up the stairs and found Laura outside, still catching her breath from her sprint up the stairs and out of the cave.

"Are you all right?" asked Tom.

"Sure, I'm fine," said Laura between breaths. "I wanted to see who took our picture."

"And did you?" Tom asked.

"No," said Laura. "He really hustled off after he took that shot. All I saw was a pair of bushy eyebrows peering at me over the camera lens."

"I saw some stubby fingers," said Tom. "But what difference does it make?"

"Why do you suppose someone wanted our picture?" asked Laura.

"I don't know why it matters," said Tom. "Maybe he just wanted a picture of a p—" Tom started to say "a pretty face," but he thought better of it and revised his words mid-sentence. "A person, to show the scale of the cave."

"But you can't even see the images on the walls from that angle," said Laura.

"Who knows why people take pictures of anything?" asked Tom. "I saw a guy in Oxford the other day taking a picture of a postcard of Christ Church College. Apparently he liked the weather in the postcard better than the weather in real life."

Laura was still looking out towards the street, as if hoping to catch a glimpse of their phantom photographer.

"Let's go back down and have a better look around," said Tom.

"If you wouldn't mind, I'd rather not," said Laura with a slight shake of her head.

"I'm sorry it wasn't the crypt you are looking for."

"It isn't that really," explained Laura. "It just seemed so smothery down there. I guess I have a touch of claustrophobia."

"That doesn't make sense," said Tom. "You could see the open air above our heads. And the exit was right there in plain sight."

"Of course, it doesn't make sense," said Laura. "That's why it's called a phobia—an irrational fear."

"Laura Hartman. Phobic," intoned Tom. "Sounds like a case for Dr. Freud."

"And I don't like it when people make fun either," said Laura, wiping a bead of sweat from her brow. "I just felt like a bug in a bottle the whole time we were down there. So when that flash bulb went off, I got spooked and decided it was time to get out of there."

Tom felt he'd seen enough of the cave, so he didn't press the issue of going back down. "I think we've seen enough," he said. "As you say, the place must have had thousands of visitors in the past several centuries. Not the best place to make any new discoveries." Tom suggested they go over to the Royston Library to see what more they could find out about the Templars. "It's too fine a day to waste underground," he said. "Besides, I'd like to chase down that fellow who took our picture," he added. Laura was just about to nod in agreement, perhaps even to smile, until Tom explained, "I think I may have been blinking last time."

## ← 5 →

*Near Hitchin, between Oxford and Royston*
*The second week of May*

The next day Tom and Laura were on a cream-colored bus again, heading back in the direction of Oxford. As Laura had suggested, they got off the bus at Hitchin, stowed their luggage in a locker at the station, and took a taxi down to Temple Despy. When they got out of the cab, though, there was no ruin in sight. There was only a pasture on one side of the road and a tall redbrick wall on the other, with iron spikes on top to discourage intruders. They walked along the wall a few dozen yards until they finally came to an elegantly wrought iron gate, with a painted family crest adorning the arch over the driveway. Peering inside, Tom saw a maze of lawns, gardens, staircases, and fountains. Further back was a redbrick mansion, with arched windows and tall chimneys, a row of dormer windows along the roof and two towering gables on either side. The building looked to Tom like one of the Oxford colleges, not like someone's private residence.

"Do you suppose it's all right to go in?" asked Tom.

The two wrought iron gates stood wide open. Laura pointed to a stainless-steel chain hanging from one gate, with an open padlock on one end. "Mr. Mirden said they would be expecting us," answered Laura, pointing to the open padlock. "I suppose this is the English-style welcome mat."

She took a few tentative steps past the gate, pausing as if waiting to hear an alarm or the barking of dogs. But nothing happened so Tom followed her in. They walked down the driveway past immaculate lawns, bright lilies floating in dark water, and little arbors covered with yellow laburnum and purple wisteria. "I feel like Dorothy in The Wizard of Oz," said Laura.

"And I feel like the cowardly lion," whispered Tom, turning his head left and right.

They finally reached the manor house, its pillared porch adorned with climbing roses in full bloom. There was a great brass knocker shaped like a boar's head, but apparently it was just for show. At one side of the massive oak door was a little white button and a printed sign that said, "Please use door-bell." Tom pushed the button and soon the door was opened by a young man of about thirty with pale skin and wispy brown hair. He was wearing a plaid sweater vest and a bow tie, but his serious demeanor did not match his sportive attire. "Yes, what is it?" he asked.

"Hello, I'm Tom McCord and this is my assistant, Laura Hartman. I'm researching a book, and we were told that Mr. William De Lott might be willing to speak with us a few minutes."

"His name is *Willem* De Lott," said the young man curtly. "He's from the Netherlands. I'm his assistant, Lionel Mirden."

"Mr. Mirden, we spoke on the phone," said Laura.

Mirden turned to Laura and smiled. "Oh, yes. You're the Americans who were going over to Royston," he said. "Why don't you step inside?"

Mirden led them into the front hall and then softly padded away. Tom and Laura looked around them at the oak-paneled walls, the crystal chandelier over their heads, the tables on both sides of the entryway covered with exotic objets d'art from all over the world—jade elephants, marble busts, alabaster vases full of flowers, and a silver chalice that could have passed for the holy grail itself.

"Impressive," whispered Tom softly, almost as if he were in church.

"Lavish at any rate," said Laura in a normal speaking voice.

Mr. Mirden came treading softly back, saying, "Mr. De Lott will receive you now." Tom and Laura gave him their coats and followed him down the hall and to the left. They came into a room that looked like a library, lined with books from floor to ceiling, though the space was larger than most drawing rooms. Sitting at a mahogany desk in front of the fire was an elegant-looking man of about forty, with blond hair combed straight back, wearing a field-gray, three-piece suit with a flamboyant silk tie of scarlet and amber. "Greetings," he said rising from his chair, "I'm Willem De Lott. And you must be our friends from America, Mr. McCord and Miss Hartman." He shook Tom's hand and made a graceful bow towards Laura. "Would you like to have a seat?" he asked, gesturing toward two leather armchairs near the fire and sitting back down at his desk.

"Tell me then. What brings you two out to our untrodden ways?" he asked. "We don't get too many visitors this far off the main road."

"Mr. McCord is writing a book on Arthurian sites," said Mirden, "Miss Hartman says he's traveling all over England—"

"Thank you, Lionel," said De Lott with a tight smile. "Actually, I was speaking to them."

Tom looked at De Lott, then at Lionel, then at Laura, and realized they were all waiting for him to speak. "Yes, that is right," he said. "I'm writing a guidebook, mainly for tourists, about all the sites associated with legend and romance."

"I'm a bit of a relic hunter myself," said De Lott. "So tell what it is your digging for?"

"You already know all the stories about the Templars and their relics," answered Tom. "Actually, I'm more interested in King Arthur, the historical figure, not the legendary one."

Mr. De Lott made a little sighing sound. Tom couldn't decide if he was disappointed or relieved. "I have something you might be interested in," said the Dutchman, rising and walking over to a glass case with a curtained canopy, almost like a shrine. Tom and Laura followed De Lott and glanced down to see an ancient book beneath beveled glass, the opened pages showing bold black quill strokes in Latin.

"You know Nennius?" asked De Lott. "*Historia Brittonum?*"

"Of course," said Tom, "the ninth-century codex that first mentions Arthur. I was just looking at the text in the British Museum a few weeks ago. Harleian 3859, I believe it is called."

"That's correct," said De Lott. "The British Museum has a fine early text of the *Historia*. As do Oxford and Cambridge. As do I." De Lott made a sweep of the hand toward his prized possession, like an impresario introducing an amazing new performer. "Can you guess why the book is opened to this page?" asked De Lott.

Tom stepped forward and peered at the script through the glass. He felt that this was some kind of entrance exam, but he was not sure what sort of school he was being invited to join. "Carolingian script, I guess," said Tom, trying to buy some time. Then he spotted the word that looked like *artur* at the bottom of the page, and the phrase *bellum in monte badonis* in the preceding line. "This is the page about Arthur's twelve battles with the Saxons," said Tom calmly, as if he'd been glancing at a newspaper. "Ending with his victory at Mount Badon."

"Very good," said De Lott. "And where do you suppose that is?"

"I know there are quite a few candidates," answered Tom. "To be honest, I haven't investigated those sites yet."

The three of them returned to their seats, while Mirden remained standing near the door.

"I'm not sure it really matters where Badon is," said De Lott, with a casual wave of the hand. "Wherever it is, I doubt if you'd find much there but some broken skulls and rusty bits of iron."

"Yes, but that would be evidence," answered Tom. "Wouldn't you like to be known as the man who proved, once and for all time, that there really was an Arthur and that you found the site of his most decisive battle?"

"That kind of research costs money," said De Lott, reaching out for a poker to stir the logs in the fireplace. "I'm more interested in making money than spending it."

Tom looked into the fire too. "Making money," he mused. "It's an odd phrase. Nobody really makes money, unless you're the government—or a forger. All you can do is accumulate money. I'd rather make history."

"Spoken like an affluent American," said De Lott, jabbing a log in the fire till it gave off a shower of sparks.

Tom was surprised at his host's bluntness, but he acknowledged the point.

"That's probably true," he said. "My grandfather made plenty of money in banking at the turn of the century. Then my father made even more money during the Depression, when everybody else was losing theirs. I can't think of anything less interesting than trying to make even *more* money. 'The world is too much with us, getting and spending,' says the poet."

"That's where you and I differ," said De Lott. "I started with nothing. Everything you see around you here, I earned all this by the sweat of my own brow." Tom looked over at Laura, who was gazing out the window at the rose garden. He couldn't quite visualize De Lott sweating much, and he knew that farmers and miners didn't end up with manor houses the size of luxury hotels.

"What sort of business are you in?" asked Tom, "if you don't mind my asking."

"No, I don't mind," said Mr. De Lott. "I'm proud of what I've accomplished. I'm originally from the Netherlands, you know. I started out as an engineer, working on the dykes. Then I moved into manufacturing and capital investments. I liquidated all my assets in Holland back in 1938, when Germany annexed Austria. I could sense trouble brewing, and thought I'd be better off over here. If things get any worse across the Channel, I might have to move again and join you all in America."

"I assumed you were a collector," said Tom.

"Oh, no," laughed De Lott, "all this is just a hobby of mine. In fact, I purchased this very property for antiquarian reasons, not investment reasons."

"And what would those be?" asked Tom.

"Probably the same reasons you're paying me a visit today," said De Lott with a sly grin.

"Temple Despy?" said Tom.

"Very good!" said De Lott. "You are a quick study! And what else can you tell me?"

"Nothing you don't already know," answered Tom. "The three Knights Templar arrested by the king. They never did let on where their treasure was hidden."

"Don't think I haven't looked for it!" De Lott exclaimed. "The old Templar preceptory was right where this building stands now. I've made probes everywhere I can think of, all around the foundations."

"Maybe my assistant here can help you," said Tom.

De Lott looked over at Laura, almost as if he'd forgotten she was there. "You know something about archeology?" he asked.

Laura just shook her head, first at De Lott and then at Tom.

"No, but she has uncanny dreams. Almost as if she's seeing secret realities in her sleep."

"Is that so?" said De Lott, leaning forward and peering into Laura's face.

"Not really," said Laura, looking down at her hands in her lap. "Mr. McCord here has a penchant for tall tales."

"Tall tales?" said Tom with surprise. "Why just last week she was describing a dream of hers. A Roman commander being executed on a battlefield for refusing to kill a prisoner. An acquaintance of ours, a knowledgeable scholar, said her dream sounded like the martyrdom of St Maurice."

"Really, Tom," said Laura. "This is just a private interest of mine. Please don't bore our host any further."

Tom could tell it was time to drop the subject, but he didn't like playing the fool. "Isn't that why you wanted to come out to Royston Cave?" he asked. "To see if it matched your vision of an underground crypt?"

Laura got up and walked over to the window, letting the sunshine outside warm her face. "Can we just drop this please?" she pleaded.

De Lott got up and joined Laura at the window. "Please don't be upset on my account," he said. "I'm a student of dreams myself. I'd like to hear more."

"Really, I'd prefer not to talk about it," said Laura, her voice quavering a little.

"Since you seem to admire my gardens, perhaps you'd like a stroll around the grounds?"

Laura nodded that she would. Mr. Mirden hurried over and opened the French doors leading to the gardens in back. De

Lott gestured for Laura to go first, then waved Tom through, following them outside. Mirden went last, keeping a few steps behind the rest of the group.

Laura began to step over to the right, where there was a brick pergola with overhanging vines of luminescent purple. But De Lott gently took her elbow and steered her to the left, toward a stone staircase leading up to formal gardens enclosed by a square green hedge. "I hope you like roses," said Mr. De Lott, pointing to rows and rows of the fragrant flowers, red and pink and yellow and white, some with small delicate blossoms, almost like primroses, others large and showy, more like posies.

"Yes, it's beautiful!" said Laura, her mood seeming to improve with every step they took away from the house. They strolled to the end of the rose beds and came to a broad lawn with rows of lilies along both sides. There was a mound of dirt about ten feet high in the middle of the lawn and a gaping hole where the grass had once been.

De Lott turned to Tom, who been walking behind them. "Mr. McCord, you should have a look at this."

Tom came up and looked into the hole, but he didn't see much except a square-cornered excavation with a pile of dirt nearby. "Problems with your septic tank?" asked Tom.

"Hardly!" said De Lott, with a laugh. "This is my latest project. I told you I'd probed everywhere under the house for Temple Despy. We found a line of stones out here in the garden. We think there must have been some outbuildings here a long time ago."

"Find anything?" asked Tom.

"Not yet," said De Lott. "We did find some dressed stone and a few pottery shards. Nothing more on this spot."

Mr. Mirden stepped forward and began explaining further. "One of the stones looked like it had a hole in it, like a cornerstone for an upright post. But which corner, we wonder? Did the building go off that direction—"

"Yes, yes," said De Lott. "We're not sure where to go next." The Dutchman looked around him for Laura, who had wandered off a few paces to admire the lilies. "Miss Hartman, I wonder if we might have your opinion?" Laura came over and joined the others, looking blankly down into the hole.

"We were just talking about Temple Despy," explained De Lott. "We're not sure where to go from here. Do you have any opinion?"

"Dig for victory," said Laura, still without much interest.

"Yes, but which direction?" asked De Lott.

Laura walked around the square hole, kneeling down once for a closer look, then rejoined the others. "I'd dig in that direction," she said firmly, pointing south.

"Interesting," said De Lott. "And why would you suggest that?"

"Because there's only more lawn to the south. Dig in any other direction and you'll disturb these beautiful flowers," she explained.

De Lott looked distinctly annoyed and Tom decided maybe it was time to go. "Mr. De Lott, it has been a pleasure to meet you. But I wouldn't want to take up any more of your time."

"Oh, it's no trouble," said the Dutchman, recovering his poise. "I hope you'll take a glass of sherry before you go." Tom looked at Laura, who gave a little shake of her head. "Perhaps I can help you with your own research," he added. Avoiding Laura's gaze, Tom answered, "Yes, I'd love a glass of sherry. Thank you very much."

The four of them walked back to De Lott's study, Mr. Mirden following the others again by a few steps. They resumed their chairs by the fire, which had died down to embers. Mr. Mirden disappeared briefly, then returned carrying a silver salver with three crystal glasses and a decanter of sherry. He poured a glass for each of them, then set the tray on a side table and stood by the door.

"So you hope to make a name for yourself," said De Lott, sniffing at his sherry and then taking a drink. "And how do you propose to do that?"

"I can't really say," answered Tom. He took a sip of sherry, which tasted to him like furniture polish and burned his throat. But he smiled appreciatively and continued. "There have been so many important discoveries over here the past few years. First they found that new manuscript of Malory's *Morte D'Arthur* down at Winchester. Then they uncovered Tristran's grave in Cornwall. Then the Saxon burial ship in Sutton Hoo. I just feel the time is ripe for another great find."

Mr. De Lott smiled indulgently, with just a hint of condescension in his eyes. "If you want to make a name for yourself, you should go over to Wales and recover the sword Excalibur."

"You're not serious!" said Tom, his eyes widening.

"Quite serious," answered De Lott. "Some people think that Arthur was no king at all, but only a daring mercenary hired by a Welsh chieftain to ward off the Saxons. When he died—as we all must—they might well have thrown his sword into a mountain pool over there someplace. Those old Celts used to do that, throw the swords of dead warriors into the water, a votive offering to the gods. Maybe the story of Sir Bedivere throwing Excalibur into a lake has some truth to it."

"I don't know," said Tom, pulling on one ear. "I think of Arthur as Romanized, a Christian commander, not a pagan mercenary. And where would you even begin to look? There are dozens of lakes and pools to choose from?"

"You just start looking," answered De Lott sternly. "Dredge. Drain. Dive. We have the technology now. You should see the miracles we perform moving water around in the Netherlands."

Tom still looked doubtful, so De Lott changed tack, moving from speculation to persuasion: "Did you know they found pewter ingots in the Thames from the Roman era stamped with the Christian symbol *chi rho*? If you can still read the markings on pewter from before Arthur's time, I don't know why you couldn't find a steel sword etched with his name. Start in the old mountain kingdom of Powys."

Tom picked up his glass and then put it back down absently without taking a drink. "I don't know," he said. "You could spend your whole life mucking around in freezing cold water."

"Perhaps your assistant here could be of some help." Turning to Laura, he asked, "Do you have any ideas, Miss Hartman? Ever have any visions of a gleaming sword buried in the mud?"

Laura had set down her glass on a side table, after just the smallest sip. She reached for the glass but didn't pick it up, just rubbed its stem as if trying to remove a smudge. She looked up at De Lott and simply shook her head.

"She does have a dream of a Celtic cross, tall and round like a lamp-post," said Tom. "I wonder if that could be somewhere in Wales." Laura glared at Tom, but he pretended not to notice. "Really, Laura, maybe Mr. De Lott could help you with this. Do you see any lakes in the scene with the Celtic cross?"

Laura shook her head. "It's in a churchyard," she said dully, "right in front of the church."

"What color is it?" asked Mr. Mirden, seeming to forget his place by the door and coming to stand in the center of the room.

"Reddish," said Laura, "Like the Pennsylvania plumstone we have back home."

"Interesting," said Mirden. "There are only a few Celtic crosses of red sandstone. Dupplin Cross up in Scotland. But it's only about six feet tall. Could be Gosforth, one of the tallest of the high crosses. Up in the Lake District."

"Dupplin. Gosforth. Or Monasterboice. Or Kildalton," said De Lott sardonically. "There are Celtic high crosses all over Scotland and Ireland."

"Yes, but they're nearly all square, not round. Gosforth is just about the only red sandstone cross—"

"Really, Lionel," interrupted De Lott, "Haven't you heard the expression, 'A little learning is a dangerous thing'? I've seen Celtic high crosses everywhere from the Inner Hebrides to Brittany."

Mirden started to answer, but De Lott continued: "Lionel, why don't you go find a glass and pour yourself some sherry?"

Mirden pressed his lips together, gave a slight bow, and left the room.

"Please excuse my assistant. Sometimes I think he spends too much time with his nose in his books and not enough time around people. Quite a knowledgeable fellow, of course. But he can get an *idée fixe* and won't let go of it. Really, I'd hate to have my poor pedantic friend send you off on a 'wild Gosforth chase.'" De Lott laughed at his own joke and poured himself another glass of sherry. He carried the decanter over to Tom and Laura, but they both shook their head no.

Sitting back down, the Dutchman leaned back in his chair, stretching his feet toward the fire. "Now, Miss Hartman, I'd like to hear some more about these dreams of yours. Maybe there's another one I can help you with."

Laura looked in Mr. De Lott's direction, but not into his face. "Oh, just a few others," she said. "A reclining king. A country church."

"A reclining king. A country church," De Lott repeated. "That's a bit vague, isn't it? Could be just about anywhere in England. Anywhere in the world for that matter."

"Yes, it really is vague," agreed Laura. "That's why I wish Tom wouldn't bring it up." Tom had become fascinated by the fire again and didn't seem to have anything else to say. Finally Laura stood up and extended her hand. "Thank you so much for your time, Mr. De Lott," she said. "We have a bus to catch up in Hitchin, so we really should be going now."

De Lott and Tom both stood up as well, and Laura began walking toward the front door without waiting to be shown the way.

"Say, I have an idea," said De Lott. "Why don't I have Lionel bring the car around and we can drive you back to Hitchin? It's a Bentley Mark V. I think you'll enjoy the ride."

Tom smiled and started to say something, but Laura spoke first: "Oh, that is such a kind offer, Mr. De Lott. But we really couldn't impose. Besides, we want to walk down and see Preston. I've heard it's such a lovely little village. We can catch a cab from there."

"As you wish," said Mr. De Lott with a graceful bow. Mr. Mirden appeared from somewhere, gave Tom and Laura their coats and opened the front door for them. After they shook hands and said their goodbyes, Tom had to walk fast to keep up with Laura, who was headed back down the driveway with a lively step. She seemed miffed about something, and Tom wasn't sure if he should say anything or wait for her to talk.

"Who says Preston is a lovely little village? I've never heard of it before."

"All these little English villages are lovely," said Laura, looking straight ahead. "The ones that don't have a factory or an aerodrome nearby."

"What's wrong with a ride in a Bentley Mark V?" Tom asked. "I could have saved cab fare."

"Oh, Tom, how could you?" said Laura, still walking stiffly and briskly, with her arms swinging.

Tom decided that his first idea of letting Laura talk first was the better one. "How could I do what?" he asked.

Still walking at parade-march pace, Laura looked over at Tom with an expression somewhere between disgust and disappointment. "How could you talk about my dreams like that? Especially to someone like him. Don't you know that's private? Now I wish I had sent you away last week at the King's Arms."

Tom sped up and walked backwards in front of Laura, so he could look into her face. "That's just it," he tried to explain. "Mr. Williams was so helpful explaining your dream about Maurice. I remember how delighted you were. I was thinking maybe this guy De Lott could be helpful too."

"So that was your idea of help?" said Laura, finally slowing down her pace. They had reached the end of the driveway and she turned right toward the little village of Preston. "Really, Tom, you can't tell the difference between Mr. Williams and Mr. De Lott?"

The two of them continued walking down the lane. There were little stone farmhouses and timbered cottages on both sides of the road, and every front yard seemed to have a flower garden more impeccably arranged than the last one. The sun was still shining, making it hard for someone who was trying to sustain a bad mood. Tom did sense a difference between the two older men, but he didn't say anything. He thought if he waited a moment, Laura would articulate it better than he could.

"Mr. Williams was trying to help," said Laura, fulfilling Tom's expectation. "He had only my interests in mind. Mr. De Lott's questions were more like an interrogation. He has no one's interest in mind but his own." Laura paused to let this sink in, and then added: "I thought it was infuriating how he treated poor Mr. Mirden."

"Well," said Tom, "I think they have sharper class distinctions over here."

"He's supposed to be his assistant, not his butler!" said Laura.

"That's a good point," said Tom, as they walked the lane more slowly. "How come you never bring me a glass of sherry?"

Laura looked over at Tom with a stony glare, and he made a mental note not to try humor the next time she was angry with him.

"I thought that was interesting advice about looking for Excalibur," said Tom, not quite sure why he was defending someone he didn't find too likeable either.

"Why is it," asked Laura, "that De Lott doesn't mind the idea of you dredging every lake in Wales, but he wants to save you the terrible trouble of riding a train up to Gosforth?"

"Yes, I'll admit that was odd," said Tom. "He wouldn't let poor Lionel get a word in edgewise. The more he kept telling us what a waste of time it would be, the more I felt like making a visit up there."

Laura looked at Tom and smiled for the first time since they had left De Lott's estate. "That's exactly what I was thinking!" she said.

"Maybe for our next field trip, we should go on a 'wild Gosforth chase.'"

Laura smiled wider. "I quite agree," she said. "But for now," she added, "Let's have a look around Preston. I hear it's a lovely little village." She quickened her pace again, and Tom had to lengthen his strides to keep up.

## ← 6 →

On a chilly May morning, Tom rode a motorcycle along a narrow road in Windermere, with a sapphire blue lake on his left and a line of gray slate cottages on his right. He was looking for the Blamore Guest House, where he had agreed to meet Laura after breakfast. He finally found the address he was looking for and parked on the grass in front of the house.

Tom climbed a dozen steep steps to the front porch and knocked on the door. It was opened by a rotund lady with rosy cheeks and tightly curled hair mostly hidden under a bright red headscarf. "Hello," he said. "I'm Tom McCord. Is Miss Laura Hartman here?"

"Yes, she is," replied the lady, taking Tom by the elbow. "We're just finishing breakfast. Would you fancy a cup of tea?"

Tom would have actually preferred to pick up Laura and get on the road, but he could tell by the pincer grip on his arm that he would not be leaving until he had finished a least one cup of tea. "That would be nice," he answered.

"I'm Mrs. Morgan," said the proprietor of the guest house. "Why don't you hang up your jacket and join us in the breakfast room?" Tom felt the leather jacket being pulled off his shoulders, so he held his arms back and let Mrs. Morgan slide it off. He followed her into a brightly lit breakfast nook, where

Laura was finishing some cereal and sipping a cup of tea. She was wearing slacks and a sweater, and her face was tanner than when he'd seen her last.

"Is this the young man you were expecting?" said Mrs. Morgan cheerfully.

Laura nodded, wiping her mouth with a napkin. "I see you've met Mrs. Morgan."

Tom saw a hefty arm pulling a chair away from the table and felt a downward pressure on his shoulder. "Yes indeed," he said, as he plopped down into his seat. "She invited me to join you for a cup of tea." He looked up and smiled at Mrs. Morgan, who disappeared into the kitchen.

"How have you been doing up here?" asked Tom.

Instead of answering right away, Laura leaned forward and whispered, "Don't ask for sugar. She's running short because of the rationing." Then she continued in a louder voice, "Oh, I've been having a wonderful time. I've always wanted to visit the Lake District, ever since I first read Wordsworth in college. So I've been to Dove Cottage, where he wrote all those lovely poems, and I've been walking all around the lakes, among the craggy rocks and daffodils."

Mrs. Morgan came in with a little pot of tea and set it down beside Tom. "Do you take sugar?" she asked.

"No thanks," said Tom, pouring himself a cup. Mrs. Morgan set down a plate with two triangles of toast and a jar of orange marmalade.

"I heard you talking about Wordsworth. I've always loved *Lady Windermere's Fan.*"

"Actually, that's Oscar Wilde. Wordsworth is the poet," said Tom.

"Oh, of course he is!" said Mrs. Morgan. "We read him in school way back when. 'I wandered lonely as a clown. . . .'"

Tom choked mid-swallow on a piece of toast. 'Wandered lonely as a *cloud*,' he thought to himself. He looked over at Laura with a smirk, but she deliberately avoided his gaze and her expression didn't change. "My favorite is 'The Solitary Reaper,'" said Laura. "'The music in my heart I bore, Long after it was heard no more.'"

Mrs. Morgan stopped to enjoy that line, almost as if hearing the music herself. Then she turned to Tom. "Laura says you're writing a book," said Mrs. Morgan, "Something about Mr. Wordsworth, I suppose?"

"No, actually it's on King Arthur," explained Tom, taking a sip of tea. "Laura is helping me. We're headed over to Gosforth today."

"Gosforth?" said Mrs. Morgan with a puzzled look. "Don't see what that has to do with Arthur."

"We're going to have a look at Gosforth Cross," explained Tom.

Mrs. Morgan gave a little shake of her head. "Don't fancy that cross much. Left here by the Vikings, you know. And it's got 'gravings of snakes on the sides."

"Really?" said Tom. "I didn't know that. Snakes on the side of a churchyard cross."

"I don't know what's wrong with a proper English cross," said Mrs. Morgan. "Gosforth is clear on the other side of the mountains. I'm surprised you'd make the trip."

Tom looked over at Laura, to see if she was going to say anything about her dreams. But she simply said, "We heard some people down south talking about it, and we wanted to have a look for ourselves."

"Speaking of which," said Tom, "we ought to get on the road, if we want to get back before dark." With a quick gulp, he finished his cup of tea and rose from the table. "Thank you so much for the tea," he told Mrs. Morgan. Turning to Laura, he asked, "You've got a warm coat, I take it?"

Laura looked a bit perplexed. "Yes," she said, "but I was thinking of just a sweater. Sometimes they turn up the heat too high on those buses."

"We're not taking the bus," said Tom.

"But the branch railway ends here in Windermere," explained Laura.

"Yes, I know," said Tom. "Come have a look."

Tom thanked Mrs. Morgan again, grabbed his jacket, and headed out the front door. Laura followed him out front and down the steps, spotting the motorcycle and its sidecar parked in front of the guest house.

"Voilà!" said Tom.

"Surely, you're joking!" said Laura, not looking pleased.

"Not at all," said Tom. "I rented it for the day from a garage just down from the train station."

"Do you even know how to drive one of these things?" said Laura.

"Sure, my cousin has one," said Tom. "I used to borrow it when we went for vacation in Colorado." He took a map out of his jacket pocket, unfolded it, and showed it to Laura. "Look," he said. "We're here at Windermere, and Gosforth is almost due west of us, near the coast." Laura looked at the wrinkled sheet of paper with a skeptical look on her face.

"I checked on the buses," explained Tom. "One makes a long northern loop, up to Keswick, over to Cockermouth near the coast, and then back down to Gosforth. The other bus goes all the way down to Oxen Park, then over to the water, then up through Bootle. Either way, a bus ride would take us nearly all day."

"And how is a motorcycle any better?" asked Laura.

Tom pointed to a little line cutting almost due west, from Windermere to Gosforth. "The shortest distance between two points is a straight line," he said.

"It doesn't look too straight to me," said Laura. "It wriggles across the map like a worm." Looking closer, Laura added, "There's a reason the bus lines go north and south. Those are the Cumbrian Mountains between here and the coast."

"Well, English mountains," said Tom. "Not much real elevation. Out West, we wouldn't call those mountains. More like mounds."

Still peering at the map and still not convinced, Laura said, "But look at the names on your route. Wrynose Pass? Hard Knott Pass? That doesn't sound good."

"Come on, Laura," insisted Tom. "Where's your sense of adventure? Think of the sunshine. The fresh air. We'll have such larks! And who cares what they name the passes?"

"I would have preferred something like Lakeview Pass or Ferny Meadow Pass," said Laura. "Maybe I should take the bus and meet you over there later," she said.

"I'll be there and back by the time you arrive," said Tom curtly.

Tom went over to the bike, opened a compartment in back of the sidecar and took out two leather caps and two sets of goggles. "Ok, here's the clincher," he said. "You get to wear these." Tom handed her the smaller cap and set of goggles and put the other ones on himself. Laura tried hers on, tucking her dark curls underneath the cap.

"You look like Amelia Earhart!" laughed Tom.

"That's really reassuring," said Laura. "Disappeared without a trace, you know."

Tom wasn't to be dissuaded, and so a few minutes later, he was riding the motorcycle up the hill, headed west, with

Laura in the sidecar, slumped down low to keep out of the wind. The engine was too loud for them to talk, but as they headed up the pass, Tom tapped Laura on the shoulder and made a sweep of his arm to point out the beautiful view. They could see green pastures down below, enclosed by blue-gray slate walls, the land rising in a graceful curve toward rocky ridges, garnished with patches of fern and yellow wildflowers. Laura nodded, but then pointed to the handlebars, indicating she would prefer that Tom steered with both hands.

They rode uphill for about an hour, mostly in lower gears, as the grade was steeper than Tom expected, and the cycle a bit underpowered to be carrying a sidecar. Finally, they reached the summit of Wrynose Pass, dipped down through a U-shaped valley and started up Hard Knott Pass. As they crossed the summit of the second pass, they came upon a startling panorama, a bowl-shaped valley strewn with rocks, stretching all the way down to the sea. There was a dark cloudbank off to the west, and Tom could see slanting curtain of rain falling down below, making the slate roofs of distant farmhouses glisten like ice. The road ahead of them was not paved, and it looked like hardly more than a piece of twine strewn carelessly among the rocky peaks and high meadows. Tom pulled his cycle over to the side and cut the engine.

Laura pulled off her goggles and sat up in the sidecar. "Now there's a view worth writing a poem about!" she said with breathless elation.

"I don't know," said Tom. "Maybe this wasn't such a good idea after all." He looked back over his shoulder and then gazed down at the road ahead of them.

"What's the matter?" asked Laura, "it looks all right to me. There's a mackintosh under the seat in here, in case you're worried about the rain," she said.

"Yeah, the guy at the garage said the weather would be 'dodgy,'" explained Tom.

"Which you took to mean what?" asked Laura.

"I guess I thought it meant I could dodge whatever rain showers came along. But this one is right across our path. I wonder if we should try and circle back."

"But don't you think we're more than halfway? It would be farther back than it would be to push on."

"I don't know," said Tom, lifting his goggles for a better look. "It doesn't look quite safe."

"Really, Tom," said Laura. "Where's your sense of adventure? I thought these were only mounds or molehills or whatever you called them."

Laura's tone was playful, but Tom still looked serious. He pulled off his cap and looked over his shoulder again. "Be honest now. Doesn't it make you feel a little bit dizzy, looking down such a steep grade? It makes you feel like you're going to pitch forward and fall off the edge of the earth."

"It doesn't make me dizzy at all," said Laura. "I think it's exhilarating." She looked at Tom's face and a little smile crept over her own. "Falling off the edge of the earth. That's not a reasoned response. Is this Tom the arch-rationalist? Tom the mountain man? Do I detect an irrational fear here?"

Tom looked at Laura, enjoying herself a bit too much, and wished he'd kept his mouth shut back at Royston Cave. He put his cap and goggles on and kicked the motorcycle engine back to life. They headed on down the pass for another twenty minutes, passing through the wall of rain that was only a drizzle once they got to it. But as they neared the bottom of the pass, coming into walled pastures again, there was a flock of about a hundred sheep walking straight up the narrow road, strolling up to higher ground. There was no one sight, just the sheep coming the other way. Tom tried to honk the horn on the motorcycle, discovering that it didn't work. The sheep now filled the whole road, passing the bike on both sides. Tom cut the engine again and came to a stop. Laura took off her cap and goggles and watched the sheep as they passed; they were just about the same height as she was in sidecar. An inquisitive ewe came up and looked Laura right in the eyes, voicing a long "Baaaah!"

"And Baaah to you too," Laura replied.

"Bah, Humbug!" said Tom. "Tell them to keep to the left. These are British sheep, and they ought to know the rules of the road."

The sheep continued to amble by at their own leisurely pace. "Say, do you want to hear a brain teaser?" said Laura, breaking the silence.

"Sure, go ahead," said Tom. "I've got time."

"Well, there was a poor shepherd who had three sons. In his will, he said he wanted to leave half the herd to the eldest son, one quarter to his second son, and one fifth to his third son."

"Ok, I'm with you so far," said Tom.

"But when the old man passed on," continued Laura, "he had exactly nineteen sheep in his herd. The three sons fell to bickering, as none of them could figure out how to divide the herd."

"Chop up a few for mutton stew," said Tom, swatting a passing sheep lightly on the rump.

"A neighboring farmer saw the three sons bickering, almost coming to blows. He knew about the terms of the will, so he brought over one of his own little lambs and donated it to the three sons. That brought the herd up to exactly twenty, so the eldest son could have one half, ten sheep, the second son one fourth, five sheep, and the third son one fifth, four sheep. That left one remaining, so the farmer gathered his own lamb back into his arms."

Tom thought about this as he watched the sheep continuing to pass by.

"My father used to tell me that one," explained Laura. "Did you get the point?"

"Um," said Tom, "I guess the point would be that you should do the math before you write out your will?"

"My dad said the point was that sometimes you have to add a little some extra to the equation to get things sorted out."

"That was going to be my second guess," said Tom. By then, the herd of sheep had passed by, and he started the motorcycle again. As they came down toward level ground, he noticed that Laura didn't put her cap and goggles back on, but just let her hair blow in the breeze. She seemed to be taking in the stone cottages and lush pastures and enjoying the faint scent of salt sea air. After a few minutes, they came back out onto paved road and headed north to Gosforth.

◁ • ▷

As they reached the edge of the village, Tom wondered if he should stop and ask directions. But suddenly he felt a tap on his shoulder and looked over at Laura, who was pointing emphatically at a village church just up the hill from the town square. He steered the bike up a side road and parked in front of the church. Not waiting for Tom to come open the door of the sidecar, Laura hopped out and hurried up to the front gate. "This is it!" she said excitedly. "This is the scene I've seen so many times in my head! Look at that Celtic cross in the churchyard. As tall as a lamppost, just like I said!"

Tom took off his cap and goggles and hurried to catch up with Laura. "I suppose there could be plenty of tall Celtic crosses in England and Ireland," he noted, "like De Lott said."

"You don't understand," said Laura. "It's the whole scene. The red sandstone cross standing right where it's supposed to be, with the same red stone used for the church behind it." Laura stepped quickly through the gate and hurried through the churchyard to the fifteen-foot-tall cross. She walked around it slowly, trying to make out its weathered carvings, occasionally tracing an image with her fingers.

Tom walked among the mossy tombstones and took a look for himself. Though the carvings were faded, he could definitely make out figures of horsemen, some upside down, as well as wolf-headed serpents and plaited designs like a basket weave. On the east face was a different kind of scene, a man with his arms outstretched with blood spurting from his side. Below him were a man with a spear and a woman holding some kind of bottle or vial.

"What do you make of it?" asked Tom. "Does anything click?" Laura didn't answer. She was looking hard at the images on each face of the cross, but she seemed to be working on some brainteaser of her own.

"Ah, I see you've come to admire our cross," came a voice from behind Tom. He turned to see a short, handsome man with glossy black hair, not much more than thirty, wearing a black frock coat and white collar.

"Admiring it, yes. And trying to understand it," said Tom.

"I'm seeing lots of wolf-headed snakes," added Laura.

"Ah, you sound like Americans," said the young cleric. Tom and Laura nodded that they were.

"I'm Father Lesaur, the rector here at St. Mary's."

Tom and Laura each introduced themselves and then turned to look at the cross again.

"We have some brochures inside that help explain the images," he said. "But perhaps you would allow me?"

"Please do," said Laura, talking a step back from the cross.

"This cross was placed here by Norsemen back in the ninth century," explained Lesaur in practiced tones. "It's been standing her for a thousand years, since before the Norman Conquest in 1066."

Tom went and unconsciously patted the cross, as if checking to see if it were still solidly planted.

"First of all, look at the overall shape," continued the rector. "It is round at the base, like a tree trunk. But as it rises, it develops four distinct faces—east, north, west, and south. It is topped off by the traditional Celtic circle around the intersection of the two beams of the cross." Tom and Laura's eyes followed Lesaur's arm as he raised it from the ground to the sky.

"This is a figure in stone of the Scandinavian mythology being replaced by the Christian myth," said Lesaur. "The base calls to mind the World Ash Tree of Nordic myth, an image of the whole cosmos. And most of the scenes you see depict the Twilight of the Gods." The rector walked slowly around the cross pointing out images of Loki, a trickster whose unbinding would bring about the end of the world. Then there was Odin, ruler of the gods, who seemed to be in desperate battle. Then Fenris, a wolf-headed serpent, swallowing the sun.

"It's a cross all right," said Laura. "But I don't remember any of those stories from Sunday school."

"Ah, but come look at the east face," said Lesaur. He pointed to the image of the man with his arms outstretched, bleeding from his side. "This one seems to portray the crucifixion. It even shows the Roman soldier piercing Christ's side and a woman, perhaps Mary his mother, waiting to anoint his body with oil."

"She has a braided ponytail," observed Tom.

"Yes," said the rector, "a distinctively Scandinavian touch. But not much different than the pictures of a milk-skinned, blue-eyed Jesus one sometimes sees in Europe."

Laura kept looking at the scene, as if searching for something long forgotten.

"Of course, some scholars argue that this isn't the crucifixion at all," continued Lesaur, smoothing back his dark hair. "They think it's another scene from Norse myth, perhaps the blind giant Hod, accidentally shooting his brother, the noble Balder, with an arrow of mistletoe."

Tom and Laura both took a closer look at the figures on the east face. "It looks more like a spear than a bow and arrow," said Laura.

"And the giant in the scene is smaller than the man who is bleeding," added Tom.

"It has been argued both ways," explained the rector. "Ultimately, I'm not sure it matters," he added with a shrug.

"Matters how?" asked Laura, to whom it did seem to matter.

"Either way, it's the dying god myth," answered the rector. "I suppose you know Frazer's *Golden Bough*?"

Tom and Laura both nodded.

"The universal story of life, death, and rebirth. Balder in Norse myth, Osiris in Egypt, Jesus in Christian myth. They're probably all personifications of the cycles of nature— vegetation that arises in the spring, flourishes in summer, fades in the autumn, and dies in winter. Then back to spring again."

This time Tom nodded but Laura didn't. "But, Father," she said, "I'm sure you'd agree the Christian account is rather more specific than that."

Lesaur took a step back from the cross and looked directly at Laura. "Yes, the specifics vary from culture to culture. But one should be careful not to make too much of them." Laura kept listening, as if waiting for more, so the rector continued:

"Birth. Life. Death," he said, pointing to the gravestones all around them. "It's the universal human experience. And everyone does the best they can to find stories that will give it all some meaning."

"But aren't some stories truer than others?" asked Laura.

Lesaur tugged at the sleeves of his coat and eyed Laura warily. "That's a big topic isn't it? I think the important thing is to cherish stories that kindle the divine spark within us, to help it blaze up into good will towards men."

"I don't recall that one from the Prayer Book," said Laura, looking away from the rector and back at the tall cross.

"Ah yes, the Prayer Book," said the rector soothingly. "People want to hear the old familiar words. It's reassuring to people in times of trial—times like these with our young men going off to war."

Laura got ready to answer, but Tom decided to cut in: "Excuse me, Father, but we can't stay too long. Do you mind if we have a look around the church and grounds?"

"No, not at all," answered the young rector. "You are very welcome. There are fragments of stone inside with some Norse markings on them. And some literature on the cross here, available for a small donation."

"Does this church have a crypt?" Tom asked. Both Laura and the rector seemed surprised at the question.

"No. No, it doesn't," answered the rector. "This is just a simple parish church."

"Any reason you would bring animals in and out of the church?" asked Tom.

Laura glared at Tom and shook her head no. The rector looked more baffled than ever. "We have a ceremony, the Blessing of the Animals, in October. But that takes place outdoors, not inside the sanctuary."

"Thank you. You've been very helpful," said Tom. "I'll think maybe we'll just take a quick look around."

Lesaur made a graceful bow and headed toward the front gate. Tom and Laura walked all around the church grounds, and then made a brief stop inside, but they didn't find anything else to detain them. Tom glanced at his watch, and said, "Anything else you want to see here? We should probably be heading back."

Laura shook her head and began walking toward the motorcycle. She seemed pensive, almost despondent, a complete change of mood from when she had first spotted the church and its enigmatic cross.

"I had a few more things I wanted to say to Mr. Lesaur," she said between tightened lips.

"I noticed," said Tom. "But I suppose everyone has a right to his opinion."

"Everyone, perhaps, but not every minister."

"I'm not sure I follow," said Tom, as he literally followed Laura back towards the motorcycle.

"When you accept a call," Laura explained, "when you agree to lead a flock, you agree to uphold certain beliefs. You don't want to be a wolf in shepherd's clothing."

"He sounds pretty well-educated to me," answered Tom. "Probably an Oxford or Cambridge man. He's studied the Enlightenment, Higher Criticism, all that. I guess he's just trying to make sense of the old beliefs in the light of modern science."

"Well, that's fine," said Laura, standing by the sidecar. "But he if can't affirm historic creeds, he should have the courage of his non-convictions and get into some other line of work."

"He seemed like a nice guy to me," said Tom, putting on his leather cap, "explaining the cross and all."

"I'm sure he's a nice enough guy," answered Laura. "It's a question of spiritual integrity. I think the serpent in this church might be the one wearing a collar."

Tom realized this was one argument he wasn't going to win, so he changed the subject. "So I guess you've had enough of mountain passes for one day. So you want to try the northern loop or the southern loop to get back to Windermere?"

The change of topic seemed to brighten Laura's spirits. "You want me to choose between places with names like Cockermouth and Bootle? Whatever happened to 'the shortest distance between two points'?"

"I thought we decided that route was too rugged."

"I loved it!" said Laura. "Besides, I'd like to get back before dark."

"It stays light out till pretty late this time of year," said Tom, "especially this far north." He was fiddling with his goggles as he spoke, as if he couldn't get them adjusted right.

"Why, Tom McCord," said Laura, with a little laugh. "If I didn't know better, I'd say these little English mountains have dimmed the divine spark within you."

Tom was glad to see Laura cheering up, but he wasn't too happy with the topic that was bringing back her sense of fun.

"By all means, let's go home the way we came," said Laura. "Full speed ahead for Hard Knocks Pass and Nosebleed Pass, or whatever they were called."

Tom still looked like he hadn't made up his mind, so Laura added the coup de grace: "I'll tell you what, Tom. If you'll show me how to drive this thing, I'll take over the bike and you can have the sidecar."

Feeling he was in danger of losing a second argument in less than an hour, Tom put on his cap and goggles and started up the engine. After a half hour on the road, they stopped for a pub lunch as they waited out a brief rain squall. Then they headed back the same way they came, this time with no delays and fewer apprehensions on Tom's part. He found that going up a steep hill was less intimidating than going down, and he already knew that the slope was gentler on the eastern side of the pass.

◁ • ▷

There was still plenty of light as they drove up to the Blamore Guest House, and Tom parked in the same grassy spot he had used that morning. When he climbed off the bike, Laura was already out of the sidecar looking up at the guest house. "That's odd," she said, "the window to my room is open." She pointed up to the left side of the house, which you could see from the road. The window farthest back was open, with lace curtains rustling in the breeze.

The two of them walked up the stairs and over to that side of the house. "That window," explained Laura, "the one with the rose bushes under it. That's my room, right behind the breakfast nook." Tom agreed that this was odd, as it was obvious from the wet grass and pavement that it had rained there in the last hour or so.

Laura went up to the front door, but it was bolted. She knocked and soon Mrs. Morgan appeared, wearing an apron and wiping her hands on a towel. "I'm sorry, dear," she said. "I didn't expect you all back so soon. I've got soup on the stove."

"We took a shortcut," said Laura. "Say, did you open the window in my room?" she asked.

"Why, no," said Mrs. Morgan. "I don't go into my guests' rooms unless they ask me to."

"We could see from outside that it's open," explained Laura.

Mrs. Morgan left the front door open and headed down the hall toward Laura's room. Tom and Laura wiped their feet and followed her past the breakfast room to the back bedroom. It was simple room, a single bed, a wardrobe, a small writing desk, and a washbasin in the corner. Tom looked at the checkered carpet, the flowery wallpaper, and the pinstriped green comforter. He wondered how the English could work such miracles of beauty in their buildings and flower gardens but couldn't seem to find any two items that matched in their guest rooms.

Mrs. Morgan went over and pulled the curtains inside and shut the window. "It's open all right," she said somewhat crossly. "I'm just glad the wallpaper and the carpet didn't get wet."

"I'm sure I didn't leave it open," said Laura. "It was anything but stuffy in here this morning." She went over and glanced out the window, and something else caught her attention. "Mrs. Morgan, what about those rose bushes?"

Mrs. Morgan and Tom both went to look out the window. "Look at the roses," said Laura. "This morning when I looked out, they were just perfect. But now half the petals are on the ground and one whole blossom is broken off."

The other two looked out and could see this was true, but they weren't sure what to make of it. Tom looked for footprints on the grass but couldn't see any. "I suppose the wind and rain could have done that," said Mrs. Morgan, still smoothing out the curtains.

"Or some animal scratching around in the flowerbed," conjectured Tom.

Laura didn't look convinced. She opened the door of the wardrobe and checked the clothes inside, then glanced at the writing desk and the washbasin. Finally, she went over to her suitcase, flipped the lid up, and let out a little gasp.

"What's the matter?" said Tom. "Is something missing?" Laura picked up a leather-bound diary on top, unhooked its brass clasp, and flipped through the pages, locating a ten-pound note tucked inside the back cover. Then she poked through several layers of clothes, pulled out a small jewelry case and checked inside.

"Everything's here," she said. "But it's not in the same place I left it."

"What do you mean?" asked Tom.

"The diary," said Laura, "It was right on top of all my clothes. I always keep it on the bottom."

Mrs. Morgan let out a little sigh, either of relief or perhaps annoyance. "So everything is there, then? Just not where you remember leaving it?" she asked.

"I never leave the diary on top," said Laura, turning to face the other two. "It's private. It just feels safer and more snug down on the bottom."

Mrs. Morgan and Tom gave each other a quick glance, as if each was hoping the other would say something. Laura spoke up instead. "Mrs. Morgan, is there some reason you needed to come into my room? Maybe straighten things up a bit? Toss some extra water out the window?"

Mrs. Morgan put her hands on her hips and answered in a lower voice: "No, young lady, I already told you I don't come into my guest's rooms unless I'm asked. I don't think I like what you're insinuating—"

"I don't mean to offend," said Laura. "Perhaps you have another guest in the house, one of the upstairs rooms?"

Mrs. Morgan shook her head. "No one is booked till this weekend. No one here now but you. It's been a slow summer, what with the war on and the petrol rationing."

"I just feel someone has been in this room," Laura insisted, going to look out the window again. "I know I didn't leave the window open, and I didn't leave the diary lying on top of my other things."

Mrs. Morgan smoothed her apron firmly with her hands. "Now see here, I run a respectable house in a good neighborhood. And I don't appreciate anyone doubting my word. So there's an end to it, and I've got to go see if my soup has boiled over." She turned and marched out the room.

"What do you think, Tom? Should I go down and talk to the police?"

"I don't think so," said Tom. "Mrs. Morgan is already pretty worked up. I think she'd be mortified if some policeman came nosing around here asking questions. Besides, what sort of charges would there be? Felonious luggage re-arranging? Wanton destruction of rose petals?"

"Oh, Tom," said Laura, pacing up and down the room. "Can't you see how upsetting this is? If you can't be serious, at least be a little bit supportive."

"What do you want me to say?" said Tom.

Laura stopped pacing and looked straight into Tom's face with searching eyes. "How about saying you believe me?" she said.

"Well," Tom stammered, "I—I believe you're upset. I believe you think someone has been in your room."

Now it was Laura's turn to put her hands on her hips. "Is that the best you can do?" she asked.

Tom thought some more and then tried again: "I believe in your character, your common sense. I don't think you're flighty at all, nor that you would jump to conclusions."

"Thanks for that much," said Laura, crossing her arms in front of her. "At least, you're being honest. That's more than I can say for a lot of guys." Tom was wondering if Mrs. Morgan needed any help with her soup, when Laura spoke again. "I just wish you would believe me. The window. The rosebushes.

My diary. If you'd believe me, maybe we could start to figure out what's going on around here."

"I'll keep thinking about it," said Tom. "But I've got to get this motorcycle back to the garage. There's a restaurant in the hotel where I'm staying. Do you want to meet for dinner later and talk this over some more?"

Laura sat down at her writing desk and looked absently at the wall. "No, I'm not really hungry," she said. "Why don't we just meet at the train station in the morning?" Tom gave her a little pat on the shoulder and left the room. He stopped in to say goodbye to Mrs. Morgan in the kitchen and apologized for any misunderstandings. Then he got on the bike and rode back toward the garage. It seemed surprisingly difficult to steer with the sidecar empty.

Tom did think about it some more, as he rode along the lake, which looked more like coal than sapphire now, as the sun had sunk behind the western mountains. Laura had said she wanted him to believe her, so they could understand what was going on. Why did that phrase sound so familiar? Tom rummaged around in his brain until a Latin phrase popped into his mind. *Credo ut intelligam*, "I believe in order to understand." That was Anselm of Canterbury. Tom could see the phrase in his own handwriting, class notes from a course in medieval literature. Tom had trouble picturing an actual intruder tiptoeing around Laura's room. But if she'd left the window open that morning, why didn't anything inside the room get wet? And why would Mrs. Morgan go snooping around Laura's room? Her denials seemed pretty convincing. And surely she would be careful to leave things where she found them. Somehow it didn't add up. Tom wasn't quite ready to believe Laura's suspicions. But he did leave a window open in his mind.

## ← 7 →

*Oxford*
*The third week of May*

Tom felt a tightness in his stomach as he walked up St. Giles Street, looking for a pub called the Eagle and Child. He was trying to remember why he had agreed to carve out a few hours on a Tuesday to meet with this group who whimsically called themselves the Inklings. Back in college, he had always felt nervous talking to his professors one on one in their offices. And here he was going to share a pint of cider with a whole roomful of distinguished teachers and scholars.

The "Bird and Baby," as they called it, wasn't hard to find. Just beyond the Ashmolean Museum there was a hanging pub sign, an eagle flying through a golden sky, carrying a young boy on its back. This must be Ganymede, Tom thought, the beautiful boy carried off to Olympus by one of Jove's eagles to serve as cupbearer to the gods. Tom studied the pub sign closely. He couldn't tell if the little boy was enjoying the ride or if he was being carried off somewhere he didn't want to go. The child was looking back over his shoulder. Was he enjoying the view or wishing he could find a way back home? As he pushed open the heavy wooden door of the pub, Tom thought he knew exactly how Ganymede must feel.

The room was dimly lit inside, with dark oak paneling, so it took a few moments for Tom's eyes to adjust. As he stood near the entrance, he couldn't help but overhear nearby conversations, as the pub was long and narrow, hardly wider than a railway car. To his left, he heard three young men talking in hushed voices about the "Royal Fusiliers" and the "Durham Light Infantry." Apparently, they were discussing which regiments they were planning to join or had already joined. On the other side was a flabby-faced man with a walrus mustache poking his finger at a copy of the *London Times* and complaining to his friend about "these bloody generals who are always fighting the last war."

Tom looked past the bar to one side and spotted Charles Williams in the back room, wearing a well-tailored, if well-worn, blue suit and setting down pint glasses on a table. Mr. Williams saw him and motioned for him to come on back, a graceful sweep of the arm that reminded Tom of a stage actor's gesture. Tom threaded his way down the aisle and found a long table in the back room, where C. S. Lewis and two other men were already seated.

"Gentlemen, Mr. McCord is here," said Williams, patting Tom on the shoulder. "Welcome to the Rabbit Room!" said Lewis in a hearty manner, setting his cigarette down in an ashtray. "This is our own little warren on Tuesday mornings," he added. "May I introduce you to Professor Tolkien and Dr. Humphrey Havard?" Tolkien rose as far as he could from behind the table and reached out to shake Tom's hand. He looked the part of the Oxford don more than Lewis, with his pipe and tweed jacket, as well as his stylish burgundy vest and carefully pressed trousers. Dr. Havard also shook Tom's hand. He had wavy white hair, black glasses, and loose jowls, giving him the wise but careworn look of a veteran physician.

"May I get you some refreshment?" asked Williams. Tom would have preferred a cup of coffee, as it wasn't quite noon yet. And he had expected to order a drink himself from the bar. But he sensed a certain ritual etiquette being enacted, so he asked for a pint of cider. "I've afraid 'we few' are indeed few this morning," said Lewis. "Professor Coghill is busy putting up a play for the Oxford University Dramatic Society. And my brother Warren has pressing business on the continent."

"His brother is a major in the army," explained Dr. Havard. "Called up for active duty last autumn. He's with the B. E. F. in France."

Williams returned, placed a glass in front of Tom, and took a seat next to him. Nodding thanks, Tom turned to Lewis again. "I trust your brother will be all right," he said.

"We were just talking about that," said Lewis. "I don't think he is in imminent danger. He's not on the firing line. He's been assigned to a supply depot in Le Havre, on the coast. We're more concerned about Tollers' two sons."

Tolkien leaned towards Tom, speaking softly but in a rapid onrush of words: "My son Michael is an anti-aircraft gunner. And Christopher is planning to be an RAF pilot." Tolkien's tone was serious, but Tom thought he detected a hint of pride mixed in with apprehension.

"May they all be under the Mercy," said Williams gently. "Not just for their safety. I pray they won't have to endure what our boys went through the last time."

"Yes, do pray for that," said Lewis emphatically, gripping his glass. "Memories of the Great War haunted my dreams for years." He paused, as if he didn't want to speak of it anymore. But the words seem almost to force themselves out: "Trenches knee-deep in water. Cratered landscapes of mud where not even a blade of grass had survived. Wounded soldiers in No Man's Land still moving like half-crushed beetles."

Tolkien fiddled with his pipe but didn't actually light it. Not looking up, almost as if speaking to his pipe, he nodded in agreement. "There is a sheer animal horror to the trenches that you could never imagine unless you'd been there." Finally striking a match and holding it to his pipe, Tolkien looked up and tried to lighten the mood. "And yet there are unexpected compensations, aren't there? It wasn't till I served in the army that I discovered the excellence of the sturdy English yeomanry. Those lads from the country were so brave, so resolutely cheerful. They always kept their wits about them, and they always knew their duty."

"Yes, it's quite true," said Lewis, his mood brightening. "I wonder if I detect something of the yeomanry in our friend Sam Gamgee. He's a simple, uncomplicated soul, but you wouldn't want anyone else at your side in the middle of a battle or on a desperate adventure."

Tolkien smiled and nodded his head. "I met a host of Sam Gamgees during the war, the privates and the N.C.O.s. I always preferred them to my fellow officers." Tolkien raised his glass and said somberly, "To those who did not come through."

The others raised their glasses in the air and touched them lightly. Then there was a long stillness at the table, as each man seemed lost in his own thoughts.

The silence was broken by an ebullient voice. "I thought I'd come to the Bird and Baby for an Inklings meeting. But I seem to have stumbled upon a Quaker meeting." Tom turned to see a cheerful-looking man with broad shoulders and curly hair dressed in a casual suit, carrying a glass of lager in his hand.

"Hugo!" said Tolkien with a broad grin. Everyone smiled, and the atmosphere in the room immediately lightened.

The man sat down and took a sip of his lager. "McCord," said Lewis, "this is Hugo Dyson, a lecturer down at Reading. Hugo, this is the young American writing a book about King Arthur." Dyson reached out and shook hands, "Good to meet you, Percival," he said.

"You're tardy this morning," said Havard.

"Couldn't be helped," explained Dyson. "Some are born late, some achieve lateness, some have lateness thrust upon 'em. The trains are all running behind schedule. They're giving priority to military traffic. I could have gotten here faster if I'd pedaled over."

"Perhaps you should get a car," suggested Havard. "The old Morris Minors are quite affordable now that the new Eights are on the street."

"I don't think so," said Dyson. "This is no time to be buying a car, with all the petrol rationing."

"Too true," said Tolkien, "knocking out his pipe in an ashtray. "I just got rid of mine. A handsome Morris Cowley, vintage thirty-two."

"Not that I wouldn't like to own a car," said Dyson wistfully. "A Morris, a Morris, my kingdom for a Morris."

Everyone at the table groaned, though there was a certain lightheartedness and buoyancy in the room that arrived the same time Dyson did.

"Get thee to a punnery!" commanded Lewis jovially, waving his arm as if banishing Dyson from the table.

"Alas, poor Hugo," added Tolkien with gusto. "A fellow of infantile jests."

Dyson leaned over to Tom and explained with a grin, "Pots calling the kettle black."

"And yet," interjected Williams, "to quote from your own book: whatever color the pots, the kettle may indeed be black."

Again, everyone at the table laughed, a complete change of mood from just a few minutes before. Finally, Dyson gestured toward Tom and asked the others: "And what about young Percival here? Has he been regaling you with tales of his knight errantry?"

"Not really," said Williams. "We've barely allowed him to get in a word. We were talking about the trenches."

"Grim-visaged war," said Dyson. "That's all I've been hearing about this morning. Let's talk about something else." The others all nodded that they were ready for a change. Dyson turned to Tom again and said, "What about this glorious son of Yanks? Tell us, Mr. McCord. Have you spoken to Merlin lately?"

Tom swallowed hard and looked around at several expectant faces. He had been fascinated by the conversation as a spectator, both the somber moments and the light banter. But he hadn't expected to participate much. Suddenly, he felt as if this were an oral examination back in college. He took a sip of cider and replied in the spirit of the moment, "No, I was told that Merlin was sleeping and didn't want to be disturbed." Tom saw several grins around the table and felt encouraged to continue. "Last week I was up in Gosforth, in the Lake District."

There were several puzzled expressions around the table, until Tolkien took his pipe out of his mouth and spoke up: "Gosforth. The high cross in the churchyard left there by the Danes?"

Tom nodded. "Exactly. I realize it's not an Arthurian site. But I had a friend who very much wanted to see it."

"Ah, Miss Hartman," said Williams. "One of her dreams. The Celtic cross as tall as a lamppost. And did she find what she was looking for?"

"Yes and no," said Tom. Turning to the others, he explained. "I met another American over here several weeks ago. Laura Hartman. She has these compelling dreams that seem to her like visions of something real."

"Oh yes," said Lewis. "Williams told us about her. Like Pauline Anstruther in his novel. But she didn't find what she was looking for?"

"The cross is the one from her dream," said Tom. "It's about fifteen feet high, standing right in front of the church. On three sides, it's engraved with scenes from Norse mythology— Fenris Wolf, Loki bound, the Twilight of the Gods. But the fourth side seems to depict the crucifixion of Christ. There's a man with his arms outstretched and blood spurting from his side. And a soldier thrusting a spear."

"I would think Miss Hartman would be delighted to find another of her dreams in the real world," said Williams.

"She was at first," said Tom. "But now she feels that questions are multiplying faster than the answers."

"Gosforth and multiply," interjected Dyson. The others ignored him this time and Tom continued. "Besides, she almost got into an argument with the local curate up there. He said the man with his arms outstretched might not be Christ at all. It might be another scene from mythology, perhaps the mortal wounding of Balder."

"That seems plausible," said Havard. "One wouldn't expect Norse mythology on three sides of a cross and Gospel narrative on the fourth."

"That's not what upset her," answered Tom. "The curate said it didn't matter if the scene depicted Christ or Balder. He said they were both just examples of the universal Dying God myth."

Lewis, Tolkien, and Dyson began exchanging glances, all three with knowing smiles on their faces.

"Am I missing something?" said Tom, looking around the table.

"The Dying God myth," explained Lewis. "That's how these two apostles helped drag me into the Kingdom, kicking and screaming, almost ten years ago." Lewis grinned at Tolkien and Dyson, and they smiled back. Tom sensed a shared memory that they all treasured, and he waited for some further explanation.

"I had a stern old tutor growing up," said Lewis, "a strict logician who doted on *The Golden Bough*. He thought that Frazer's research had proven, once and for all, that every culture has its myth of the god who must die for the people. Osiris in Egyptian myth. Balder in the Norse epics. So he dismissed the story of Christ's death and resurrection as just one more version of a universal myth—just an expression of our culture, not a bedrock reality."

Tolkien took up the story: "Hugo and I had supper one night with this poor old sinner and got to talking about myths and fairy tales. Lewis took the Frazer line, that Christianity was just one dying god myth among many. We tried to reframe the issue," he said, looking over at Lewis and placing his hand on his shoulder. "We argued that myths are not just well-wrought lies; they are actually real though dappled shafts of the Divine light falling on human imagination. We believe that the great and universal myth, the Dying God who sacrifices himself for the people, shows everyone's inborn awareness of the need for redemption. As we understand it, the Incarnation was the pivotal point at which myth became history."

"What a night that was," said Lewis, looking at Tolkien and Dyson, "and what a new dawn the next day!" Turning to Tom, Lewis added, "You can't imagine the liberation! In this view, Christianity becomes the True Myth to which all the others are pointing. It is a faith grounded in fact, the myth that unfolds itself in history."

Tom was impressed, but still skeptical. He couldn't help but enjoy the zest with which these three men recalled a night that changed one of their lives—perhaps all their lives— forever. But Tom still had plenty of questions. He felt himself outnumbered, a whole tableful of believers, and every one of them a formidable intellect. Yet, in all honesty, he couldn't pretend to be won over to a whole new way of looking at things from ten or fifteen minutes of conversation. "That's a wonderful story," said Tom, "and such a beautiful, hopeful way of looking at things." He wished someone else would take up the conversation, but apparently he still had the floor, whether he wanted it or not.

"Of course, there are still some tough questions," he said, trying to sound as offhand as possible. "You all were talking a few minutes ago about the horrors of the last war. And now, here we are twenty years later, and it looks like we may have to go through the whole thing all over again. Don't you think an all-good, all-powerful God could fashion a world where humans don't inflict so much pain and suffering on each other?"

Tom expected a barrage of caustic rebuttals, but everyone around the table nodded that this was indeed a question worthy of careful thought. "It's true," said Lewis at last. "With the Apostle Paul, we see in a glass darkly and only in part." He paused and then asked Tom a series of questions "Suppose God did decide to intervene whenever he saw suffering or injustice here on earth? What would that look like?" He gave Tom a moment to think about this, then offered some specifics: "We believe that the world was once a paradise, and that the scales will again be balanced on the Last Day. But what about this blighted earth of ours now? What should God do about our wars and our pain? What if he turned every bullet into a puff of air and every bayonet into a flower?"

"That would be a start, I suppose," answered Tom, not sure he wanted to travel down this road.

"Yes, but only a start," continued Lewis. "Why would a good God even allow things to get a far as bullets and bayonets?

Shouldn't he go back a step further? Perhaps every time someone got ready to tell a lie or utter a hateful word, God could paralyze their tongues or disturb the air in front of them so their words wouldn't carry?"

"Better still," said Tom weakly, feeling that he was headed into deep water.

"But not the best," said Lewis. "Why not go back a step further? Don't stop with harmful deeds or hateful words. Why not erase bad thoughts from people's minds, so that neither their words nor their deeds can hurt anyone else?"

Checkmate, thought Tom. "Because then they would cease to be people," he answered. "That would cancel out their free will." Tom still wasn't convinced, but he was disappointed in himself for not putting up a better fight. Lewis reached over and patted him on the arm. "I'm not fool enough to think that settles it all," Lewis said. "'Great we confess is the mystery of our faith.' It's a vast topic. We should talk about it more sometime," he added in a friendly tone.

"Yes, it is a vast topic," said Dyson, "a subject for endless argument, if you're not careful. I agree with the old wisdom: 'When pain is to be borne, a little courage helps more than much knowledge, a little human sympathy more than much courage, and the least tincture of the love of God more than all.'"

"Well said," boomed Lewis. "That cuts right to the heart of the matter. Who wrote that?"

Tom saw several smiles around the table, though he couldn't for the life of him see anything humorous in the quotation.

"Really, Dyson," continued Lewis. "It sounds so familiar. Is it Augustine? Boethius?"

"That is Mr. C. S. Lewis," Williams explained with a grin. "A forthcoming book of his called *The Problem of Pain*. He's been reading it to us on Thursday nights."

Everyone around the table laughed—even Lewis, who already ruddy, actually blushed a shade redder.

"How is it," asked Tolkien, "that you can remember everyone's writings verbatim, except your own?"

Everyone laughed again and then paused to catch their breath. "Really though," whispered Lewis slyly, "It was well said, wasn't it?"

Everyone laughed again, an unexpected mood for a group discussing the problem of evil.

"And what can we expect from you next?" asked Williams, looking over the rims of his glasses and adopting a tone of mock severity, "after you've solved *The Problem of Pain* in a hundred pages or so?"

"This indefatigable man!" interjected Tolkien. "He's probably got three half-finished projects setting on his desk right now!"

"Since you asked," said Lewis. "What would you think about this? I was sitting in church last week and an idea popped into my mind. It would be series of letters between two devils, one a senior tempter and the other an apprentice, trying to practice his infernal trade on an unsuspecting human subject."

"Brilliant!" said Williams enthusiastically, raising his glass.

Tolkien had a more doubtful look. "I don't know," he said. "More popular theology. I sometimes wonder if these questions are not best left to those with formal training—a clergyman, I should think."

"Or publicans perhaps," added Dyson whimsically. "Recall your A. E. Housman: 'Malt does more than Milton can/ To justify God's ways to man.'"

"Perhaps it's not one or the other," said Lewis, taking up Dyson's quip as if were a matter for serious reflection. "Perhaps both malt and Milton have their place in justifying God's ways."

Lewis looked around the table to see if anyone wanted to develop his theme, but the others waited to hear him amplify his own thoughts.

"I wonder if I should write a companion book," continued Lewis. "*The Problem of Pleasure*, it might be called. I have an intuition that all earthly pleasures are just foretastes of the gladness that awaits all those who choose to walk with God." Lifting his glass, Lewis went on. "We enjoy our malt in the here and now. But we always thirst again—for the living water. And the great pleasure I take in reading Milton. Is it only an echo of all the songs and hymns to be sung in heaven? This very fellowship, this Company, as Charles would call it. Couldn't it be just a glimpse, a reminder of something else? Think of all the images of heaven our Lord gave us—banquets and wedding feasts, 'pleasures forever more.' I suspect that all earthly pleasures, when rightly practiced and rightly understood, are whispers of a wind from beyond this world, the fragrance of a flower we've never seen. Recall a verse from the Book of Revelation: 'And I shall give you the morning star.' The Bible talks about 'the beauty of holiness.' But let's not forget about the *joy* of holiness."

Everyone around the table nodded, each one seeming lost for a moment in his own glad reverie. But no single mood prevailed for very long in a gathering like this. So it wasn't long before Dyson said, "Speaking of pleasures, when shall we Inklings meet again? In thunder, in lightning or in rain?"

"This Thursday evening in my rooms, as usual," answered Lewis. "We're hoping that Tollers will favor us with the latest installment of his New Hobbit." He looked at Tolkien, who nodded with a modest smile that he did indeed have some new chapters to read. The conversation turned to Tolkien's dwarves, in contrast to the banal dwarfs in the Disney film *Snow White*. From there, the talk raced on to any and all topics—mechanized warfare, country pubs, the fiction of James Joyce, the thorny West Midland dialect, the indomitable Winston Churchill, and the question of whether a noble Roman such as Virgil might be received into heaven.

Tom gave up trying to follow the rapid-fire conversation and just sat back to enjoy the camaraderie around the table—the witty banter and hearty laughter, the prevailing winds of agreement with occasional gusts of disagreement. The tilting of glasses and the curling plumes of tobacco smoke. *What a gift of friendship these men have*, Tom thought to himself. He heard Tolkien utter the phrase "a feast of reason and a flow of soul," and he thought that described perfectly this band of brothers in the back parlor of a cozy pub.

The meeting began to break up a little after one, with men rising and shaking hands. There was an elevation of spirit among them all that Tom hadn't felt when he first joined them an hour earlier. Each one shook Tom's hand, and thanked him for joining them, as if the privilege were theirs.

As he took his leave, Tolkien added an intriguing word of parting. "It was good of you to join us," he said. Then he added as an afterthought: "I've been pondering your friend's dreams. I think I might see a scarlet thread that knits them together." Tom was eager to hear more, but Tolkien took out his watch and glanced at it. "I'm sorry, but I'm already late for a meeting at Pembroke," he said. He thought a moment and then had an idea: "I have pupils come to my study at home for tutorials. Perhaps you could come for a visit some morning next week? It's a topic that merits more than a sentence or two."

"I'd happy to come see you next week," said Tom. "Would it be all right if I brought my friend Laura along? I'm sure she will want to hear about this firsthand."

"Yes, that would fine," answered Tolkien. He gave Tom a kind of salute, holding his pipe to his brow and drawing a J in the air, then hurried out the front door.

Tom wished he could continue the conversation one on one with either Lewis or Williams, the last two to leave, but both were gathering up their things. And there seemed to be an unspoken rule that once an Inklings meeting was over, it was over for everyone. So he contented himself with a last sip of his glass and a last round of handshakes, thanking Lewis for asking him to join in. Then he headed for the door, noticing how quiet and glum the other tables seemed, compared to lively and learned repartee he had been enjoying the past hour.

As he pushed opened the front door, Tom had one last look at the Eagle and Child pub sign over the sidewalk. He decided that Ganymede's wide-eyed expression was one of delight, not fear. After all, he thought, how often does a young man get carried aloft on the wings of eagles?

← 8 →

*Oxford*
*The end of May*

Tom stood and gazed at the Martyr's Memorial, a Victorian monument that looked like a church spire rising out of the ground. The inscription explained that it was a tribute to the Protestant bishops executed in the reign of Queen Mary. Tom was equally amazed that people could die for something as speculative as religion—or to kill for it.

"Ah, there you are!" he heard Laura call out, as she crossed St. Giles and joined him. She was wearing a floral dress, with a lacy hat and white gloves, and carrying an elegant umbrella.

"You look like you've just come from church!" said Tom.

"A lady wants to make a good first impression," said Laura. "It's not every day she gets to meet an Oxford don and a well-known author." Laura looked at Tom's casual slacks and short-sleeved shirt and added, "And you look like you've got on your Sunday attire as well," she said. "All set for the golf links."

Tom grinned and they started walking north. In less than a block, they came to the Eagle and Child, and Tom stopped to admire the pub sign. "This is where I took a drop with Lewis, Tolkien and the Inklings last week," he explained. "Charles Williams was there too."

Laura kept looking up at the pub sign.

"What are you thinking?" asked Tom finally.

"I think those old Greeks were dangerously lax in their child safety laws," Laura replied. Then she looked up and down the street and added, "Which way to Professor Tolkien's house?"

"This way," said Tom, taking a few steps north, away from the town center. They walked up Woodstock Road, then took a right in front a group of stately Victorian buildings behind an iron fence. "This is St. Hugh's," said Laura, "one of the women's colleges." She had been walking in her usual brisk stride, and Tom was surprised to see her stop, grip the railings and peer into the college courtyard, almost like a child at the zoo hoping to see a tiger come out of its den.

"It's still several more blocks," prodded Tom gently.

"Of course," said Laura, shaking off her reverie and resuming her stride. "I appreciate your inviting me along for this meeting," she added.

"Tolkien said he thought he saw a pattern in your dreams. A scarlet thread, he called it. He said there was quite a story behind it, and I thought you'd want to hear it for yourself."

"Thanks, Tom," she said, touching him lightly on the arm. "That was thoughtful of you. And, yes, I certainly do want to hear the story for myself." After a few more steps, she asked, "Tell me, what's he like? What should I expect?"

"He and Lewis are great friends," said Tom. "Lewis is the one who encouraged him to submit *The Hobbit* for publication."

"Like two peas in a pod then?" asked Laura.

"Not really," replied Tom. "Lewis has a big, round face and a booming voice. And he's a slovenly dresser. His manner is hearty and self-confident, but he's a bit clumsy and fumbly with his hands. He makes lighting a cigarette look like a real chore. Tolkien has an oval face and is quieter when he speaks. But he looks the part of the dapper don, and he seems more agile and athletic. They say he was quite the horseman and the marksman in his younger days."

"How much does he know about my dreams?" asked Laura.

"I just mentioned two of them briefly," answered Tom with diffidence, recalling Laura's fury after their talk with Willem De Lott. "The one we discussed with Mr. Williams, the soldier being martyred. And the one that took us up to Gosforth, the high cross in the churchyard. I figured you would want to decide for yourself how much else to say."

Laura nodded her approval and gave Tom a soft look and a dimpled smile. He had an impulse to reach out and interlace his arm with hers as they walked, but he was learning that discretion had its own rewards. They continued on till they came to Northmoor Road, a street of expansive red brick homes built close to the road. "We're looking for Number Twenty," Tom explained. The sky cleared overhead, and Tom felt a sudden rush of pleasure—the burst of sunshine; the comfortable-looking, well-kept houses with their flower gardens; his walking companion and their destination. How good is it to be alive on this planet, he thought.

About halfway up Northmoor Road, they decided they were in about the right place, but couldn't spot a house number. They were approaching a large, vine-covered home with leaded windows and a gray slate roof. There was a spacious garden in back—tomatoes, beans, squash, even a few small fruit trees and a grape arbor. Alongside the house was a small cylindrical aviary, with brilliantly colored canaries and parakeets flitting about inside. A girl of about ten or eleven stood in front of the vegetable garden, tossing kernels of dried corn to a half dozen hens from a denim apron with big pockets. She had rosy cheeks and curly hair under a blue scarf.

"Excuse me," said Laura. "Does Professor Tolkien live here?"

"Yes, he does," said the little girl with crisp English diction. "And so do I. My name is Priscilla."

"Pleased to meet you, Priscilla," said Laura. "I'm Miss Hartman and this is Mr. McCord."

Priscilla nodded to both of them and brushed a few stray kernels of corn off her hands, shooing the hens away, as if she had found something more important to do.

"This is quite a farm you have here," said Tom.

"It's not a *farm*," said Priscilla. "It's just our garden. A Victory Garden. We grow as much food as we can, because of the war."

"Chickens even!" said Tom.

"Yes," said Priscilla, glancing over her shoulder. "Mum says hens don't ask to see your ration book."

"Do you know if your father is at home?" asked Laura.

"Yes, I believe so," said Priscilla. "Why don't you go knock at the front door?" With that, Priscilla suddenly bolted away and disappeared behind the house. Tom and Laura walked up to the front porch and knocked on the door. After a brief interval, the door opened slowly. There was Priscilla again, though she had taken off her scarf and apron.

"Good morning," she said a slight curtsy.

"Good morning," said Tom. "We just met your twin sister in the garden."

"That was *me*," said Priscilla with a giggle. Tom couldn't tell if she realized he was joking or if she thought he was a bit thick. He had the same problem with females his own age.

"Is your father in?" asked Laura.

"Please follow me," said Priscilla said. She turned and led them down the front hall, walking on her toes to seem as tall as she could, and adopting her best hostess demeanor. She knocked on a side door and then opened it. "Papa, some Americans are here to see you," she said. Then she gestured for them to enter the room and skipped off toward the back of the house again.

Tom followed Laura down the side hallway, so crammed with bookshelves and piles of books that it seemed almost like a tunnel. He emerged to find Professor Tolkien sitting at his desk, jotting something in a florid script on the back of an old blue book with a dip-pen. After he finished the sentence he was writing, Tolkien set down the pen and rose to greet his visitors.

Tom offered brief introductions and then all three sat down in leather chairs. As he settled into his seat, Tom couldn't help letting his eyes wander around the room—rows of dark leather-bound books from floor to ceiling, a big black coal stove glowing with embers, and Tolkien's desk strewn with books and papers. There was a ceramic jug shaped like a jolly fat man, used for holding the professor's favorite pipes. Right next to it were a wooden tobacco jar and an ashtray the size of a cereal bowl. In general, the room was rather dim and plain, furnished for comfort and not for show. But there was a splash of color near Tolkien's desk—a little shelf with samples of stationery in a variety of pastels, plus a rainbow collection of inks and sealing waxes to go with the paper.

"I'm glad to see you're so delighted with my study," said Tolkien in a soft voice.

"Excuse me?" said Tom.

"You're smiling like the Cheshire cat," explained Tolkien.

"I'm just admiring the room," explained Tom. "With all due respect, when I came through that tunnel of books and emerged into your study, I thought I might meet Bilbo Baggins in the flesh!"

Tolkien laughed and picked one of his pipes out of the mug. "I don't deny it," he said good-naturedly. "I am essentially a hobbit in everything but size. I like good, simple food and plenty of pipe-weed." Tolkien took a pinch of tobacco out of the jar and carefully pressed it into the bowl of his pipe. "And I love trees and gardens, anywhere I can get away from cities and machines. I try to avoid travel or adventures, and I dress plainly. But I do have a fondness for splendid waistcoats." Tolkien glanced down at his leaf-green vest, which was indeed a bit gaudy compared to his beige jacket and gray flannel trousers.

"Have you had occasion to slay any dragons lately?" asked Tom.

"Oh, I've slain a few dragons in my day," answered Tolkien, putting his pipe into his mouth. "But not the kind you're thinking of."

Tom waited for the professor to explain, but Tolkien went on to a new topic: "One of the first stories I ever wrote was about a dragon. When I was six or seven, I recall writing about a 'green great dragon.' My mother told me the phrase should be 'great green dragon.' I wondered at the time why that should be, and I'm still wondering."

"I read your address to the British Academy," said Tom. "The one about reading *Beowulf* as a work of literary art, not just a linguistic artifact. I suppose that's where you got the idea of taking that epic story of a dragon-slayer and transposing into a comical, fairy tale setting."

Tolkien looked puzzled. "Which fairy tale are you referring to?" he asked.

"I was thinking of *The Hobbit*," explained Tom, a little crestfallen.

"Oh, *The Hobbit!*" said Tolkien, leaning back in his chair and chuckling to himself. "Bilbo as a pint-sized Beowulf! Your theory is both ingenious and plausible," he said. "And also completely wrong. That's the way it is with Source Criticism. Lewis and I have both noticed that theories about the origins of someone's creative work have a remarkable quality of always being mistaken."

Tolkien found a match and lit his pipe, taking a few puffs and then setting it down. Then he opened the coal stove and stirred up the embers. "Are you two warm enough?" he asked. They both nodded that they were and waited for him to continue. But he began looking at the sheaf of papers on his desk, almost as if he'd forgotten they were there.

"So how did *The Hobbit* get started?" Laura asked finally.

Tolkien looked up, blinked once or twice, then picked up the thread of the conversation again: "Yes, yes, of course, I was sitting right here at this desk. I had spent most of the day marking essay examinations. After laboring through pages and pages of youthful scribbles, I turned the leaf of one examination book and found it blank. Ah, what a glorious sight that was! I think all students should leave an empty page once in a while, just to relieve the monotony for their examiners!"

Tom and Laura both smiled, and Tolkien continued: "I just rested my eyes on that blank page, and it began to look like an empty canvas waiting for the painter's brush. And a sentence came to me all at once: 'In a hole in the ground there lived a hobbit.' I had no idea what a hobbit was, and decided I'd have to write a story to find out."

"Did you visualize the hobbit as someone like Bilbo Baggins?" asked Tom.

"No, not at first," explained Tolkien, picking up his pipe again. "Most writers I talk to tell me their stories begin with an image or an idea. But mine nearly always begin with a word. The shapes and sounds of words seem to affect me the way colors or melodies affect other people. So I had this word 'hobbit' in my head, and I knew I had to find out what sort of creatures they were and what sort of life they lived."

"I'd say you answered the question admirably in your book!" said Laura.

Tolkien smiled graciously and nodded. "Thank you," he said. "But I wouldn't say I've got my answer yet." Gesturing with his pipe toward the scribbled notes in front of him, he added, "I don't think I'm finished with these hobbits. Or rather they're not finished with me." Tolkien leaned forward and tried to decipher his own handwriting on the back of the blue book. "I've started a 'New Hobbit,'" he explained. "And I've been reading it to my friends, the Inklings, on Thursdays nights."

"More adventures of Bilbo Baggins?" asked Tom.

"He comes into the story," said Tolkien. "But this one is more about his nephew, Frodo. His seems to be a darker journey than Bilbo's. I've got Frodo and his friends to a crossroads inn where they've met some sort of walker in the woods."

"Friend or foe, I wonder?" asked Tom.

"I wonder too!" exclaimed Tolkien. "Who is this fellow hanging back in the shadows? I don't even know his name. Is it Strider or Trotter?" Tolkien looked at Tom and Laura as if hoping one of them might know the answer. Then he looked back down at the paper in front of him and made a quick note to himself. "I'll just have to do some more digging and find out." Tolkien said this as if it were a matter for further research, not a matter of making up more of his own story. Then he knocked the ash out of his pipe and set it down on the ashtray, not having gotten more than a few puffs out of his tobacco. He seemed to use the pipe more to emphasize his points in conversation than for smoking. After dipping his pin and jotting down another quick note, Tolkien turned abruptly toward Laura and said, "Tom here tells me you've been having uncanny dreams."

Laura cleared her throat and leaned forward in her chair. "That's right," she answered. "And he said you might have some ideas about them."

"If I understand correctly," said Tolkien, "there was one about a Roman general who was executed for refusing to obey the emperor's command."

Laura nodded.

"And one about a high Celtic cross of red sandstone."

Laura nodded again.

"From the details I've heard," Tolkien continued, "I would agree with Charles Williams. Your first dream certainly sounds like the martyrdom of St. Maurice, who refused to execute fellow Christians after a battle. And the second dream certainly does sound like the cross at Gosforth. So there's your link." Tolkien said this matter-of-factly, as if the answer was plain to see.

"That's just it," said Tom. "Both dreams seem to be about real things, but we don't see what connects them."

"Why, the spear of course!" said Tolkien.

Tom and Laura looked at each other, both still baffled, then back at Tolkien.

"The spear of Longinus," Tolkien explained, "the spear that pierced the side of Christ on the cross."

Laura nodded slowly, as if she was remembering something. But Tom suddenly felt left out of the secret.

"In John's Gospel," Tolkien went on, "it says that after Jesus had died on the cross, a Roman soldier stabbed him in the side to make sure he was dead, and out flowed blood and water. The soldier isn't named in the narrative, but he has long been known as Longinus."

"That explains the cross at Gosforth," said Tom, "but I don't see how it relates to St. Maurice."

"The spear of Longinus has a fabled history," Tolkien continued. "Much older than stories about the Holy Grail. Longinus himself is said to be one of the earliest Christian converts, and he passed the spear on, a sacred remembrance from one generation to another. Maurice is one of those who is said to have possessed the spear in his time, though he gave it up willingly."

"And where did it go from there?" asked Tom.

"Oh, there's nothing so clear as a direct line," explained Tolkien. "The spear shows up and then disappears from the historical record over and over again. And, of course, there are many versions of the story." He got up to check on the stove, explaining, "Have to keep a close eye on this infernal contraption. Almost burned the house down once." Rather than taking his seat, Tolkien begin pacing back and forth in front of the stove, giving an impromptu lecture. "The old romancers say Joseph of Arimathea brought the spear to England, along with the Grail," he explained. "You recall the bleeding lance seen at the Grail Castle of Carbonek. Some commentators associate that with Longinus' spear."

"I thought you said the legends of the spear went back much further than Grail stories," said Tom.

"They do," answered Tolkien, still pacing in front of the stove. "In the fourth century, the Emperor Constantine announced that he had the spear, given to him by his mother Helena after her famous pilgrimage to the Holy Land. Constantine claimed he could never lose a battle, so long as he possessed the spear. That's why it gathered such an aura about it. People began calling it the Spear of Destiny. After that, all the conquerors seem to lay claim to it. Charlemagne said he had the spear, adding that it always brought him victory and even allowed him to read the thoughts of his enemies."

As Tolkien warmed to his topic, his words came out in erratic bursts and his voice grew quieter, almost as if he were just thinking aloud. Tom and Laura both leaned forward in their seats, trying to take in all of the professor's words. Without looking over at them, Tolkien continued pacing and continued talking: "Napoleon knew all about the spear, and he wanted it for himself. During his campaigns in Germany, he rode to Nuremburg to get his hands on the ancient spear on display there called the 'Heilige Lanze,' the Holy Lance. But the relic was carried off to Vienna when word got out that he was on his way."

"Did anyone ever find it?" asked Laura eagerly.

Tolkien looked across the room, as if surprised to find visitors in his study. "Oh, yes," he answered, "the same spear was on display in the Hofburg Museum for many decades."

"*Was* on display?" asked Tom. "What happened to it?"

Tolkien looked genuinely surprised, as if he thought this were common knowledge. "Why, Adolf Hitler has it!" he explained simply. "He saw it in the Hofburg when he was a young man, and it cast a spell on him. He felt that if he could ever claim that talisman of power, he would hold the destiny of the world in his hands."

Tolkien let these words sink in a moment, and then he continued: "And now he *does* have it in his hands. The first thing Hitler did after Germany's annexation of Austria was to take the Holy Lance from Vienna and carry it off a secret crypt in Nuremburg."

Laura nearly jumped at the word "crypt," but Tom leaned back in his chair and smiled. This seemed to him the same sort of yarn as the Holy Grail being buried under the Chalice Well in Glastonbury.

"How much stock do you put into all this?" Tom asked.

Tolkien quit pacing and went to sit down in his chair again. He looked over his collection of pipes, then picked out a meerschaum. "I'm just answering your question about the spear of Longinus," Tolkien explained calmly. He lit his pipe and gave it a few puffs. "I certainly believe the Gospel account," he said. "But the rest are just traditions. You are welcome to believe as much as you want or as little as you want."

"Do you really think Hitler has gotten hold of something called the Spear of Destiny?" asked Tom.

"I believe he's got the spear they call the Holy Lance," replied Tolkien. "And I believe it is the ancient spear that was on display in the Hofburg for over a century," he added.

Tolkien then set down his pipe and leaned forward in his chair, as if telling Tom and Laura a secret. "And I also believe he's got the wrong spear!" Tolkien added, with an almost elven twinkle in his eye.

Laura leaned back and let out a sigh. But Tom sat straight up with the same skeptical look on his face. Tolkien studied both their expressions and then continued: "I've seen pictures of the spear that was at the Hofburg," he explained. "Of course, the wooden handle has longed since turned to dust. But the part that is left, the spearhead, looks medieval to me, not Roman."

Neither Tom nor Laura pretended to know much about ancient weaponry, so Tolkien explained: "Roman spears were pretty simple affairs, a sharp iron point fastened to a wooden shaft. But the spearhead they had on display at the Hofburg is long and broad, probably from the late Middle Ages. It even has decorative flanges, not the sort of tip you would see on the lance of an ordinary Roman soldier."

"So where is the real spear?" asked Laura.

"I'm not saying there *is* a real spear," answered Tolkien. As I said before, I believe the Gospel account. But the rest is pure speculation. Some make claims for a spear at the Vatican, but the Holy See does not argue for its authenticity. Others say the spear made its way to Antioch or even to Krakow Actually, if you are going to argue there is an authentic Spear of Longinus, then we English can put in as good a claim as anyone."

"Do you think the Grail Castle, with its bleeding lance, might actually be somewhere here in England?" asked Tom.

"No, no, no," said Tolkien, with a hint of irritation in his voice. "Not the Grail Castle, and not Arthur. Nothing to do with the Celts. Doesn't anyone recall the Anglo-Saxons? The romances say that Arthur established a community of Christian chivalry at Camelot. But the Saxons achieved the real thing, or something very like it, under Alfred the Great and his successors. They beat back the Danes, nourished faith and scholarship, even translated Scripture into their own tongue."

"But why would they have the spear?" asked Tom.

"I assume you know William of Malmesbury," replied Tolkien.

"Of course," said Tom. "The twelfth-century chronicler who insisted that the historical Arthur ought to be distinguished from all the tales and legends."

"That's right," said Tolkien. "This same William insists that Athelstan, grandson of Alfred the Great, received the Spear of Destiny from the Count of Paris. Do you recall the passage about all the gifts that were sent to Athelstan to honor him as 'first king of all England'? Tolkien closed his eyes and began quoting fluently in Latin. Tom caught the word *lanceum*, "lance," *invictissimus*, "invincible," and maybe something about defeating the Saracens.

"As you can see—" continued Tolkien, waving his pipe in the air.

"May I interrupt a moment?" said Tom. Though he had studied Latin for four years in school, Tom was astounded that these Latin words could come rolling so easily off the don's tongue the way a child in America might recite a nursery rhyme. He was also struck by how much more clearly and resonantly Tolkien spoke when reciting than in ordinary conversation.

"Excuse me, sir, but my Latin's a little rusty," said Tom, swallowing his pride. "Could you go over that again in English?"

Tolkien looked a little surprised, but said he'd be happy to translate. Reviewing the passage in his head a moment, he recited the passage in English as fluently as he had in Latin, explaining that Athelstan had received the lance of Charlemagne, who always emerged as victor whenever he brandished it against his enemies. "In general," Tolkien continued, "William is regarded as one of the earliest of true historians, in the modern sense. And he says that Athelstan himself was a great believer in sacred relics, and pilgrims came from all over Christendom to see the treasures on display at Malmesbury. And Athelstan chose to be buried in Malmesbury Abbey, near his beloved relics, rather than with the rest of the royal family at Winchester. It does give you pause, doesn't it?" asked Tolkien impishly.

"Do you suppose that Hitler ever worries that he might have the wrong spear?" asked Tom.

"I don't know," answered Tolkien, gripping his pipe tightly in his teeth. "The man is a beastly little ignoramus when it comes to anything besides tyrannizing his neighbors. He has taken the noble Northern spirit and twisted it into his perverted master race theories. The great Teutonic myths were first refined and Christianized right here on our own island. I sometimes wish there were a literary genius to create a national epic for England, the way the Finns have their *Kalevala*. Someone to go back and finish what the Saxons had begun before they were trodden down by those rapacious Normans."

Tolkien's fist came down on the arm of his chair, as he spoke of "those rapacious Normans." Tom was astonished that someone could still feel so much anger and sorrow over a conquest that happened almost nine centuries earlier.

Suddenly an alarm clock on Tolkien's desk clanged urgently, as if warning of some new invasion. Tolkien reached over and turned it off and then rose from his chair. "Mr. McCord. Miss Hartman. It has been a pleasure talking to you," he said. "But I'm afraid I have other business to attend to."

"Thank you very much," said Laura, shaking the professor's hand. "You have been most helpful."

"Yes, thank you for your time," Tom added. Priscilla appeared in the door of the study, as if the sound of the alarm clock were her cue. She took Laura's hand and said, "I'll show you the way out."

"Thank you, Priscilla," said Tolkien, offering a friendly nod and then returning to his desk and taking his pen in hand again.

Priscilla walked them down the hall and opened the front door. "It was a pleasure to make your acquaintance," she said, letting go of Laura's hand.

"It was good to meet you too," said Laura.

"I hope we haven't made your father late for another engagement," said Tom.

Priscilla had a puzzled look on her face, so Tom continued. "The way that alarm clock went off. I got the feeling your father has somewhere else he needs to be."

"Oh that!" said Priscilla. "He'll be home all day today, I think. He just sets the alarm clock before a meeting, so it doesn't go on longer than he wants it to."

Tom and Laura smiled at each other and nodded once more to Priscilla, as she made a little wave and then closed the front door. They turned back down Northmoor Road toward the town center. The sky had clouded up again, and a few drops of rain were beginning to fall. Laura opened the umbrella she was carrying and asked, "Would you like to share?"

"That's all right," said Tom. "I don't mind a little rain." As soon as he had spoken, Tom wished he could take back those words. One side of him thought it was unmanly to hide from a few harmless raindrops. But then he realized he'd missed his chance to walk shoulder to shoulder with a winsome young woman in a summer dress.

"What do you think?" he asked.

Laura closed her umbrella, as those few drops of rain seemed to be all there was to the momentary shower. Already, the sun was peeking out from behind the clouds again. "I'm encouraged!" she replied. "As soon as Professor Tolkien said the word 'spear,' I knew he was onto something. The way the noble captain—Maurice—lays down his lance and sword in my dream. It is so grand and formal, almost like a sacrament. I think Mr. Tolkien has explained it perfectly. I feel like the pieces of the puzzle are beginning to fall into place."

"It's too bad you didn't get to ask him about your other dreams," Tom said.

"Maybe some other time," said Laura. "But I feel like we're on the right road," she added brightly. "We just need to do some digging, as Professor Tolkien says."

"Tell me honestly now," said Tom. "How much of his Latin did you catch?"

"Hardly a word," said Laura with a laugh. "But I'm just a simple American girl over here to keep her aunt company. I thought that *you*, a rising authority in the field—"

"Yes, I saw you over there finding bliss in my ignorance," said Tom, with a grin. "Even if he were just showing off, I would have to be impressed. But the amazing thing for me is that he *wasn't* trying to show off. I can see why he and Lewis get along so well."

They walked in silence some more, until Tom thought of something else to say: "Maybe we should stop at the Ashmolean on the way back into town," he suggested. "Have a look at some authentic Roman spears."

Laura nodded.

"Maybe we could go someplace for lunch afterward?" Tom offered.

Laura began to smile, but then she thought a moment and shook her head no. "Today's not a good day for me," she said. They walked on a silence for a while. The sound of nothing but their steps on the pebblestone pavement began to feel uncomfortable, until Laura spoke at last: "Thank you again for asking me to come along, Tom. Isn't Priscilla just a little darling?"

"Yes, she is," said Tom. "And now I know where we can find some fresh eggs around here." They walked on in silence some more and Tom tried to think of something to say. His brain was a blank slate, so he just contented himself to listen to the not unpleasing syncopation of his footsteps mingled with hers.

"You know where I *would* like to go sometime," said Laura at last.

"Where's that?"

"Malmesbury."

"Today's not a good day for me," said Tom. He meant that as a quip, but Laura nodded that she understood, as if she would have been ready to jump on a train that very afternoon, if Tom had been willing.

The spear is a legitimate part of Arthurian romance too, Tom thought to himself. Before he and Laura had gotten more than a few blocks away from Tolkien's house, Tom already had a pretty good idea about where this puzzle would take them next.

# ← 9 →

*On the train to Malmesbury, west of Oxford*
*Early June*

Tom peered out the train window, but the swirling fog prevented him from seeing much beyond the line of telephone poles that ran alongside the tracks. He looked at Laura, who sat across from him reading *Middlemarch*. Tom felt disappointed not to enjoy the view on their way into Malmesbury, but there was something snug and cozy about sitting in the well-appointed railway car, with wood-paneled walls and padded seats, looking at the fog outside and listening to the steady clack-clack-clack of the wheels passing over the tracks.

"*Middlemarch*," said Tom. "I had to read that in Victorian Lit. Do you want me to tell you what happens?"

"No thanks," said Laura, "without looking up. "This is the third time I've read it."

"Really?" said Tom. "You're re-reading it of your own free will?"

Laura looked up and turned her head all around the car, which was empty except for the two of them, then went back to reading. Tom took this as her wordless way of saying, "Why else would I be reading the novel again except my own choice?" After a few seconds, she looked out the window at the fog. "I was hoping to see more of the Wiltshire countryside," she said.

"We're only a few hours from Oxford," said Tom. "Maybe you could make another daytrip later on this summer. You'd see a lot more on foot," he added. "Jack says he doesn't like watching the landscape from a moving train. Everything goes by too fast. He says it's like reading only the first page of a hundred books one right after the other."

"Jack? Which Jack are we talking about?" asked Laura.

"Jack Lewis. C. S. Lewis, that is."

"Oh, 'Jack' is it? So you two are poker buddies now?" said Laura, closing the cover of her novel, but keeping her hand on the page she had been reading.

"Hardly," said Tom. "For one thing, he doesn't play poker or any game of that sort. He says he'd rather just gaze into a fire than play cards."

"The man sounds like an endless font of intriguing opinions," said Laura, looking out the window again. Then turning to Tom, she asked, "But how do you get 'Jack' Lewis from C. S. Lewis?"

"Actually, I wouldn't call him that to his face," said Tom a bit sheepishly. "Apparently, he's been called that ever since he was a little boy. When he was three or four, he pointed to himself, announced he was 'Jacksie,' and wouldn't answer to any other name. Eventually it was shortened to Jack."

"And what does the C. S. stand for?"

"Clive Staples."

"Oh, dear," said Laura, with a smile. "No wonder he prefers 'Jack.' And he calls you Tom?"

"He just calls me 'McCord,'" explained Tom.

"Not even Mister McCord, like those starchy old school-teachers?"

"Nope, just McCord. He calls most of his friends by their last names. Barfield. Dyson. Coghill. He says it's actually more personal that way. He says he knows lots of Toms but only one McCord."

"Another intriguing opinion!" said Laura, smiling some more. "And what about Tolkien?"

"Same thing. 'My good friend Tolkien,' he says."

"Then what does the J. R. R. stand for? More Christian names best kept secret? Something like Jasper Rasputin Rumplestiltskin Tolkien?"

"It's stranger than that," said Tom.

Laura paused and then said, "Really, I can't come up with a name any stranger than that."

"I asked Lewis what the 'J. R. R.' stood for. It was the same time we were discussing 'Clive Staples.'" And he scratched his head and said he really couldn't recall! He thinks one of the R's might stand for Ronald."

"But he can't tell you what the J stands for?"

"Nope. He said it is always just Tolkien. Or 'Tollers.'"

"Now that is strange!" admitted Laura, shaking her head and smiling some more. "Why does that seem so quintessentially Oxford to me?"

Tom just shrugged his shoulders. "You seem to be in a jaunty mood today," he said.

"Am I?" asked Laura. "As opposed to my usual grim demeanor?"

"No, I didn't mean that," said Tom quickly. He was on the verge of explaining himself, when he realized she was just kidding. This was something new in her; he was seeing more playfulness in those dark eyes than he was accustomed to.

"You might be right," Laura continued. "I had something on my mind, something I was worried about. But it seems to have taken care of itself."

"Anything you'd like to talk about?" asked Tom.

Laura shook her head. "No, we don't need to talk about it," she said, "just a load off my mind."

"Now you've piqued my interest," said Tom. "Can I at least try and guess?"

"Ok, I'll give you exactly one guess," said Laura, holding up her index finger. "And after that, we drop the subject."

"Let's see now," mused Tom aloud. "What could it be? Last week I recall quite a few sighs and faraway looks. But today you seem to find almost everything amusing."

"Just the guess please," said Laura. "I can do without the commentary."

"Hmm," said Tom, rubbing his chin in imitation of deep thought. "You inherited a castle in Surrey?" he guessed. "Turns out you're a long-lost countess?"

"Hardly," said Laura, with a dismissive wave of the hand. She acted as if that was the end of the subject, but then she suddenly tossed her head back. "If you really must know, I've been jilted!" she explained breezily.

"I must say, you're taking it awfully well," said Tom, both perplexed and amused.

"I got an aerogram from Timothy," Laura explained. "I guess he's tired of waiting. Feels the two of us have been drifting apart."

"I'm sorry to hear that," said Tom. He didn't really mean it, but it seemed like the right thing to say.

"Oh, don't be sorry," said Laura, closing her book again. "It's all for the best. I've been feeling the same way. He's looking for a pastor's wife, and I'm not sure that is me. Coming over to England has made me realize how much I'm still getting to know myself."

Laura looked out the window, then added quietly, "Dear old Timothy. Trying so hard to let me down easy. 'I feel that there is more than an ocean separating us . . .' he wrote. Very poetic for him."

"Hmm. Sounds to me like your young man was about to get a Dear John letter just before he sent off his, uh, Dear Jane letter, or whatever you would call it."

Laura sat up straighter in her seat and tugged at the lapels of her jacket. "I hope you don't think this changes anything between us," she said firmly. "I just was explaining because you were asking about my mood. But I wouldn't want you to get the wrong impression."

"Of course not," said Tom, holding up his hands, as if in surrender. "Just friends." That didn't sound quite right, so Tom cleared his throat and tried again: "Really, I appreciate all your help with my research."

Laura nodded and then seemed to find a sudden fascination in the map she was carrying. She unfolded it and checked on something, folded it back up, then opened it up again, tracing her finger along a line. "We must be nearing Malmesbury," she said.

"Yes, we are," answered Tom, looking out the train window. The fog was beginning to lift, he could see a city on a hill up ahead, rising like a green island out of a milky sea. Laura turned and looked out the window. "I can see why they call it 'The Queen of the Hilltop Towns,'" she said. The train pulled into the station ten minutes later and the two of them got out and walked toward the abbey ruins, a great wall of stone on the highest elevation of the city, dominating the town like a medieval fortress.

Once they had reached the top, they walked all around the abbey, noticing foundations of the old building that extended far behind the walls that were still standing. Yet what remained was imposing enough, a section of the sanctuary that still had its roof, supported by square pillars and elegant flying buttresses, with pointed finials reaching to the sky like a row of spears. Tom and Laura went in through the South Porch, a great rounded arch with intricate carvings of biblical scenes on both sides of the entryway. They entered the main sanctuary and were surprised to find this "ruin" well maintained and still in use as a parish church. Sharing a brochure, they looked around the high-vaulted nave and tried to figure out which features corresponded to the *triforium* and the *clerestory*.

"Are you students of architecture?" Tom heard from behind him. He turned to see a slender woman in her thirties with horned-rim glasses and her hair swept back in tight curls.

"Not really," said Tom, "We're more students of literature. But we can't help but admire this beautiful building."

"What you see here is only about one quarter of the original abbey," the woman explained. "The building was shaped like a great cross, with a lofty spire like the one at Salisbury. William of Malmesbury called it 'the fairest thing in all England.' But the tower was struck by lightning, and it came crashing down, taking most of the abbey with it, except for the part you see here."

"That's too bad," said Tom, not sure what else to say.

The woman gave a musical little laugh. "Oh, that's all right. That happened back in the fifteenth century, so we're over it now."

"It's a splendid remnant," said Laura politely.

"You're Americans, I think?" the woman said.

"Yes, we're over here from the States," he replied. "I'm working on a book."

The woman looked at Laura, but Laura didn't seem to feel the need to explain herself. "And this is my assistant," Tom added. Laura looked up at him, and apparently decided the time had come to speak: "I'm over here staying with my aunt in Oxford. Tom and I have a number of interests in common."

"Ah, Oxford!" the woman said. "I was at Somerville College. Took a degree in classics. So many fond memories." She extended her hand. "Tom, is it?" she said. "I'm Margaret Ashbrook. I'm a docent here at the abbey. Feel free to ask if you have any questions."

Laura reached out her hand and introduced herself as well. Tom wasn't looking for a conversation, and he thought Miss Ashbrook was being a bit forward, wondering again where the British ever got their a reputation for being aloof and reserved. He suspected he was going to be asked for a contribution before their visit was over.

Laura apparently had no such reservations, as she was gladly accepting help from Miss Ashbrook, learning that the triforium was the second storey of the abbey wall and the clerestory the third. Tom followed Miss Ashbrook's arm as she pointed out distinctive features of the abbey's design, when he noticed a stone compartment jutting out from the wall, with windows cut out on all three sides. "What's that?" asked Tom.

"I was coming to that," said Miss Ashbrook, seeming peeved that he was getting ahead of her lecture. "That's called the Watching Loft. It's one of the most distinctive features of the abbey here at Malmesbury."

"It looks like the box seat at the theater," said Tom.

"Yes, it does look like that," agreed Miss Ashbrook. "And that is one theory as to its purpose. Some scholars think that it served as a kind of 'box seat' for special visitors on high holy days. Others think it was more like a guard booth."

"I was wondering, Miss Ashbrook—" Laura began.

"You can call me Margaret, if you like," the woman said.

"Yes, all right. I was wondering how you get up there?"

"There's a staircase behind the triforium," Margaret

explained. "It's closed to the public now. It's not entirely safe anymore, I'm afraid."

"And what were they guarding?" asked Tom.

"That's open to debate as well," Margaret answered, pushing her glasses up her nose. "I think the best theory has to do with the relics. The great king Athelstan was a devoted collector of sacred relics. Besides the bones of many saints, it is said he donated to this abbey a fragment from the crown of thorns, the Sword of Constantine, and—"

"The spear of Longinus," said Tom.

"Why yes, that's right!" said Margaret. "You know about that, do you? Well, if they had pilgrims coming from all over England to visit these relics, it stands to reason that they might want to have someone standing guard over them, someone up high to keep a lookout."

Margaret made a wide sweep of her arm to indicate how someone in the Watching Loft could keep an eye on the whole sanctuary. Just then something else caught Laura's eye. "And what's that over there?" she asked, pointing to a white marble monument in the north side of nave. Without waiting for an answer, she strode swiftly across the center aisle. Tom excused himself and followed her, and then Margaret followed them both, though with a more dignified step. The three of them made a strange procession in a room where most of the people were standing still or treading about lightly at an unhurried pace.

Laura came up to a tomb-chest, an ornate marble box about the size of a coffin. On top was the figure of a king lying in state, seeming to sleep through the centuries with a lion at his feet. "This is my king!" exclaimed Laura, having trouble keeping her voice down. "This is the sleeping king with the lion at his feet!" Laura touched the marble figure lightly and reverently, as if she wanted to make sure it wasn't just a dream. "A monument, of course. How could I have not recognized it?"

"I see you've discovered Athelstan," said Margaret, as she joined the other two.

"This is the king who collected all the relics?' asked Tom.

"Oh, he was so much more that!" exclaimed Margaret. "His grandfather Alfred stemmed the tide of the Danes in the ninth century, preserving Wessex for the Saxons. But it was Athelstan who drove the Norsemen back, clear out of the country, in fact. He was the first king to be called *Rex Totius Britanniae*, 'King of all Britain.'" Margaret rested her hand on the shoulder of the king, almost as if she hoped to wake him up. Then she turned to Laura. "I wonder why you called him 'my king'?"

Laura looked up at the vaulted ceiling, as if seeking guidance about how much she should say. "That's a long story," she said at last. "I keep having extraordinary dreams. I seem to see things in my sleep that I've never seen in waking life. And this is one of them—'my sleeping king,' I call him."

Margaret smiled and moved closer to the monument. "It's odd that you say that. I used to call Athelstan 'my king' too. My father used to bring me here when I was a little girl and tell me about all the king's wonderful deeds. I used to think of him as sleeping too. *Ego dormio sed cor meum vigilat.*"

Laura glanced at Tom to see if he'd ask for a translation, but this time he was up to the task. "I sleep, but my soul wakes," he said. Margaret nodded her head thoughtfully. "That's from the Songs of Songs, is it not?" Tom asked. Margaret nodded again, still looking fondly at the sleeping king.

"I wish he *would* awaken," said Margaret pensively. "We could use his strength right now, with this new invasion looming. Margaret turned to study the faces of both Tom and

Laura. "Did you hear Mr. Churchill on the wireless this week?" she asked. "We shall fight on the beaches, we shall fight in the fields and in the streets, we shall fight in the hills. We shall never surrender!' Now that's the spirit of Athelstan! How it would have warmed my father's heart to hear that!"

Tom noticed Margaret's use of the past tense, and she must have seen the questioning look on his face. "My father was killed at Passchendaele in the Great War. June 1917—twenty-three years ago this week."

"I'm sorry," Laura said simply.

"Thank you," answered Margaret. Then she took her hand away from the monument and stood up straighter. "And why do you suppose you would be dreaming about Athelstan?" she asked.

"I didn't know it *was* Athelstan until a few minutes ago," explained Laura. "Just a sleeping king with a lion at his feet. But, strange as it may sound, all my dreams seem mixed up somehow with the spear of Longinus."

"I suppose you know the Bosch think they have it now," said Margaret, spitting out the word *Bosch* like a bad taste in her mouth. "Hitler thinks he found it at Vienna."

"That's right," said Tom. "But we know an Oxford don who thinks the Führer has got hold of the wrong spear. He wonders if the real one might be down here somewhere."

"That's always a possibility," said Margaret. "We've already mentioned all the holy relics that Athelstan brought to Malmesbury."

"I don't suppose you'd let us pry up the lid of this tomb-chest and see what's under it?" said Tom. He planted a wide grin on his face, to make it clear he was joking.

Margaret gave a token smile. "It wouldn't do any good if you did," she explained. "This abbey was begun in the twelfth century, two hundred years after Athelstan's time. This isn't actually a tomb-chest; his bones aren't here. It's only a memorial."

"Yes," said Laura, still studying the figure of the king. "I had a sense that he wasn't here anymore. It's odd: I feel in some ways like I've been here before. But other things don't feel quite right."

"What sort of things?" asked Tom.

Laura looked at the figure of the king, then glanced around the nave. "In my dream, there was slanting light falling over him. I didn't expect to find him over here in a dark corner. I would have thought he'd be over there by the windows."

Margaret's eyes widened and she actually took off her glasses and cleaned them with a handkerchief. "That's remarkable!" she said. "This piece *did* rest beneath those windows for many centuries. It was only moved during some renovations in the twenties." Tom looked at Laura as if she'd just made a pigeon appear from underneath a handkerchief. But Laura just nodded as if she already knew this. "And there's something about the windows themselves that doesn't seem quite right." Laura crossed over to the south wall of the nave again and looked up at three stained-glass windows. On the left was a window labeled "Faith," showing a vigorous young man with a staff and shield. In the middle was "Courage," a gentle-looking king with his hands on the hilt of his sword. On the right was "Devotion," a helmeted soldier resting his lance so that he could fold his hands in prayer.

"I don't see anything wrong with these windows," said Margaret. They are among of the most prized possessions of the abbey. They were designed by the famous pre-Raphaelite artist Sir Edward Burne-Jones."

"Beautiful," said Laura, gazing up at windows. The golden light was falling on her face as she spoke, and Tom had the same adjective in his mind. "But what about the titles?" asked Laura. "I don't see why a mild-looking king should make us think of courage."

"How intriguing that you should ask that!" said Margaret. "I spoke a moment ago about the renovations back in the twenties. That's when they changed the titles on the windows to make them more broadly applicable."

"Do you remember what the older titles were?" asked Laura. Margaret closed her eyes as if trying to see something in her mind. "Yes, I can recall them myself from when I came here as a girl. The man on the left with the shield was called 'St George.' The one in the middle was 'St Ethelbert,' a famously devout king. And the one on the right was called 'The Centurion.' Laura nodded again, as if she'd known this all along. Tom looked at her as if she'd made that magic pigeon disappear.

"We seem to keep coming back to that centurion and his lance," said Tom. "What do you suppose happened to all the holy relics collected by Athelstan? Especially the spear of Longinus?"

"No one can say," answered Margaret, walking slowly back toward the figure of the sleeping king. "Some claim that, before his death, Athelstan passed the spear on to Otto of Saxony, the Holy Roman Emperor, who used it to gain victories over the Mongols. Others assume that all the relics were hidden away in the sixteenth century, when Henry the Eighth dissolved the monasteries and confiscated their property."

"If you had the time and inclination, where would you look?" asked Tom. Laura shot him a disapproving glare, as if he sounded too much like those rapacious Normans whom Professor Tolkien talked about. But Margaret accepted the question as if she'd given it some thought herself.

"I would think they must be buried somewhere," she said. "You wouldn't want to carry them across the sea, because ships can sink. But you wouldn't cache them away in a closet, as castles can be ransacked and churches fall down. If I'd had the relics, I would have sealed them up tight and put them underground."

By this time Margaret had led the other two back to the figure of Athelstan.

"I know what you're thinking," she said to Tom with a smile. "You're thinking, 'Britain is a big island. *Where* underground?'"

That's exactly what Tom was thinking, but he refused to admit it. "I was just listening and hoping to learn," he said. "I'm doing research for a book on King Arthur. As my associate here can attest, we came down here on the train today with books and notepads, not picks and shovels."

"Explanation accepted," said Margaret, still smiling. "As long as I know you're not an unscrupulous treasure hunter, I might give you one more clue." She reached up and touched Tom lightly on the temple as she said this, as if she were getting ready to plant a valuable thought in his mind. Tom couldn't tell if Margaret was just being emphatic or slightly flirtatious. He looked over at Laura for some help, but Laura just stood there smiling too, with her arms folded across her chest. Tom wished someone would write a guidebook about this sort of thing, not just about triforiums and clerestories.

"If I were hunting for buried treasures," Margaret continued, "I'd go prospecting out on the King's Heath, outside of town."

"Why there?" asked Tom.

Margaret went back and rested her hand on the figure of the king. "Athelstan wasn't just a warrior," she said. "He was a just and merciful ruler, a big-hearted man. He looked after the commoners, built almshouses for the poor. And after his great victory over the Danes, he gave away plots of land to common foot soldiers, a reward for faithful service. There are about five hundred acres southwest of town, still called the King's Heath. Those little farms were passed from father to son for many generations, given to families out of the king's largesse. I think if any of Athelstan's followers were going to hide his remains or his sacred relics, they would probably go out to the heath."

"Five hundred acres," said Tom. "That's still a lot of land. I don't think I'll go rent a metal detector just yet."

Margaret didn't seem to hear him. She was still looking down at the sleeping king. "Noble Stone," she said under her breath.

"Yes, it is handsome marble," mumbled Tom, not sure what else to say.

Margaret looked up at him, no longer smiling. "Noble Stone." she said, "That's what the name Athelstan means." Margaret went up and gently touched the hand of the marble statue. "Athelstan the Glorious, some have called him. Last of the great Saxon kings." Her voice trembled as she spoke these words. She stood directly over the sleeping figure and breathed a long sigh. Tom wondered if she were seeing the face of a little-known king, but also a lost father.

"Who was that?" Laura said suddenly.

Tom and Margaret were both startled, and they both turned around. Laura was pointing up at the Watching Loft. "There was someone up there!" Laura exclaimed.

"That couldn't be," said Margaret. "The Watching Loft has been closed off for decades."

"I'm sure I saw someone up there," said Laura. Turning to Tom, she added: "I think it was the same lout we saw in Royston."

"*You* saw," corrected Tom. "I just remember a flashbulb going off. And I didn't see anyone this time either."

"Neither did I," said Margaret. "Unless I saw a shadow pass across the window of the Loft. I didn't think anyone could get up there anymore."

"Could we go have a look at the staircase?" asked Laura.

"I'll go check with the verger," said Margaret, hurrying off toward the front entrance to abbey.

"Laura—" Tom started to say.

"That's all right," said Laura, "I know that you didn't see anything. And I know that I did."

That pretty much summed up the case, so they just looked around while they waited, tacitly agreeing that there wasn't any point in replaying the conversation they had had up in Windermere about the intruder in her room.

Margaret came back about fifteen minutes later, a bit out of breath. "The verger and I went and had a look at the staircase. He wouldn't let me climb the stairs, as there's a lot of loose masonry in the ceiling."

"What did he see?"

"He didn't find anything unusual. It's a stone staircase, so somebody could go up and down without leaving any tracks. The door at the entrance isn't locked, but it's a great oaken door, and would take a lot of muscle for someone to open and close it on his own."

"The guy I saw up there looked big and burly. If somebody could manage it, I would think it would be him."

"But why would someone climb clear up there just to spy on us?" Tom asked.

"I don't know," said Laura. "All I know is that I saw someone up there. And I think it was the same bushy-browed fellow who took our picture in Royston."

Margaret touched Laura lightly on the forearm to get her attention. "I don't know about any of that," she said. "But I think I may have seen a shadow up there."

Laura nodded thanks and the three of them stood in silence for a moment. Tom glanced at his watch, and suddenly became animated. "I'm sorry to interrupt, but I just looked at the time. We've got to get down to the station if we're going to make it back to Oxford before the trains stop running."

Laura seemed glad to get out of the abbey, and she and Tom both thanked Margaret for her help. Margaret walked with them back to the South Porch entrance, then waved goodbye to them as they made their way through the churchyard. Tom thought she looked a little forlorn standing there by herself under that massive arch.

◁ • ▷

The two of them walked back toward the station without saying much at first. Tom was trying to gauge her mood as they walked, and Laura seemed to read his thoughts: "I'm not upset with you, Tom. If you didn't see anything, it's good to be honest about it. I'm just glad Margaret saw a shadow at least. That should keep you from trying to have me committed."

"Fair enough," said Tom, glad to hear some playfulness in Laura's voice. "Though I'm not quite sure what to make of Miss Ashbrook."

"What do you mean?" asked Laura, turning to study Tom's face as she walked.

"Was she serious about digging around the King's Heath looking for relics?" asked Tom.

"I don't know," said Laura. "Maybe she was trying to give you a reason to come visit Malmesbury again. I noticed how she touched your head when she was talking about giving you another clue."

"I noticed that too," said Tom. Absently brushing his hair with his hand, he asked, "Why is it that I keep finding myself in awkward situations, while you're standing off to the side having a good laugh?"

"I read on one of the plaques that Athelstan had flaxen hair. Maybe you remind her of him," said Laura, running her fingers through her own hair.

"She's not my type," said Tom flatly. "Too old for one thing."

"What's the other thing?" asked Laura, as they turned the corner and headed toward the station.

"I'm not sure how to put it," said Tom. "Let's just say she didn't wear her learning lightly."

"What do you mean?" asked Laura.

"Well," explained Tom, "she certainly didn't waste any time letting us know about her Oxford degree. And she seemed to go out of her way to sprinkle some Latin into the conversation."

"She has a degree in classics, Tom!" said Laura. "I thought you admired that sort of thing in Lewis and Tolkien."

Tom sensed a difference between the two cases, but he didn't have a ready answer. As they continued walking, Laura pressed her case: "Do you remember the first time we met? In Blackwells?"

"Vaguely," said Tom, trying to act as if their first meeting had almost slipped his mind.

"Remind me: how long did it take for you to let me know that you had a master's degree? That you were going to have lunch with C. S. Lewis?"

"That was different," insisted Tom. "I was just trying to explain why I needed to have a look at that book." Tom wanted to add that the rules are different when a young man is trying to impress a young lady, but he decided against that line of defense. So he tried to get the conversation back to Miss

Ashbrook. "Honestly," he said, "Are you going to tell me you didn't find her a little pretentious?"

"Not for her situation," answered Laura, pulling up her collar and flipping her hair over the back of her coat.

"What does that mean?"

Laura turned and looked at Tom. "You asked me to be honest, so now I'll ask you the same thing. Do you notice anything strange over here sometimes when people first hear your American accent?"

"Yes, they usually want to sell me something," said Tom.

"Come on, now, think harder," said Laura. "You could pass for an Englishman until you open your mouth. But then what happens?"

"Ok, I will be honest," said Tom. "This doesn't happen all the time. But once in a while, as soon as someone hears me speak, I detect a slight change of expression in their face, an adjustment of demeanor. I might feel a bit of reluctance in their handshake or catch a note of condescension in their voice."

"And why would that be?" asked Laura.

"As you said before, we Americans don't have the best reputation around the world. Too much swagger and too much money, I suppose."

"How about here in England?" asked Laura.

"Really, most of the people over here have been just fine. But I do run into a certain sort, especially when I'm doing research. I think their notion is that it was all the riffraff of England and Ireland who went sailing off to America. So they look at me, and they're wondering how somebody with so little brains to spare could have so much money to spare."

"Exactly," said Laura. "So you want to prove yourself right away. You want to let them know you can follow their Latin and quote your sources too."

"Yes, I suppose I'll admit to feeling some of that over here.'

"Over here," repeated Laura. "And only for the past few months, while you were in England. But don't you think Margaret feels that every day of her life? Before she even opens her mouth, she can feel men thinking, 'Why isn't she home looking after her kids? Why does she want to read books?'"

"So now she's a mind-reader too?" asked Tom.

"It's not that hard to read men's minds," said Laura. "You know, with her degree, Miss Ashbrook might be back at Oxford herself if it wasn't for—"

Right in mid-sentence, Laura was interrupted and Tom was almost knocked down. A bicycle rode right in between them, and a hand reached down and snatched the notebook out of his hand. Tom watched as a slender figure dropped the notebook into a basket over the handlebars and pedaled down the sidewalk as hard as he could. Tom gave chase, but when he turned the corner, the thief was already half a block away. Tom began to run after him, but the bicycle had turned into an alley and out of sight. Tom jogged down to the alley for twenty yards or so, then gave up the chase.

He jogged back to rejoin Laura and found her almost running herself to catch up. "Are you all right?" she asked, grabbing Tom hard by the arm.

"Of course, I'm all right," said Tom, still panting. "I just thought he might turn down a cul-de-sac and I could catch up with him. Or at least get a better look. But he took off at full speed, and he seemed to have his escape route planned in advance."

"You shouldn't go chasing after crooks like that," said Laura, gradually loosening her grip on Tom's arm. "They might turn and have a go at you."

"He looked pretty scrawny to me," said Tom. "I think I could have taken him in a scrap."

"But he might have had—" Laura started to say. But she was beginning to relax now. She had caught her breath and she could see for herself that Tom was all right.

"Who looked pretty scrawny?" Laura asked ingenuously.

"Why, the guy on the bicycle, of course," said Tom.

"What bicycle?" said Laura. "I didn't see anything," she said with her tell-tale dimples showing.

Tom was just catching his breath and just catching on: "Ok, ok, I get it," he told Laura.

"Do you think we should go down to the police station?" asked Laura.

Tom put his hands on his hips and thought about it a few seconds. "It was an odd snatch and grab," said Tom. "Just some scribbles of mine about Athelstan and Malmesbury. I wonder why he didn't go for my wallet or your purse?"

"Maybe the same reason somebody would go through my luggage in Windermere and not steal anything," Laura said.

Tom thought about this and had to admit he did sense a connection. "I don't know if it's worth our going down to see the police. I think we'd just fill out some forms and answer a lot of questions, and never hear about it again. Nobody got hurt, and nothing of real value was taken. So I'd just as soon we make it in time for the return train to Oxford."

They were just a few blocks from the station and the sky was beginning to darken. Tom noticed that Laura wasn't quite gripping his arm as they walked, but she was still lightly holding on to the sleeve of his jacket.

"Why would anyone want my 'umble little notebook?" Tom asked out loud. Laura shook her head that she didn't know.

"Let me offer my apologies. Now it does seem likely to me that there was someone in your room up in Windermere. Maybe the same person who snatched my notepad. And while I'm at it, I guess I'm ready to believe that someone has been shadowing us, though I can't think why. But maybe you really did see Quasimodo, or whoever it was, up there in the Watching Loft."

Laura let go of Tom's arm and laughed out loud. Tom looked over at her in surprise.

"What's so funny? Me? I didn't think I was that funny."

"No, you're right," said Laura, still chuckling, "you're not that funny."

Tom had to smile too, just see her smile.

"You seem to be in fine spirits again," Tom said, "for someone who got spied on an hour ago and nearly run down a few minutes ago."

Still grinning, Laura nodded that she was in a surprisingly good mood. "For one thing," she explained, "I saw my sleeping king. I don't know how he relates to the spear, but I know now who he is. A Noble Stone. That's a big relief in itself."

"And what else?"

"The other thing," said Laura, looking up at Tom and taking his arm again. "The other thing is: you don't know how good it feels when someone decides to believe you."

# ← 10 →

*Oxford*
*Mid-June*

C. S. Lewis read a pocket-sized book as he leaned against the railing of the Rainbow Bridge, northwest of Oxford.

"I hope I'm not late," shouted Tom, as he crossed the bridge to join Lewis on the far side.

"I wouldn't know if you were," said Lewis, putting his book in the side pocket of his coat. "I don't carry a watch. I always forget to wind the confounded things."

To Tom's eyes, the portly don didn't look like he was dressed for a morning walk along the Thames. Lewis was wearing a tweed jacket, a sweater vest, and even a tie. But this formal effect was more than offset by his baggy pants, scuffed shoes, and rumpled felt hat. The hat looked as if Lewis had dropped it into the water a few minutes before, grabbed it and wrung it out, then scrunched it back down onto his head.

Tom shook hands with Lewis and the two of them walked up the footpath along the Thames.

"Will Mr. Dyson be joining us?" Tom asked.

"He's been detained in Reading this morning," said Lewis. "He said he'll join us for lunch upriver, at the Trout Inn."

"It's a beautiful morning for a stroll," said Tom.

"Yes," replied Lewis, "What's that line from Milton? 'Vernal delights able to charm all sadness but despair.'"

They began walking along some boathouses, with dozens of long, narrow cabin cruisers moored on both sides of the river.

"I never saw boats like those till I came to England," said Tom. "They look the offspring of an American yacht and a Venetian gondola."

Lewis smiled at this description. "My brother Warren owns a canal boat like one of these," he said. "*The Bosphorus*. The last time I was on this stretch of the Thames was in his boat last September. We were motoring up to the Trout when we got the word that Germany had invaded Poland."

"That must have been a shock," said Tom.

"Tensions had been building all summer," explained Lewis. "But one always hopes for last-minute resolution of the difficulties. So when the news came, yes, it was a shock. I remember a long silence, when you could hear nothing but the water lapping against the sides of the boat. Then someone said, 'At least this lessens the chance that we'll die of cancer.'"

"And how is your brother?" asked Tom. "I heard he made it out of France."

"That's right," said Lewis. "He was one of the thousands evacuated from Dunkirk before the Germans closed in. He's been posted in Cardiff for now. He says he might be allowed to leave active service and join us back here in Oxford as part of the Officers Reserve."

"I'm glad to hear it," said Tom. "'The Miracle of Dunkirk,' the papers are calling it."

"Not the best kind of miracle," said Lewis. "We're grateful for all the men we got back, including my brother. But they had to leave all their equipment behind. Of course, a successful evacuation is not the same as victory."

As they passed the boathouses and moved out into open country, Lewis looked visibly buoyed up by his surroundings.

He seemed to take an almost childlike delight in the sunshine and the cool breeze, the birdsong coming from a nearby ash tree or the plop of a bullfrog jumping into the river. "Look at that eyelash of trees along the ridge," he said, pointing to an evergreen copse on the hill. Tom nodded, taking as much pleasure in Lewis's delight as he did in the scene itself.

As they passed around a bend in the river, Lewis asked, "And what is the latest chapter in your pilgrim's progress?"

"My friend Laura and I went down to Malmesbury last week," said Tom.

"Malmesbury?" asked Lewis. "I know William of Malmesbury mentions King Arthur. But couldn't you have consulted his books at the Bodleian here in Oxford?"

"It wasn't Arthur who took us down there," explained Tom. "It was Athelstan. We were talking about the Spear of Longinus with Professor Tolkien. He quoted a passage about how Athelstan received the spear when he came to be recognized as King of All England."

"That sounds like Tollers," said Lewis with a rumble of laughter. "How very like him to think, 'If anyone in England ever had the spear, it would be those noble Saxons.'"

Tom wasn't quite sure he got the joke. "Of course, William of Malmesbury is one of the best historians of his time," Tom said. "And he makes it plain that the spear that pierced the side of Christ was the same one given to Athelstan."

"That's true," conceded Lewis. "Along with the Sword of Constantine and a piece of the crown of thorns. Which seems to me one too many gifts for a minor king who's just barely established control over our turbulent little island."

"Then you don't believe the spear was ever at Malmesbury?" asked Tom.

"I don't believe or disbelieve," answered Lewis. "It's all just speculation. But I would think Glastonbury has as good a claim as Malmesbury."

"I was in Glastonbury this spring," said Tom. "That's where I ran into those ruffians who didn't like me researching King Arthur. I still don't know what they thought I was after."

"Something to do with Joseph of Arimathea, perhaps," said Lewis. "According to the romances, he brought the sacred spear and the holy chalice to England and started the Christian church here long before missionaries arrived from Rome."

"Yes," said Tom, "and those same romances tell us that Merlin moved Stonehenge from Ireland to Salisbury with one wave of his hand."

"Are you saying he didn't?" asked Lewis with a look of feigned surprise. "Actually, the stories about Joseph aren't as far-fetched as they sound. The Roman Empire was more cosmopolitan than many people realize. Archaeologists have found lead ingots in Rome stamped with the word *Britannicus*. So it is not out of the question that a wealthy merchant from the Middle East might travel all the way to Celtic lands. As late as the sixteenth century, John Calvin, in his *Admonitio de Reliquias*, talks about rumors that the Spear of Longinus is hidden somewhere in Glastonbury."

"It sounds like I should make another junket down there," said Tom.

"If you think it will help you write a better book," said Lewis. "Of course, there might be a danger . . ." he began to say, his words trailing off in midsentence.

"Yes, I was thinking about that," said Tom. "I don't need another run-in with the locals down there. And lately both Laura and I have a sense that we're being followed for some reason."

"That sounds ominous," said Lewis. "But I was thinking of another kind of danger."

"Of what sort?" asked Tom.

"Perhaps it's not something you want to hear," answered Lewis in an unusually soft voice.

"Please," said Tom. "I do want to hear."

Lewis walked along in silence for a while, brushing his hand along the tassled heads of some tall stalks of grass that grew alongside the path. Finally, he spoke: "When you and I first met," said Lewis, "I remember the zest with which you quoted Tennyson."

"I recall that too," said Tom. "I started declaiming a passage from 'The Passing of Arthur' and you finished it."

"Yes, that's right. I remember thinking that day, 'I've just discovered a new friend.'"

Tom's heart glowed when he heard these words. But he also sensed an admonition in the air.

"But there is always a danger of losing one's first love. You might begin studying literature for the sheer joy of it, a love of imagination and word-craft. But after a time, something else sets in. The lover becomes the pundit. You pick up your Tennyson in order to examine his syntax and his stanza forms. Your interest in the *manner* of his writing begins to overshadow your interest in the *matter*."

"Yes, I know what you mean," said Tom. "I've had teachers who seemed more interested in the footnotes of books than the actual texts."

Lewis nodded. "Yes, I have colleagues like that too. They have become 'professional' in the worst sense of the word. A tell-tale sign is when they consider you a bore for wanting to discuss literature outside of work hours. They seem to say, 'Lewis, didn't you hear the whistle blow? Our workday's over;

we don't have to keep discussing books.'" Lewis looked over at Tom, and then continued: "But one can slip even further. At some point, the scholar may continue his work not for the reader's love of the subject or even the pedant's fascination for details. He may continue his work simply to build his reputation, to achieve eminence." At that point, he's twice removed from his original purpose. And therein lies a danger to the health of his soul."

Tom felt a pang, as if Lewis could see into his own heart. He did indeed feel a gnawing hunger, a restless craving for renown. He wanted to get his book on King Arthur into print, at the very least. But there was something else that was driving him. Could he be the one who proved, once and for all, there was a historical Arthur? Could he uncover a lance in England that proved to be *the* fabled Spear? Tom knew down deep that his real grail quest was to escape anonymity, to become Somebody in the eyes of the world.

Tom could admit this to himself, but not to Lewis. "I appreciate the word of caution," he said. "But, really, I just want to do the best job I can in writing this book. I want to do justice to the subject." Feeling a growing pressure in his chest, Tom decided it was time to change the topic. "I'll try to remember your 'word to the wise,'" he said, "though I still think Laura and I ought to make another call on Glastonbury."

"Your friend with the dreams?" said Lewis, who also seemed relieved to change to subject. "And how is she getting on?"

"Pretty well," answered Tom. "In one of her night-visions, she sees a sleeping king with a lion at his feet. And she found exactly what she was looking for at Malmesbury: the figure of Athelstan on top of a tomb-chest."

"Intriguing," Lewis said quietly.

"It's uncanny really," said Tom. "She seemed to know as much about the abbey as the docent there, though she'd never set foot in Malmesbury until last week." Tom reached down for a round, flat stone in the path, picked it up, and skipped it across the river. "I envy her," he said. "She's on a kind of quest. And she's found the king she was looking for."

They heard a cacophony of bird cries overhead and stopped to watch a flock of geese circling overhead. The V-shaped squadron circled once around a wide spot in the Thames, then circled again a little lower. Then they all came down at once, landing together in a riot of splashing and honks.

"I'd like to see the RAF try that maneuver," said Tom.

Lewis smiled, choosing that odd moment to straighten his tie. "We should probably keep moving," he said. "Dyson may start to wonder what's become of us."

The two of them continued walking along the river, with woods and pastures on both sides, hardly a road or a building in sight. "I'm sorry my brother couldn't be here," Lewis said. "We all love Dyson and his wit, but none more than my brother. When he's in his best form, Dyson is a roaring cataract of nonsense."

They passed by the gray stones of an abandoned barn and Lewis stopped again to take in the view. "Look at that ribbon of cloud above the barn," he said. "It almost looks like a winding road that leads to the other side of the horizon." Tom looked too, and it did indeed look like a floating byway across the sky. "It reminds you of Bifrost, doesn't it?" said Lewis. "The 'tremulous bridge' to Asgard, home of the gods." Tom nodded and smiled, but Lewis turned away from the scene with what sounded almost like a sigh. The two of them resumed their walk along the river.

A few minutes later a mother duck climbed out of the river and waddled across the path, followed by six ducklings. Lewis and Tom stopped and let them pass, like pedestrians at a crosswalk.

"I think that is what makes a walk in the country so soothing," said Lewis. "All creatures acting in obedience to their nature, as their Maker intended."

"That's one way of looking at it," answered Tom, watching the parade of ducks disappear into the bushes. "But what other people see is 'nature red in tooth and claw.' The insects eat the leaves, the little birds eat the insects, and the big birds eat the little ones. A ceaseless struggle for survival."

"You are a Darwinian then?" asked Lewis, looking over at Tom.

"I'm not educated enough in the sciences to know what I am," answered Tom. "But it's easier for me to see nature in terms of random survival than in terms of a kindly Gamekeeper in the sky."

"Do you consider yourself an atheist?"

"Not exactly," answered Tom. "That sounds too much like an actual philosophy, as if I'd proven to my own satisfaction that God doesn't exist. I don't sit around all day grinding my teeth at believers."

"An agnostic?" offered Lewis.

"That's closer, I suppose," said Tom. "But even calling yourself an agnostic implies you have sifted the evidence. To say you don't know implies a positive decision, that you've examined the evidence for both sides and found it wanting."

"I quite agree," said Lewis. "Saying you can't decide is a kind of deciding. Both the theist and the atheist would disagree that the evidence doesn't point in either direction. But what do you call yourself then?"

"To be honest, I hadn't thought about it much until this summer." He shoved his hands into his pockets as they walked along, and tried to think how best to explain himself. "Perhaps I would call myself an Apatheist," he said at last. "Someone who just hasn't put much thought into religious questions. I've been too caught up in the here and now to be concerned with the not-here and after-now," he explained.

Lewis smiled and nodded his head. "I admire your candor," he said. "And don't think you are alone. If all you Apatheists get organized, I'm sure you will quickly become one of the largest congregations in England and America."

Tom kept his hands in his pockets, and he kept his head down as he talked. "I still have trouble believing that a good God could create a world with so much evil and suffering," he said. Looking at Lewis, Tom added, "I remember what you said at the Bird and Baby about God respecting humans' free will. But, really, is this the best he can do? *This* is the best of all possible worlds? Hitler's vicious persecution of the Jews, the Nazis running roughshod all over Europe. Don't you think God could invent a new, improved model of human beings who don't abuse their free will so atrociously?"

"Believe me, I sympathize with your position," said Lewis. "When I was your age, I used to quote the Roman poet Lucretius:

Had God designed the world, it would not be
A world so frail and faulty as we see."

Tom nodded: that summed his position perfectly. "And yet," continued Lewis, "there's a catch. If some amoral brute created the world, he also created our minds. And how can we trust moral judgments given to us by this same amoral brute? If you reject God because there is so much evil in the universe, you need to explain where you obtained your standard for discerning good and evil."

"Better to give up the idea of God altogether, I guess," said Tom, almost under his breath.

"Yes, I tried that too," said Lewis, reminiscing more than arguing. "But there always seems to be a fifth columnist in our souls. When you try to believe, part of you keeps asking questions. And when you doubt, part of you thinks it would make more sense to believe. I tried my best to be an atheist, but it seems that every set of answers generates its own set of questions. If you think this physical world is 'the whole show,' you have to wonder why it is here at all. Why it seems to obey such orderly principles. How it got started. Even what it is made of. Lately these physicists can't decide if the basic 'stuff' of the universe is particles or waves, or neither or both. When I read these modern physicists, they sound to me like the old Church doctors trying to sort out free will and predestination. No matter which direction you go, you seem to knock your head against these unavoidable paradoxes."

They walked past a hawthorn hedge, with a little sparrow pecking at some red berries, as if trying to decide if they were edible or not.

"But don't you think science can give us the best picture of reality?" asked Tom.

"Within limits," answered Lewis. "Science studies Nature, the material world. But it can't tell us if there is anything behind Nature. I think some of the best clues as to the ultimate meaning of things are the ones closest at hand. We've already talked about the moral law within, a general consensus about right and wrong. But we all have to acknowledge as well that we're not living up to that moral law. We all must admit that our very best behavior isn't all that good. I think that's why the Dying God myth appears in so many cultures. Everyone feels the need for redemption."

Tom was amazed how smoothly all these points fit together in Lewis's mind. He had run into Christians before, and they always seemed to rely on memorized Bible verses, dogmatic answers or catechism-style formulations of truth. He had never talked to anyone before who spoke so effortlessly about his faith, who made it sound like little more than sanctified common sense.

"I think there was another clue to the meaning of things just back down the river a few minutes ago."

Tom didn't recall seeing any tablets of stone or angels with shining swords, so he waited for Lewis to explain. "Do you remember when we were walking by the stone barn? The cloud that looked like a bridge to the beyond?"

Tom nodded that he remembered.

"As I looked at it and thought of Asgard, it created a peculiar sensation in my breast, a painful sort of pleasure. I didn't want to just look at the cloud and imagine it as a bridge. I wanted to cross over the bridge, to join the gods and slain heroes waiting on the other side of the sky."

"Yes, I know what you mean," said Tom. "That why I threw a stick into Dozmary Pool. I knew it was a silly thing to do. But I didn't want to just imagine the Lady of the Lake; I wanted to enter into the story myself. There's a kind yearning that comes over you that is also an ache. It's as if you've found the door to Eden, but you're not allowed to go in."

"That it's precisely!" boomed Lewis enthusiastically. "I've been having that experience ever since I was a child. I call it 'Sweet Desire,' or sometimes just 'Joy.' It's an ache for the infinite, a sense of some lost paradise calling out to us. Sometimes I hear 'the horns of elfland' in the call of birds flying overhead. Sometimes it can be just a phrase from a book—'The Well at the World's End.'"

Tom nodded again. He had had these experiences all his life as well. But he had supposed they were just a quirk of his own psychology. He had never known till now that anyone else had them, or treasured them, the way he did.

"Don't those experiences make more sense if you think of them as a kind of homesickness for heaven? As Augustine said, 'Our hearts are restless until they rest in Thee.' If the Christian view is right, we are all exiles from paradise."

Lewis's analogy seemed perfectly timed, for as they passed a stand of alder trees, they came to a bridge leading to a crowded pub on the other side of the river.

"And here's the Trout," said Lewis. Tom could see a large, two-story inn with a slate roof and two tall chimneys. "I'm sure Dyson will be glad to see you again," said Lewis.

Tom stopped at the bridge and looked across the river at the people sitting outside, eating and drinking, talking and laughing. He wasn't feeling hungry, and he wasn't really in the mood for "a roaring cataract of nonsense."

"Would you think me terribly rude if I decided not to join you two for lunch?" Tom asked.

Lewis looked surprised but not upset. "That would be quite all right," he said. "Dyson plus one makes for a full table!" he added affably.

"It has been a real pleasure walking with you," said Tom, shaking Lewis's hand. "You've given me plenty to think about."

"Delighted to talk to you," said Lewis. He crossed the bridge and stopped at the entrance of the pub, looking back over the river and giving Tom a friendly nod. Tom nodded back and thought about changing his mind, about going on over to join the others for lunch. But he didn't feel up to it.

Not quite ready to turn back for Oxford, Tom decided to continue walking up the Thames. The pub across the river had a large outdoor patio, which was mostly full of young men and women, enjoying the food, the drink, the river, the sunshine.

Tom envied their carefree laughter, but he felt the need to keep walking. He continued up the footpath, quiet water to his left, green pastures to his right.

Tom kept walking till the sound of human voices faded away. He found a little willow tree not far from the river and decided just to sit and watch awhile, to let his own thoughts flow where they may. He gazed at the water sliding by and listened to its soothing ripples of sound. He watched a goose dozing in the grass, its head tucked under its wing. Even the slow drone of an insect flying by had a drowsy sound to it, as if all nature were ready for a nap.

How could the world around him seem so serene, so complacent? Couldn't it hear the riot in his head, that whole unruly throng of thoughts and feelings all shoving their way to the forefront of his mind? He felt a kind of vertigo and put one hand down on the ground. He'd felt dizzy that time on Hard Knott Pass, when he and Laura came suddenly upon those wide and unexpected vistas. But this time it wasn't just the landscape that seemed to be tilting. He felt as if his whole world might be turning upside down.

What if? The great Perhaps. What if his life, all human life, were not just a Darwinian accident in a vast, empty universe? What if the cosmos, with all its jeweled stars and tasseled galaxies, were only the hem of a garment, the robe of infinite majesty? "The heavens declare the glory."

Then came a more troubling question: what if his soul were not his own? What if he were under orders? What if the great quest, the abiding question, were not how to find renown but rather how to find—and do—the will of Another?

Tom felt a great surge within, but whether it was gladness or fear he could not tell. Then he did something that reminded him of childhood: he offered up a kind of prayer. Closing his eyes, he spoke the words aloud: "I *do* feel the longing, God. I do wonder if I'm made for something else. And I get so tired of myself. It would be so good to know I'm a child of yours, and I don't have anything to prove. My heart *is* restless, God. I'm looking for some peace."

Tom felt like saying, "I hope to hear from you soon." But that didn't sound right, so he just ended with "Amen." He looked up and everything was just the same: the river, the grass, the mild sky. He felt foolish, but he also felt better. It was as if some nameless burden had begun to melt away. He reached up to wipe his face and discovered something else that reminded him of childhood: his cheeks were wet with tears.

# ← 11 →

That bluish mound on the horizon. The one beyond the zigzag hedgerow. That's Cadbury Castle. It's one of the best candidates for the real Camelot."

Tom and Laura were standing on top of Glastonbury Tor, and Tom was pointing southeast. Shielding her eyes from the midday sun, Laura nodded that she could see where he was pointing. "When I was down here in Somerset this April, I stood on that very hill and could see where we're standing now, the Tor and St. Michael's tower here." Tom glanced back over his shoulder at a great square tower, a hollowed-out ruin, with castellated battlements, like a giant chess piece.

"Did you come up here last time too?' asked Laura.

"I came to Glastonbury," Tom replied. "But I never made it up here. I cut my visit short. This is where I met those tough guys I told you about. Let's just try to blend in this time, to look like tourists."

"I hope we can still go have a look at the abbey."

"Of course," said Tom, making a you-first gesture with his arm. They started down the winding path, surrounded by green pastures dotted with grazing sheep. Besides the yellow buttercups and purple thistles, there were bright red poppies scattered all over the hillside.

The two of them kept walking until they reached the outskirts of Glastonbury. They were headed in the direction of the abbey ruin when Laura stopped suddenly and put her hand over her mouth. "What?" asked Tom, looking at the old abbey barn at the side of the road.

"Tom," Laura said excitedly, "This is it! This is the one in my dream. The church with the animals going in and out!"

"Are you sure?" said Tom. "This isn't a church. It's the abbey barn, where the monks kept the crops and livestock."

"Well, that explains the animals!" said Laura eagerly. She walked toward the gate and took a closer look. "This is definitely the building I've been seeing in my dreams!" Laura exclaimed.

As he joined Laura at the gate, Tom could see why someone might mistake the abbey barn for a church. It had dressed stone walls with sturdy buttresses and cross-shaped window slits. There was even a mullioned window on one end and a little cross on top. But it looked even more like a barn—its broad gabled roof, its great square door in the middle, and muddy barnyard out front, surrounded by a stone wall. There was even an old stone watering trough, though it was covered with moss and half crumbled to dust.

"I don't know what there is to see here," said Tom. "It just looks like someone has been using it as a regular barn—at least until a few years ago."

"I'm going in!" said Laura firmly.

"We're trying not to call attention to ourselves," said Tom nervously. But Laura didn't seem to hear; she lifted the latch on the gate and looked back to see if Tom were coming too. Glancing quickly left and right, and then behind him, Tom cautiously stepped inside the gate. The wooden gate was hard to budge. When they finally swung it open, it made an eerie creak, almost like a groan. They walked along a raised cart path, overgrown with grass, that led up to the main door of the barn, a wide arched portal right in the middle of the front wall. One of the great barn doors was open and the other was missing entirely, so they had no trouble looking inside.

When they stepped in, they found it dimly lit by the doors in front and back, and from narrow window slits on both ends. Once their eyes had adjusted to the faint light, they could see that the building was mostly empty, with only a few sagging bales of hay stacked here and there, blackened with rot and age. The cobblestone floor was mostly bare, except for a few charred logs where someone had built a fire, vagabonds perhaps, taking shelter from the rain. In the south corner of the barn was a cart with spoked wheels, the kind drawn by a horse or mule in the old days. Near it lay a wooden ladder along the wall, stacked beside some portable scaffolding. These must have been for hoisting haybales into a loft, though the upper platform had long since collapsed.

The most impressive thing about the barn, besides its dressed stone walls, was its elegant wooden rafters, thick oaken beams supporting the stone roof, with graceful arches and vertical posts that rested on stone piers. "This barn is more beautiful than some churches I've seen in America," said Tom, looking up at those artfully engineered rafters. "That's no joke trying to hold up a slate roof," he added. He felt they'd seen everything there was to see and he started toward the barn door from which they had entered.

"Look over there," said Laura, pointing. "That cart."

Tom looked and saw that unremarkable old cart piled high with loose hay, with two yoke-poles sticking out front.

"Yes, one haycart. One pile of hay," he said.

"Nothing else in here has been used for years," said Laura.

"Why would someone be loading the cart with fresh hay? Let's go have a closer look," insisted Laura, walking over to the corner of the barn.

Tom reached out to grab hold of Laura's shoulder, but she was beyond his reach. He went and peeked out the doorway to see if there was anyone else around, then followed her over to the corner of the barn. By the time he got there, Laura had already walked completely around the cart and was ready to report.

"Ok, Tom, let's test your powers of investigation. What's odd about this scene?"

"Besides the two of us standing here?" Tom said, still keeping an eye on the door.

Laura made a little frown, the way a mother responds to an obstinate child, and offered her own observations. "Listen, I've been to my grandparents' farm in Lancaster County dozens of times. First of all, you leave the hay in bales until you take it out to where you intend to feed the livestock. You don't pile a cart with loose hay."

"Should I be taking notes?" Tom asked.

"Second," she said, "the pile should be loaded over the wheels, for balance. But it's all piled in the back." Pointing to the front of the cart, she added, "Look. One of the yoke poles has been tied down, anchored to an iron ring in the floor, to keep the cart from tipping over backwards."

Tom walked over to the cart and grabbed a handful of hay. He pulled it out of the pile and gave it a sniff. "Smells like hay," he observed. But then he looked back at the cart and saw something that genuinely surprised him. "Hey, Sherlock," he called out. Laura came around to the side of the cart and looked where he was pointing. Beneath the spot where he had grabbed some hay, there was something darker, more solid.

They brushed away the surface layer of hay and discovered it was covering a pile of moist earth, strewn with cobblestones and mud-encrusted rocks.

"No wonder the cart is to tethered to the floor," said Tom, "that pile of dirt must weigh at least a ton."

"Where'd it all come from?" asked Laura. Tom looked around the barn and could see nothing but the empty cobblestone floor, with a few piles of hay scattered here and there.

"Look over here in the corner," said Laura, "behind the cart. Isn't the straw distributed too evenly? The same way the hay in the cart is covering the load of dirt."

"We really shouldn't be in here," said Tom, peering out a narrow window slit to see if there was anybody outside. Again, Laura seemed not to hear him. "This whole corner has a familiar feel to it," she said. "The herring-bone stonework. The way the walls don't quite meet at a right angle." Tom came up beside her to see what details had caught her attention this time. She took a step toward the corner to get a better look, but she pulled her foot back quickly as soon as it touched the layer of straw. She threw her arm in front of Tom and held him back. "Don't take another step!" she shouted, "it's a trap!"

Tom didn't like her peremptory orders, but he didn't mind her arm across his chest.

"What are you talking about?" he asked.

"The footing isn't solid," explained Laura, "it's soft underneath. "She kneeled down and brushed away the surface straw, revealing a piece of coarse cloth. Tom kneeled down too and they carefully brushed away the straw, exposing a canvas tarp, about ten feet square, that had been stretched out and staked down at all four corners. Laura pushed down on it softly, and Tom could see it give.

"You see?" Laura said, "there's nothing solid under there."

"Curiouser and curiouser," said Tom. He felt the ground for himself, but he mainly kept his eyes on the open barn door.

"What should we do?" asked Laura. "Should we have a look?"

"I don't think so," said Tom. "This would be a bad spot to be in if somebody blocked the entrance."

Laura laughed a little at Tom's caution. "Come on," she said, "Where's your sense of adventure? I didn't see any No Trespassing signs. And we can put everything back the way we found it. And there's a back door right over there." Laura pointed to a little wooden door in the opposite corner of the barn. Tom felt relieved when he spotted the second exit, so he cautiously nodded his head.

Quietly and carefully, they pulled out the two stakes nearest the hay cart and threw it back like a bedspread. Beneath it they found a hole about six feet across, as if someone had been trying to dig a well. They couldn't see to the bottom in the dim light of the barn, so Tom took off his rucksack and pulled out a flashlight. Shining its beam down into the hole, they could see that it was about ten feet deep, exposing thick, rough-hewn foundation stones beneath the ground level. There was a slight recess between two weight-bearing piers, but Tom couldn't see how far back it went. Moving around the rim, he shined his light on the other side of the hole, revealing a wooden ladder, leading up to the back of the haycart, which had its tailgate down.

"Now we know where all the dirt came from," Tom said. "Somebody went to a lot of trouble to dig out this hole and pile the dirt in that cart," he added.

"But why?" asked Laura.

"Maybe the foundation is crumbling on this end," suggested

Tom. "Maybe there's been a crew out here to shore it up. There's some scaffolding over there, with a block and tackle, to hoist some buckets up from the bottom."

"I don't see anything wrong with the foundation," said Laura. "And if it's just a work crew, why not leave the scaffolding up? Why hide the hole and the dirt underneath a layer of straw?"

"All good questions," said Tom. "Maybe we should go into town and ask around."

"Or maybe we should go down there and have a look," said Laura.

Tom handed her the flashlight, gestured toward the ladder, and said, "Ladies first!"

Laura handed the flashlight back and said simply, "Claustrophobia." Then she added earnestly, "Please, Tom. Do this for me. This has the real-life feeling of my visions. It feels like I've been here before. Couldn't you just go down and take a quick look?"

Tom sighed and took one last look at the door. Then he stepped down the ladder, and shined the light around, while Laura looked down eagerly from the rim of the hole.

"What do you see?" she said.

"Mostly dirt," said Tom. He took a closer look at the exposed stones. "You're right about the foundation," Tom said. "These stones look like they'll be here for another thousand years." When he shined his light on the recess, he took a closer look. "Hmm," he said. "This niche goes back a ways."

"How far?" asked Laura, eagerly.

"Just a few feet. It looks like there might have been a little chamber here, maybe even a tunnel. But the roof has collapsed so you can't go back very far." Tom reached down and pulled away a few loose stones, but he could tell there was nothing underneath but more dirt, dust, and rubble. "I wonder if this is what the workmen are trying to excavate," he called back over his shoulder.

"They're being awfully sneaky about it," Laura replied. She moved around to a different angle to get a look at the recess Tom had been exploring. Suddenly, she got excited again and said, "Shine your light on that wooden beam. The one embedded in the stone a few feet into the niche." Tom did as he was told and saw a thick, twisted oaken beam, crusted with dirt, running from over his head to a thick stone base at its feet. It was mortised to a crossbeam that ran from the edge of the recess back into the tunnel and out of sight.

"It looks like a support beam," Tom said, "probably to hold up the ceiling of the chamber. Like the ones up there on the barn roof.

"Look really close!" said Laura, almost shouting. She disappeared for a moment, then returned with an old hand spade she'd found behind the cart. "Here, use this!" she said, tossing the shovel down into the hole."

"Be careful! You might put somebody's eye out," Tom said. He picked up the little shovel, with its wooden handle and dented blade, then shined his light back up at Laura. "Use it for what?" he said. "I'm supposed to dig out a pile of stone and rubble with this?"

"Oh, Tom," Laura said. "Quit being infuriating! Forget about the tunnel or whatever it is. The wooden beam. Scrape it as clean as you can." Tom went over and knocked off what might have been centuries of dirt and mud. He found underneath just what he had expected, a thick flat beam, crooked and cracked with age, but just about as solid as the stones surrounding it.

"What do you see?" Laura called down.

"Nothing," said Tom, "just an upright post holding up a crossbeam."

"Look closer, Tom. Any writing on it?" Tom could find nothing but a few ridges and grooves, just the scars of hand tools left by builders who knew their work was not for show. He ran his hands across the wood, as if trying to read Braille. But they revealed nothing more than his eyes could see.

"Nope," he said. "Just wood."

Laura disappeared from sight for a few moments, then reappeared with a piece of a charred log and a large coarse rag in her hands. "Use these," she said.

"At the risk of being infuriating: Use them for what?" asked Tom.

"Clean off the upright timber as best you can," explained Laura, like a teacher supervising a student. "Then rub it up and down with the charred piece of wood."

Tom did as he was told, and soon the timber was black from top to bottom, as if he'd painted it with charcoal.

"Ok, now take the rag and brush away the residue," said Laura.

Tom began rubbing about face level and saw nothing but the natural grain of the wood and a few adze-marks. "Say, this is sort of like brass rubbing," he said. "We did this once—"

"Do you see any letters?" Laura shouted down. She had moved around the top of the hole opposite him, so she could see his work directly.

When he got down about chest high, Tom noticed a black mark on the left side of the beam that looked like something more than just a random scratch. He leaned and rubbed it gently, uncovering something that looked like a curvy Y. Rubbing further down, he uncovered another figure, a rough oval about two inches wide.

"It's writing, isn't it?" shouted Laura from up above. "I can see some figures from up here."

Tom stepped back and shined his light upwards into Laura's face. Her curly hair was hanging down, and she had a smudge of dirt on her forehead. The flashlight beam glinted in her eyes, and Tom forgot what he was going to say. What he was looking at seemed to him so much more interesting than some charcoal scribbles on a piece of gnarled old wood.

"What are you stopping for?" asked Laura impatiently. "Tell me what it looks like from down there." Tom turned back to the two figures and traced each one with his fingers. A curvy Y and a fat oval. "The one on top looks sort of like rabbit ears," he said. "And the second one is round."

Tom worked his way down the beam and uncovered three more figures beneath the other two. One looked like a Y on its side, the next like an X and the last like the number three that wasn't quite finished. Tom studied the five figures arranged from top to bottom, about halfway up the left side of the timber.

$$\begin{array}{c} \rotatebox{90}{$\lambda$} \\ \rotatebox{90}{$\acute{o}$} \\ \rotatebox{90}{$\gamma$} \\ \rotatebox{90}{$\chi$} \\ \rotatebox{90}{$\acute{\eta}$} \end{array}$$

Tom moved out of the way so Laura could see it from above. "That's all I can find," he said. "I'm not sure if they're even figures, or just accidental dents in the wood."

"Oh, Tom!" Laura shouted excitedly, "Don't you see?"

Tom looked back at the shapes he'd uncovered and then back at Laura. He didn't see.

"Unbend that stiff neck of yours! Look from a different angle!" Tom turned his head to the right, brushed a smudge on one figure and traced his finger over another. Suddenly they did begin to look familiar:  λ ό γ χ ή

"It's Greek to me," he said. "Literally. These are letters: Lambda. Omicron. Gamma. Chi. Eta. . . . . *"Logche!"* he cried out. "That means *spear* in Greek!"

"I knew it!" shouted Laura, "this is all like my dream. This is the crypt with the writing!"

"But why Greek?" Tom wondered aloud. "All the monks knew Latin but in the old days, but not many knew Greek."

"Maybe it was the 'not many' who etched the letters in the wood," said Laura.

"I wonder if that really means somebody's spear is hidden further down this tunnel? If we could get the permit for a dig, we could—"

"Forget the tunnel," said Laura. "Concentrate on the wood."

"Ok, but you keep an eye on the doorway," answered Tom.

Tom looked at the wooden beam again, kneeling down for a better look and tracing each letter with his finger one by one. *"Logche.* Spear," he said to himself quietly.

"Try pressing down hard on the center of the omicron," Laura instructed from above.

Tom had gotten used to taking orders by now, so he pressed his finger on the o-shaped symbol on the post. To his surprise, it responded to his finger, retreating into the beam slightly, like an elevator button. Tom heard a dull click behind the wood, and then the section of the beam with letters on it popped open sideways, like the wooden panel over a wall safe.

"You were right!" shouted Tom excitedly. "A little door just popped open! How did you know?" he added.

"I don't how I knew," said Laura, her voice trembling. "Just tell me what's inside!"

Tom carefully opened the little door and found the beam hollowed out inside, with a bundle wrapped in coarse cloth stuffed into in the hidden chamber. It was about the length of his forearm and looked like it been resting in that hollowed out beam for centuries. Tom reached out to grab the bundle, but then hesitated. Stepping back and shining the light up at Laura, he looked up at her and asked, "What next?"

Laura, who had seemed so sure of herself till now, seemed to share Tom's sense of awe and caution. "I don't know," she said. "Could it be something dangerous? Some sort of booby trap?"

"I doubt it," answered Tom. "Who would hide a booby trap inside an old timber ten feet underground in an abandoned barn?"

"All the same, I guess we should go into town and report this to the authorities," said Laura. "This could be something really important."

Laura's caution had the wrong effect on Tom, making him feel bold and reckless. His ambition, his sense of adventure, and his general aversion to authority all conspired against Laura's sensible advice. "I suppose you're right," admitted Tom. But his hands seemed unconnected to his brain; they reached out and laid hold of the bundle. "Let's just have a quick look," he said.

"Tom, be careful!" Laura shouted from above. And he was careful, cradling the bundle in his arms, and slowly peeling off the outer layer near the top. It was coarse and brittle, like ancient parchment, and it crumbled to pieces as soon as he touched it. The layers underneath were in better shape, rough like burlap, but supple enough to be folded back. Underneath these layers was a much finer fabric, shiny and finely woven like samite. Tom could begin to see a hard, triangular shape just beneath the satiny cloth, like a spearhead, and he paused before peeling back the last few folds. He had the odd sensation of pulling back a blanket to look into a baby's face.

Suddenly doubts began fluttering through Tom's head like bats in a cavern. Perhaps there was truly something sacred here, something upon which he was utterly unworthy to gaze. Or could it be something unspeakably evil, a talisman that that would drive him mad or turn him to stone? Tom took a deep breath, tried to empty his mind of all the superstitions and myths he had been collecting since boyhood, and surrendered himself to the moment. After all, he told himself, he had a right to look. He was an accredited researcher, investigating an abbey barn in Glastonbury, examining an unusual artifact he himself had discovered among the foundation stones.

Tom slowly lifted the final layer near the top of the bundle, exposing what looked like the tip of a lance, a dull metallic gray, but with an edge that looked sharp enough to cut his finger. There was something hypnotic about the sight, though the part he saw was no larger than an arrowhead. At that point Tom seemed to have lost the strength to unwrap the bundle any further. It felt impossibly light, as if it might float into the air unless he held on tight. But it was also impossibly heavy, more heavy than gold, as though it would plunge down to the very center of the earth if he didn't hold onto it with all his might.

Tom stood with his eyes affixed, not moving, his mind empty. Suddenly he heard Laura's frantic voice above. "Someone's coming!" she said in a hoarse whisper. "I just caught the sound of that creaking gate out front!"

Tom felt his heart jump in his chest. He thought about clambering up the ladder, but he knew there wasn't time for that. "No sense our both getting caught," he whispered from the bottom of the hole. "Why don't you slip out the side door and head into town? I'll just keep quiet down here. We can rendezvous later at the market square."

"I can't just abandon you down there," said Laura.

"Listen, if I get into trouble for this, I'll need someone on the outside to post my bail. You need to get out of here."

Laura thought for a moment, then looked over her shoulder, as if she could hear the steps getting closer. She looked back down at Tom, stuck down in that hole, and he saw an expression on her face he'd never seen before—apprehension, certainly, but also something like pity, perhaps even tenderness. "Good luck!" Laura whispered, "holy luck!" She made a little wave and then hurried away toward the side door of the barn.

◁ • ▷

Tom turned off his light, stepped as far back into the niche as he could, and tried to take soft, shallow breaths, despite feeling suddenly short of air. Hard-soled shoes clicked on the stone floor of the barn. The sounds stopped for a few seconds, then the footsteps got louder. Tom leaned as far back as he could into the darkness and held his breath. Suddenly, though, there was a beam of light shining down the hole, revealing the tips of his boots sticking out.

"Fee, fie, foe, fum. I see the boots of an American," Tom heard a pleasant voice say from up above. "Is that Mr. McCord perhaps?" The beam of light circled around the bottom of the hole. "And Miss Hartman? Are you down there too?"

Tom couldn't think of any other option, so he stepped out into the light. At first he was blinded by the bright beam shining in his face. "Ah, I see it *is* you, Mr. McCord! Whatever are you doing down there?" Tom recognized the voice, but he still couldn't place it. Finally, the man at the rim of the hole turned off his flashlight, and Tom recognized Willem De Lott, the owner of the manor house at Temple Despy. He was as stylishly dressed as ever, wearing a navy-blue suit and a gray fedora, as if he'd just come from a dinner party.

"I was just looking around. More research for my book," said Tom, trying to sound as casual as possible.

"Oh, come now, Mr. McCord. Researching your book at the bottom of a hole in an abandoned abbey barn?"

"Well," Tom replied, in the most casual voice he could muster. "I figured if someone went to all the trouble to dig this hole, I should at least have a look around."

"And what did you find?" asked De Lott.

"Nothing, really. Just rocks and dirt. There's some sort of niche or chamber down here. I thought it might be tunnel back towards the abbey. But it looks like it caved in centuries ago."

"Yes, that's about as far as I got too. I was hoping your girl-friend might be able to help me out from here. But I see she's not down there."

"She's my assistant," said Tom stiffly. "I sent her back to town, to see if anyone there knew something about this dig. Maybe to ask about getting a permit for a proper excavation."

Mr. De Lott's habitual smile disappeared. "Sent her back? When?" he asked.

"About an hour ago," said Tom. "I told her to stay in town and I'd meet her later. There's really nothing more to do here today."

Tom stepped forward to climb the ladder, but he heard a sudden, "Halt!" He looked up to see De Lott with a Luger in his hand, pointed directly at him. "Please, Mr. McCord. Quit playing the fool. The last thing we need is to have any local authorities involved. This is my private little dig, and you are— what would you Americans call it?—a claim jumper. Now you just stay down there."

"Really, Mr. De Lott, I have no idea what you're taking about. I was just looking around and my curiosity got the better of me—"

"Come, come, Mr. McCord," interrupted De Lott, making circles in the air with the barrel of his pistol. "Enough of your 'Innocents Abroad' routine. I know what you're looking for and you know what I'm looking for."

"Honestly, Mr. De Lott—"

"Dishonestly, you mean," broke in De Lott. "Really, young man, I'm getting tired of your mendacities. I found out that you and your girlfriend headed up to Gosforth right after you met me, even though I told you it wouldn't be worth your trip."

"What do you care?" asked Tom. "Since when does it matter which tourist sites we visit?"

"It matters because you're here to steal the very thing I've spent the past two years looking for," said De Lott between his teeth. Suddenly De Lott switched back to his usual friendly tone, as if they were just two old friends talking about their common interests. "Now, where is that young lady again? She's the one I need to talk to."

"Like I said," answered Tom. "She went back to town. If you'll let me climb up, perhaps we can go find her."

"Stay there!" De Lott commanded, again pointing his Luger straight at Tom. "I'm sure we're looking in the right place. We just need one more piece of the puzzle—a piece Miss Hartman better have, for your sake."

"I don't understand," said Tom, feeling as curious as he was afraid. "Of all the places in England, all the conflicting legends, what makes you so sure there's anything so special down in this hole?"

"Miss Hartman's notebook," explained De Lott slyly. "She likes to make drawings of her dreams. The 'country church' with animals going in and out. The stonework on this wall, the hidden tunnel down there. It's all just as we see here." De Lott pointed his pistol at the recess behind Tom. "She's got a lot of natural talent," added De Lott. "But she needs to work on her perspective. Too much foreshortening."

"I'll be happy to pass that along next time I see her," said Tom. "So you did sneak into her room at Windermere then?" asked Tom.

"Not me personally," explained De Lott. "I guess it wouldn't hurt for you to know. It was that fool Mirden. I had to let him go. Neither reliable nor discrete."

"I'm sorry to hear he wasn't up to your standards," said Tom with wasted irony.

"Almost got caught at Windermere," mused De Lott. "Then there was that bicycle snatch in Malmesbury. It was the young lady's diary I wanted, not your dry old notes about Athelstan."

"So you fired him?" asked Tom, trying to buy time.

"I'm sorry to say he got 'pinched,' as you Americans say." Suddenly, De Lott straightened up and took a look around. "And I will be too if I spend all day around here making pleasantries."

"Well," said Tom, "if you'll put that pistol away, I have an idea for you. Pull up the ladder, and you'll be long gone before anyone finds me down here."

"A capital suggestion," said De Lott. But then he looked at the haycart and shook his head. "But I'm afraid it won't do. First, I have an aversion to manual labor. You know, it was some associates of mine who dug this hole, not me. And second," he hissed, "you know too much. You keep getting in my way."

Tom's mouth was dry as he tried to read the genial, ruthless face above him. "Surely, you wouldn't shoot me over some old relic you've got your heart set on."

"My heart has nothing to do with it," explained De Lott calmly. "And you have no idea of the value of what I'm looking for. Armies depend on it. Nations depend on it." De Lott paused, then resumed again in his usual bantering tone. "But you needn't worry about my shooting you." The Dutchman holstered his pistol and Tom felt momentarily relieved. "Gunshots make too much noise," explained De Lott. "And besides, if you had a bullet wound, even these local dullards would discover some foul play."

"I'm not stopping you," said Tom. "Feel free to take your leave."

"Just one last thing," said De Lott, smiling and holding up the pocketknife. "Just a quick slice of the cord in front of the haycart. That will send it tipping backward, all those tons of dirt and rock down upon your sorry head. A tragic accident, I'm afraid. A young American mucking around where he shouldn't have been, an unstable load of earth, and you'll be buried. That seems a fitting way to go, don't you think?" De Lott lifted the knife and began to step toward the front of the haycart.

"Wait!" said Tom, "what if I already found what you're looking for? What if I turned it over to you?"

De Lott's eyes widened, but his lips tightened. "Another fabrication," he said. "If you think I'm going to come down there—"

"No, no," explained Tom, "I could toss it up to you. Then you could pull up the ladder and clear out. You could be long gone before anyone could give chase."

"An interesting proposal," said De Lott. "That is, if you're telling the truth. Actually, I've already made arrangements to leave the country. But it would be ever so much more pleasant for all concerned if I had a little something to take with me."

De Lott held up the pocketknife and said, "All right, show me what you've got. And if this is a trick, a curse upon your head—along with two tons of earth."

Tom turned around, disappeared into the niche, and then knelt down a few seconds.

"What are you doing down there?" yelled De Lott. "Be quick about it!"

"All right, all right," muttered Tom. "It's wrapped in a bundle. I need to tie it in a knot before I can toss it up." Tom turned around, cradling a bundle in his arms, a solid object wrapped in coarse cloth. "Maybe it would be safer if I carried it up?" he suggested.

"No," commanded De Lott, "Stay where you are. Just toss it up and I'll catch it."

Tom took the bundle in both hands and flung it upwards. He saw De Lott reach out his arms, but suddenly the Dutchman made a sound like "ungh!" and tumbled forward. The bundle arched over his head and landed somewhere out of sight. De Lott came plummeting down, and Tom stepped aside just in time to avoid being hit. The Dutchman was stunned, but not seriously hurt, and he immediately rolled over to see what had happened. There at the rim of the hole stood Laura, her arms still extended in front of her.

Tom reached for the pocketknife, but De Lott recovered himself quickly and took a wild swipe in the air with the blade. "Climb up the ladder!" yelled Laura. That seemed to Tom as good a plan as any, so he grabbed the highest rung he could reach and began scrambling up. He felt something sharp rip through his pants leg and graze his thigh. "Come on!" yelled Laura. She grabbed some stones and dirt clods out of the haycart and started heaving them down at De Lott. That erstwhile gentleman, his suit now torn and soiled, put his hands over his head and shouted incongruously, "Be careful there! You're hurting me!"

Tom made it to the top rung and looked for something to grab onto to crawl out of the hole. Just then he felt two strong hands grab onto his ankle. He kicked wildly, holding onto the top rung with all his strength. "The ladder!" yelled Laura, "it's falling backwards!" Tom could feel himself tilt backward and saw the top of the ladder swinging away from the edge of the hole. Without thinking, he lunged forward and grabbed onto the tailgate of the haycart, like a falling mountain-climber reaching out for whatever handhold he could find. For a moment, Tom thought he had a good grip and he started kicking again, trying to get De Lott to let go of his leg. Suddenly, though, he felt a downward jolt, and there was an avalanche of dirt sliding down his back. It only took him a second to realize that the cord in front of the haycart had snapped, and all that dirt and rock was pouring back into the hole. Tom got plenty of dirt down his collar, but he was halfway under the tailgate, and most of the dirt was going over him. De Lott was not so lucky, as he was getting the full force of all that rock and rubble. He clung to Tom's legs, trying to climb up as high as he could to avoid being buried alive.

It only took a few seconds for the cart to empty its load back into the hole. Tom's legs were buried from the knees down, but the soil was loose enough that he lifted his feet and crawled under the tilted haycart, spitting dirt out of his mouth. Laura rushed over to give Tom a hug, and then quickly remembered herself. "I'm so glad you're all right!" she said with an awkward formality. Tom untucked his shirt to let some dirt fall out, then turned around to see about De Lott. The Dutchman was trapped behind the haycart, covered to the armpits with dirt and rock, with only his head and his outstretched arms sticking out. His face was nearly black with dirt, and he was bleeding in several places.

"Help me!" shouted De Lott. "Get me out of here! I'll pay you whatever you want!"

Tom went over to the Dutchman and brushed some dirt clods out of his blond hair. He noticed the fedora De Lott had been wearing sitting near the edge of the hole, and he placed it on the gentleman's head. "There now. Is that better?" he asked.

"Hold it right there!" came a shout from behind them. Tom and Laura turned to see five men, two in black uniforms and three in civilian dress. "Stay right where you are!" shouted a man in a three-piece suit, his heavy eyebrows underscoring his look of stern authority. "Put your hands up!" Laura and Tom both raised their arms in the air; De Lott's predicament had him obeying this command even before it was given. Tom looked at Laura and mouthed wordlessly, "Bushy Brows!" Laura nodded her head in agreement.

"Thank God you've come, officers! These two young people were trying to kill me! Arrest them at once!" De Lott shouted, almost hysterically.

"I'm Inspector Javett of MI5," said the stocky man with the caterpillar eyebrows. Tom recognized the two other in civilian dress. "Those are the two that accosted me last time I was down here," Tom said quietly to Laura.

"That's right, Mr. McCord," said the tall man. "I'm Inspector Huffman of the Glastonbury Constabulary. And this is Detective Sergeant Durham." The sergeant made a polite tug of his cap to Laura, ignoring Tom completely. "I wish you'd taken my advice last time," said Huffman. "You are all under arrest for espionage." Huffman nodded at the two men in uniform, who went over to dig out the half-buried suspect. "Be careful, there," said Tom, "he has a knife. And he's got a pistol in his holster."

It took several minutes for the constables to dig De Lott out of the hole. They didn't find the knife, but they did discover the Luger at his side, disarming him and making him empty his pockets. "This is an outrage!" shouted the Dutchman, trying to brush the soil off his suit as best he could. "Why haven't you taken these two into custody?"

"There's plenty of time for that," said Javett. "Let's try to get this sorted."

"I'll have you know I am Willem De Lott, a Dutch refugee from Nazi tyranny. Ask about me in Hertford. They'll tell you who I am!"

"As a matter of fact, we have been asking about you," answered Javett. "You are Wilhelm Brandt of Nuremburg, an agent of the Third Reich. You are under arrest for crimes against the King. We're just trying to figure out who these confederates of yours are. How did two Americans fall into league with a Jerry?"

"In league?" said Tom, "Hardly! We're over here doing research. I've only met this man once before today, up at his estate in Temple Despy." The inspector looked at Javett, who shook his head in confirmation. "That's true enough," he said. "Though I suppose you didn't know Brandt's been following you all over England."

"As have you," said Laura, putting her hands down. "I saw you first in Royston. And then again in Malmesbury."

The inspector looked at the Javett and shook his head, suppressing a little grin.

"Well, yes, we have had you two under surveillance. We've been trying to figure out how you got mixed up with a bad apple like this one." Javett nodded at De Lott, who simply sulked and wriggled in the officers' grip.

"We're no friends of his!" said Tom. "Look at us." The policemen looked Tom up and down. He was covered with dirt and had a gash on his chin. De Lott looked even worse, with one eye almost swollen shut and with a bruised knob on his forehead the size of a walnut.

"Well, I have to admit, it looks like there's been some sort of falling out here." He surveyed the digging, the tilted haycart, and then looked back at the three suspects. "So what exactly were you fighting about?" he asked.

"Shall I show you?" said Tom. Huffman glanced at Javett and then nodded. Tom took a few steps forward. "This is an archaeological excavation," he explained. "He's the one who dug the hole—illegally, I suspect—but we're the ones who found what he was looking for." Tom walked over and retrieved the cloth bundle that had landed on the ground next to the cart. He carried it over to the others, who leaned in close to watch him open it. De Lott tried to take a step forward to get a closer look, but the constables held him back. Even so, he strained his neck forward, opened his mouth and licked his lips.

Tom untied a loose knot in the coarse fabric, then pulled back several folds. Finally he peeled back the last layer, revealing an old hand spade wrapped in soot-covered cloth. All five policemen stood there utterly baffled. De Lott glared at Tom with murder in his eyes. Laura bit her lip to keep from smiling. Tom held the little shovel in both hands, holding it up for inspection as if it were a jeweled crown. "It may not look like much," Tom said cheerfully. "But the wooden grip fits right into your hand. And there's hardly any rust on the blade." Patting the hand spade like a little puppy, Tom added, "You know, they just don't make them like this anymore."

Huffman looked at Javett and Javett looked at Huffman. Neither of them knew what to say. Finally, the inspector barked out an order: "Let's take them all down to the station," he said. "And bring along the, uh, evidence." Durham let Tom and Laura walk on ahead of him, but the policemen led De Lott away in handcuffs.

"Foreigners," muttered Durham under his breath. "It's seems like there's only two types left in the world these days— mad dogs and Englishmen."

# ← 12 →

Laura Hartman crossed the street in front of the Eastgate Hotel wearing a satiny blue dress, with white gloves and a matching purse.

"My, don't you look . . . respectable this evening!" said Tom.

"And so do you!" said Laura. "I've never seen you in a coat and tie before!"

"When in Rome," answered Tom. "I'm sure the other gentlemen will be dressed more formally. I believe these Brits wear a necktie when taking a bath."

Tom opened the door for Laura, and they entered the main dining room of the Eastgate. It was more luxurious than either of them expected, with plush carpeting, linen tablecloths, and upholstered leather chairs. "Who's paying for this?" asked Laura.

"I think I am," said Tom. "I invited the others to have supper with us before we go back to the States. I wanted to get their advice about the spear."

They walked toward a table near the window, where Lewis, Tolkien, and Williams were already sitting, each with a glass of sherry. Williams was talking animatedly, both hands carving figures in the air, and the other two were listening intently.

"I hope we're not interrupting," said Tom.

198 Looking for the King

"Of course not," said Lewis. All three men rose to their feet. Tom introduced Lewis to Laura, and she shook hands with the others. As Tom had predicted, all three wore ties. Lewis and Tolkien had on tweed jackets, though Tolkien's was in considerably better condition. Williams wore his usual dark blue suit.

As Tom and Laura took their seats, Lewis explained: "Mr. Williams was just telling us about his next book of Arthurian poems, *The Region of the Summer Stars.* Hardly a year goes by that we don't get something new from him—poetry, plays, novels, books of history or theology. I wonder if later generations will call this 'the Age of Williams.' Lewis turned to Williams and said, "Why, Charles, I ought to box your ears! The rest of us will end up as footnotes in your biography." Lewis let out a guffaw, and everyone around the table laughed. Tom once again had the image of Lewis as a jovial farmer sitting around a pub with his cronies, not as a distinguished Oxford don.

After the waiter had come and taken their orders, Tom started the conversation: "I'd like to thank you for all the help you've been to us this summer, and for agreeing to meet with us tonight. I hope this meal will serve as a small token of my gratitude."

Laura glanced over at Tom with a smile, amused perhaps by how his formal tone matched his formal attire.

"You're going back to the States soon?" asked Williams.

"Laura is leaving tomorrow," said Tom. "I've booked passage for next week."

"You've finished researching your book then?" asked Lewis.

"I had hoped to stay all summer," said Tom. "But both my parents and Laura's are quite insistent that we come home. With all this talk of the Germans invading Britain, they don't want us anywhere near a battle zone."

"I understand completely," said Tolkien. "If I had the power to take my sons out of harm's way, I would certainly do so. We've had children in our home since last September, evacuees sent up from London."

"So have we," said Lewis. "They're charming creatures, though they don't know how to entertain themselves. I was thinking there might be a story in that—children sent away from London who have a series of adventures in the country. I started something a few months ago."

"And how's it coming?" asked Williams. "A book for the Inklings to hear some Thursday evening?"

"Not quite yet," said Lewis. "I've only written one paragraph so far!" Lewis and Williams chuckled, but Tolkien seemed preoccupied, perhaps still thinking about his sons.

"Do you know what you will be doing back home?" Williams asked the two young Americans.

"I'll be living with my parents in Haverford for a while," said Laura. "I have a job waiting for me at a nearby library. But I'm thinking about pursuing a master's degree in literature." The others were willing to hear more, but Laura seemed suddenly shy, and she looked at Tom to signal it was his turn.

"I'm going to look for a teaching job," said Tom.

"Back in California?" asked Williams.

"I'll start there," said Tom. "But there are a lot of colleges and universities in eastern Pennsylvania. I made a few inquiries and have gotten some encouraging replies. So I'm not sure where I'll end up." Tom looked over at Laura to gauge her response, but he she was resolutely buttering a piece of bread and didn't look up.

Once the meal was served, Tom took up his main topic for the evening. He explained in vivid detail what had happened in Glastonbury—how Laura's dreams had led them to the abbey barn, the digging they had discovered, the spear hidden inside the wooden beam, and the confrontations with Willem De Lott and the police.

"It sounds like a Williams novel!" exclaimed Lewis.

"I'm glad you're both all right," added Tolkien, more somberly.

"What happened to the spear?" asked Williams, with the light from a brass lamp glinting off his gold-rimmed glasses.

"That's what I wanted to talk to you about this evening," explained Tom. "I'm still wondering about the spear. When Laura first heard the footsteps approaching the barn, I just had time to put the spear back inside the post and close the door. And the hole got filled back in with a cartload of dirt. So I believe the spear is well concealed back where I found it."

"Did you tell the police about it?" asked Williams.

"Only in general terms," said Tom. "I told them there might be a Roman artifact buried down there. I wasn't sure how much I should say until I had talked it over with some of you."

"What did they say?" asked Lewis.

"They just shrugged it off," Tom replied. "The inspector said people find Roman relics in England all the time, the way we find arrowheads in America. As far as I could tell, they were happy to have their man. They didn't seem to have any plans to go back to the abbey barn."

"And what about Willem De Lott? Or Brandt, was it?" asked Tolkien. "Don't you think he'll go back to there the first day he gets out of jail?"

"Right now I think his main concern is avoiding the noose," said Tom. "He's an enemy alien caught spying in wartime. That's a capital offense."

"I asked Inspector Javett about that," interjected Laura. "He said Brandt seemed to him more like a fortune-hunter than someone trying to steal military secrets. He said something under his breath, that the gentleman might be more useful somewhere else than in front of a firing squad."

"One way or another, I think he'll be behind bars, or under close surveillance, for a long time," said Tom. "Even if he did reopen the pit, I don't think he'd find the spear. I was standing right in front of it, but I couldn't have found its hiding place if Laura hadn't told me where to look." Tom peeked over at Laura, and this time she returned his glance with a smile.

"Which brings me to my question," said Tom. "Everyone around this table helped me find that spear—whatever it is—down in Glastonbury. So I would like for us to decide together what we should do with it. Should we just leave it where it is, to let it lie in hiding until the end of the world? Or shall I go to the authorities and make it more clear what I think might be hidden down there?"

There was a long pause as everyone pondered the question. All Tom heard for several seconds was the clinking of silver knives and forks upon china plates. Oddly, Lewis chose that moment to pick up a Brussels sprout with his fingers and pop it into his mouth. After washing it down with a sip of wine, he spoke first: "Aren't you forgetting another option? Why not go back to Glastonbury and dig up the spear? You might have it authenticated as a genuine Roman spear by an expert here in Oxford and make quite a name for yourself: 'The man who found the *True* Spear of Destiny.' Or at least the man who found a legitimate English claimant for that title."

Tom looked down at his plate a moment. Then he looked directly into Lewis's eyes. "I thought about that," he said, "but not for very long. Whatever it is, I have held it in my hands, and I could tell it didn't belong there. I felt like it wanted to fly away or to bury itself in the ground. I leave it to others to decide what to do with the spear."

Lewis smiled and lifted his glass into the air, as if he were going to propose a toast. "In the spirit of St. Maurice," said Williams, "you would rather give up the spear than use it for your own gain."

"It's easier for me," said Tom, with a weak grin. "I'm not surrounded by executioners."

"We indeed endure things," Tolkien quoted aloud. "But the martyrs endured and to the end." The others around the table gave Tolkien a questioning look, and so he explained simply, "It's an elvish saying."

"I think Tom's instincts are exactly right," said Williams. "None of us knows what this spear is. But it seems to have found a proper resting place. Recall the fate of Sir Balin in the grail stories. He is entrusted with the Bleeding Lance, which I understand to be the spear of Longinus. Balin has heard rumors of an Invisible Slayer. So when he senses a presence in the murky night, he thrusts the spear blindly into the dark and accidentally maims the Fisher King. It is this Dolorous Stroke that eventually leads to the destruction of Camelot. It is a potent image of the Fall—trying to clutch at sacred mysteries and use them for our own purposes."

Tolkien nodded slowly and made sound like "hmmm" in his throat.

Tom wasn't sure he followed all this, but he understood well enough that Williams thought they should leave the spear where it was. Lewis and Tolkien glanced at each other, then back at Williams, and Tom felt an unspoken consensus had been reached.

"What about you, Miss Hartman?" asked Williams. "This all began with your dreams. What do you think?"

"I agree," said Laura. "I never wanted the spear. I didn't even know my dreams were about the spear. I just wanted to understand them. So I've already fulfilled my quest." She touched the corners of her mouth with a napkin, and then added: "One by one, the dreams have disappeared. After we talked to Mr. Williams, I stopped dreaming about the martyred soldier. After we visited Gosforth, I stopped seeing the tall cross. When we returned from Malmesbury, I ceased to see the sleeping king. And now, no more dreams about the abbey barn. I don't suppose I'll ever understand why this happened to me."

"I still wonder," ventured Tom, "if you once read a book about the Spear of Destiny and then forgot about it. But it stayed in your unconscious."

"That's possible," said Laura. "But how could any author know about the abbey barn and the secret vault inside a wooden post?"

Tom acknowledged that he didn't have an answer. He looked around the table and asked, "In this day and age, do we still believe in dreams and visions?"

There was a long pause, until Lewis finally spoke up: "I can't say I've had visions, but I've dreamed dreams." Everyone around the table, including Tolkien and Williams, were surprised to hear him say this, and they listened for more. But Lewis just smiled broadly and added, "But all the saints and sages agree: dreams and visions aren't what counts. What matters is that each day we are becoming being transformed more and more into His likeness."

"I have one recurring dream," volunteered Tolkien. "I have an image in my head of a huge green wave coming our way, vast and unstoppable. If it ever reaches us, it will wash everything away. I call this dream my 'Atlantis Haunting.'" Tolkien gazed into each face around the table, as if wondering if there might be a Daniel present to interpret his dream.

"I wonder if that could be an unconscious symbol?" said Tom. "Maybe an expression of fears about an impending German invasion?"

"Mr. McCord," said Tolkien, with a wry smile. "You seem to have a gift for theories that are both ingenious and incorrect! Yes, I am anxious—we all are anxious—about an impending invasion. But I've been having this dream nearly all my life, long before our present trials."

Laura patted the back of Tom's hand, as if congratulating him for a valiant effort.

"My brother Warren says they've taken down road signs all over the south of England," said Lewis. "So that if the Jerries drop airborne troops, they won't be able to get their bearings."

"What if the Germans really do invade?" asked Tom. "Do you think you can resist the army that has swallowed up most of Europe?"

"Mr. Churchill says we will never surrender, and I believe he means it," said Lewis. Tolkien lifted his head and spoke solemnly and sonorously:

"Hige sceal þe heardra, heaorte þe cenre
Mod sceal þe mare, the ure maegen lytað."

Lewis rested a hand on Tolkien's shoulder, and repeated the same words for all to understand:

"Will shall be sterner, heart the bolder, spirit the greater as our might lessens."

After several minutes of general conversation, Laura cleared her throat and said, "Gentleman, I'm sorry to excuse myself. But I told my Aunt Viv I wouldn't be back too late. I have an early start tomorrow." She rose from her chair, as did all the others. Laura thanked Tolkien and Lewis and shook each of their hands. She reached out to shake Williams' hand as well, but then went around the table and gave him a hug instead. Tom also shook each man's hand and offered his own thanks.

"If you are ever in Oxford again," Lewis told Tom," please don't hesitate to give me a call."

"If I return to England any time soon," said Tom, "I expect I'll be in uniform." When she heard these words, Laura widened her eyes and blinked several times. The same remark brought smiles and one last round of handshakes from the three other men.

"You'll all be in my prayers," said Laura, as she turned toward the door.

"And in mine," added Tom. "May you be under the Mercy."

◁ • ▷

When Tom and Laura left the Eastgate, there was still plenty of light left on that long day in late June.

"Shall we stroll awhile?" asked Tom.

Laura nodded and they walked along the High Street toward the town center.

"Were you being sincere back there or just polite?" Laura asked.

"I paid the bill, didn't I?" said Tom.

"Not about that," said Laura, folding her arms as she walked. "About praying for them."

"Quite sincere," said Tom. "Quite sincere," he repeated again more softly.

Laura unfolded her arms and studied Tom's face, so he tried to explain. "I'm not clever enough to be insincere," he said, fumbling for words. "But I'm smart enough to know how much there is that I don't know."

"I'm a bit rusty in epigrams," said Laura. "Could you translate that for me please?"

Tom relaxed a little, and he tried again. "I had always thought that faith meant believing in the unbelievable," he said. "I didn't think educated people were willing to take for granted so many things they couldn't prove. But this summer I've been talking to some of the best-educated people I've ever met—brilliant, I should say. And for them it is the skeptics who take too much for granted."

Laura kept listening, as she took off her gloves and put them into her purse.

"Do you remember the puzzle-story you told me that day on Wrynose Pass? The one about the three sons arguing how to divide their herd of nineteen sheep?"

"Of course, I do," said Laura.

"The neighbor donates one more sheep, and suddenly all the numbers work out," said Tom. "I guess faith is like that," continued Tom. "You have to add something to the equation, to believe in something you can't see in order to understand what you do see. As Lewis said to me once, 'You can't look directly at the sun. But by its light, you can look at everything else.'" Tom paused and then lowered his head. "You must think I'm such a fool," he said, "trying to explain this faith growing inside me in terms of a brain teaser."

Laura stopped walking, grabbed Tom's arm, and looked into his face. "I don't think it's foolish at all," she said quietly. She was smiling, but her eyes sparkled with tears.

Laura quickly wiped her face, started walking again, trying to recover a lighter mood. "Where exactly are we going?" she asked.

"I was thinking of a place in Christ Church Meadow," Tom answered. They walked on without saying much. When they came to Magpie Lane, they turned left, walking a short way until they reached an open meadow. Looking across the fields, Tom spotted what he was looking for, a wooden bench underneath a solitary oak. "Let's go sit under that tree," he suggested. Laura agreed, and they made their way over the emerald-green grass. When they were about half way to the oak, they came to a little brook, about three feet wide, still and blue as if a mountain lake had been stretched into a ribbon. Someone had dropped a thick plank over the brook, but Tom took a running start and leaped over the water, landing somewhat awkwardly on the other side. "Now it's your turn," he told Laura.

"I prefer to use what amenities are available," she said, taking a step out onto the plank. She seemed a bit unsteady, holding both hands out like a tightrope walker. "It's wobbly," she said, reaching out one hand towards Tom. He stepped to the bank and helped her across. When they turned back toward the tree, Tom couldn't quite let go of her hand and she didn't quite let go of his. But after a few seconds, she pulled away and turned around to see the view of Oxford. "Look!" said Laura, "you can see the tops of the Radcliffe Camera and St. Mary's Church over the chimneys of Merton!"

"They're taller than I thought," Tom said. They both looked on in silence as the westering sun lent a warm glow to the ancient walls. What a pair they made against the sky, thought Tom. St Mary's, with its sky-piercing spire, spoke of spiritual aspiration—a restless quest, perhaps even dangerous. Radcliffe Camera didn't reach so high; its plump metallic dome rested on a broader base and found its peace on earth.

When they reached the bench, Tom brushed off a few stray leaves and the two of them sat down. Laura seemed content to just enjoy the scene in silence, but Tom had some questions he wanted to ask. "So, once we're both back home, I guess it would be all right if I wrote you once in a while?" he said. He looked at Laura, but she kept gazing at the city they were soon to leave.

"Sure, that would be fine," she said. "I'd like to hear how your book is coming along."

"And maybe include a few personal things too?"

"That would be nice," said Laura still watching the slanting shadows creep over domes and spires.

"If I did end up in Pennsylvania," Tom added, feeling his way along carefully. "I suppose I could pay you a visit?"

"Yes, that would be all right," said Laura, much too interested in that heap of old buildings across the grassy meadow. "I'll probably be staying with my parents for a while. But you could drop by. Maybe we could rent a motorcycle and go see Amish country. Get some sunshine and fresh air. We could have such larks," she added playfully.

Encouraged by her tone, Tom decided to take another step: "So, if we both ended up around Philly. If we were visiting back and forth . . . I wonder if we might have an 'understanding'?"

Laura finally stopped gazing at the city and turned to look Tom in the eyes. Then she gave an enigmatic smile, leaned forward and kissed him lightly on the cheek. "You're sweet," she said, in a tone that could mean a dozen different things.

"Was that a Yes?" asked Tom.

"That was a peck on the cheek," said Laura, turning to look at the city again.

Tom thought he'd better let it go at that. He leaned back and put his hands behind his head. "Philadelphia. I've never been there before. Independence Hall. The Liberty Bell." After a few seconds, he suddenly sat up straighter, "All those historic buildings from Revolutionary days. I wonder if there's an original copy of the Constitution stuffed away in an attic somewhere. . . ."

Laura reached out and cupped her hand over Tom's mouth. From underneath her hand, Tom got out some muffled doggerel: "He who's silenced against his will/ Is of the same opinion still."

Laura turned to face Tom and pressed both her hands over his mouth. Tom still got out a garbled phrase, something about "First Amendment rights. . . ."

Laura withdrew her hands from Tom's mouth and replaced them with her lips.

Tom had nothing more to say.

# SOURCE MATERIALS

Whenever I read a work of historical fiction, I can't help wondering which parts are history and which parts are fiction. Assuming that readers of *Looking for the King* may feel the same way, I have listed my source materials here. When I have used exact phrases from Lewis, Tolkien, or Williams in the novel, I have supplied the source, citing also particular facts or opinions that readers may be inclined to call into question.

Of course, I have taken artistic liberties throughout the novel, paraphrasing comments from all the Inklings' books as if they might have uttered the same opinions in conversation in the first year of World War Two. C. S. Lewis's close friend Owen Barfield remarked that Lewis's written words in his letters were remarkably similar in tone and cadence to his actual speaking voice in conversation. I think that is generally true of all the Inklings, and so I have freely adapted quips and opinions from their books and letters into spoken dialogue. I have taken some minor historical liberties, such as altering a few place-names and simplifying geography. But in general I have tried to place the scenes from the novel into their proper historical and geographical context.

## I
### COLLECTIVE BIOGRAPHICAL STUDIES
### *of* THE INKLINGS

Carpenter, Humphrey. *The Inklings: C. S. Lewis, J. R. R. Tolkien, Charles Williams, and Their Friends*. Boston: Houghton Mifflin, 1979.

Duriez, Colin. *Tolkien and C.S. Lewis: The Gift of Friendship*. Mahwah, NJ: Hidden Spring, 2003.

Glyer, Diane. *The Company They Keep: C.S. Lewis and J.R.R. Tolkien as Writers in Community*. Kent, OH: Kent State University Press, 2007.

Poe, Harry Lee, and James Ray Veneman. *The Inklings of Oxford*. Grand Rapids, MI: Zondervan, 2009.

## II
### SELECTED BIOGRAPHICAL AND INTERPRETIVE MATERIALS
### *on* C. S. LEWIS

Barfield, Owen. *Owen Barfield on C.S. Lewis*. Ed. by G. B. Tennyson. Middletown, CN: Wesleyan University Press, 1989.

Como, James T., ed. *"C. S. Lewis at the Breakfast Table" and other Reminiscences*. New York: Macmillan, 1979.

Downing, David C. *The Most Reluctant Convert: C.S. Lewis's Journey to Faith*. Downers Grove, IL: InterVarsity Press, 2002.

Gibb, Jocelyn, ed. *Light on C. S. Lewis*. New York: Harcourt, Brace and World, 1965.

Gilbert, Douglas, and Clyde S. Kilby. *C. S. Lewis: Images of His World*. Grand Rapids, MI: Eerdmans, 1973.

Green, Roger Lancelyn, and Walter Hooper. *C.S. Lewis: A Biography*. New York: Harcourt Brace Jovanovich, 1974.

Hooper, Walter. "C. S. Lewis: The Man and his Thought" in *Essays on C. S. Lewis and George MacDonald*. Cynthia Marshall, ed. Lewiston, NY: Edwin Mellon Press, 1991.

Hooper, Walter. *Through Joy and Beyond: A Pictorial Biography of C.S. Lewis*. New York: Macmillan, 1982.

Jacobs, Alan. *The Narnian: The Life and Imagination of C. S. Lewis.* San Francisco: HarperSanFrancisco, 2005.

Keefe, Carolyn, ed. *C. S. Lewis: Speaker and Teacher.* Grand Rapids, MI: Zondervan, 1971.

Kilby, Clyde S., and Marjorie Lamp Mead. *Brothers and Friends: The Diaries of Major Warren Hamilton Lewis.* New York: Harper and Row, 1982.

Lewis, Warren H. *C. S. Lewis: A Biography.* Unpublished typescript available at the Marion E. Wade Center, Wheaton College, and the Bodleian Library in Oxford.

Sayer, George. *Jack: C. S. Lewis and His Times.* New York: Harper and Row, 1988.

Schofield, Stephen, ed. *In Search of C. S. Lewis.* South Plainfield, NJ: Bridge Publishing, 1983.

## III
### Selected Biographical and Interpretive Materials on J. R. R. Tolkien

Carpenter, Humphrey. *Tolkien: A Biography.* New York: Ballantine Books, 1977.

Garth, John. *Tolkien and the Great War: The Threshold of Middle-Earth.* Boston: Houghton Mifflin, 2003.

Gilliver, Peter, Jeremy Marshall, and Edmund Weiner. *The Ring of Words: Tolkien and the Oxford English Dictionary.* New York: Oxford University Press, 2006.

Shippey, T. A. *The Road to Middle Earth.* Boston: Houghton Mifflin, 1983.

Tolkien, John and Priscilla. *The Tolkien Family Album.* Boston: Houghton Mifflin, 1992.

## IV

### Selected Biographical and Interpretive Materials
### *on* Charles Williams

Cavaliero, Glen. *Charles Williams: Poet of Theology.* Grand Rapids, MI: Eerdmans, 1983.

Hadfield, Alice Mary. *Charles Williams: An Exploration of His Life and Work.* Oxford: Oxford University Press, 1983.

Heath-Stubbs, John. *Charles Williams.* London: Longmans, 1955.

Howard, Thomas. *The Novels of Charles Williams.* San Francisco: Ignatius Press, 1991.

Huttar, Charles A., and Peter J. Schakel, eds. *The Rhetoric of Vision: Essays on Charles Williams.* Lewisburg, NY: Bucknell University Press/London: Associated University Presses, 1996.

Shideler, Mary McDermott. *Charles Williams: A Critical Essay.* Grand Rapids, MI: Eerdmans, 1966.

## V

### Selected Works *by* C. S. Lewis

*The Abolition of Man.* New York: Macmillan, 1973. Orig. pub. 1943.

*The Allegory of Love.* London: Oxford University Press, 1973. Orig. pub. 1936.

*All My Road Before Me: The Diary of C. S. Lewis, 1922-1927.* Walter Hooper, ed. San Diego: Harcourt Brace Jovanovich, 1991.

*Christian Reflections.* Walter Hooper, ed. Grand Rapids, MI: Eerdmans, 1973.

*The Collected Letters of C. S. Lewis, Volume 1: Family Letters 1905-1931.* Walter Hooper, ed. London: HarperCollins, 2000.

*The Collected Letters of C. S. Lewis, Volume 2: Books, Broadcasts, and the War, 1931-1949.* Walter Hooper, ed. London: HarperCollins, 2004.

*The Collected Letters of C. S. Lewis, Volume 3: Narnia, Cambridge, and Joy.* Walter Hooper, ed. London: HarperCollins, 2007.

*Dymer.* London: J. M. Dent, 1926. Rpt. Macmillan, 1950.

*God in the Dock: Essays on Theology and Ethics.* Ed. Walter Hooper, ed. Grand Rapids, MI: Eerdmans, 1970.

*Letters to Malcolm: Chiefly on Prayer.* New York: Harcourt Brace Jovanovich, 1964.

*The Lion, the Witch, and the Wardrobe.* New York: Collier/ Macmillan, 1970. Orig. pub. 1950.

*Mere Christianity.* New York: Macmillan, 1969. Orig. pub. 1952.

*Miracles: A Preliminary Study.* New York: Macmillan, 1968. Orig. pub. 1947.

*Out of the Silent Planet.* New York: Macmillan, 1968. Orig. pub. 1938.

*The Personal Heresy: A Controversy.* London: Oxford University Press, 1965. Orig. pub. 1939.

*The Pilgrim's Regress.* New York: Harcourt Brace Jovanovich, 1960. Orig. pub. 1933.

*The Problem of Pain.* London: Collins, 1972. Orig. pub. 1940.

*Rehabilitations and Other Essays.* London: Oxford University Press, 1939.

*The Screwtape Letters.* New York: Macmillan, 1960. Orig. pub. 1942.

*Spirits in Bondage: A Cycle of Lyrics.* New York: Harcourt Brace Jovanovich, 1984. Orig. pub. London: William Heinemann, 1919.

*Surprised by Joy: The Shape of My Early Life.* New York: Harcourt Brace Jovanovich, 1955.

*That Hideous Strength: A Modern Fairy-Tale for Grown-Ups.* New York: Macmillan, 1968. Orig. pub. 1945.

*The Weight of Glory and Other Addresses.* Grand Rapids, MI: Eerdmans, 1965. Orig. pub. 1949.

# VI

## Selected Works *by* J. R. R. Tolkien

"Beowulf: The Monster and the Critics." *Proceedings of the British Academy* 22 (1936), 245-295.

*The Book of Lost Tales, Part One.* Christopher Tolkien, ed. London: Allen & Unwin, 1983.

*The Book of Lost Tales, Part Two.* Christopher Tolkien, ed. London: Allen & Unwin, 1984.

*The Hobbit: or There and Back Again.* London: Allen & Unwin, 1937.

*The Lays of Beleriand.* Christopher Tolkien, ed. London: Allen & Unwin, 1985.

*The Letters of J. R. R. Tolkien.* Humphrey Carpenter, ed. Boston: Houghton Mifflin, 1981.

*The Lord of the Rings.* [*The Fellowship of the Ring.* London: Allen & Unwin, 1954; *The Two Towers.* London: Allen & Unwin, 1954; *The Return of the King.* London: Allen & Unwin, 1955.]

*A Middle English Vocabulary.* Oxford: Clarendon Press, 1922.

"On Fairy-Stories." In *Essays Presented to Charles Williams.* C. S. Lewis, ed. London: Oxford University Press, 1947.

*The Silmarillion,* Christopher Tolkien, ed. Boston: Houghton Mifflin, 1977.

*Sir Gawain and the Green Knight.* Edited with E. V. Gordon. Oxford: Clarendon Press, 1925.

## VII
### Selected Works *by* Charles Williams

*Arthurian Torso.* C. S. Lewis and Charles Williams. Oxford: Oxford University Press, 1948.

*The Descent of the Dove: A Short History of the Holy Spirit in the Church.* London: Longmans, 1939.

*Descent into Hell.* London: Faber and Faber, 1937.

*The Greater Trumps.* London: Victor Gollancz, 1932.

*He Came Down from Heaven.* London: Heinemann, 1938.

*Many Dimensions.* London: Victor Gollancz, 1931.

*A Myth of Shakespeare.* London: Oxford University Press, 1928.

*The Place of the Lion.* London: Mundanus (Victor Gollancz), 1931.

*The Silver Stair.* London: Herbert and Daniel, 1912.

*Taliessin through Logres.* London: Oxford University Press, 1938.

*Thomas Cranmer of Canterbury.* London: Oxford University Press, 1936.

*War in Heaven.* London: Victor Gollancz, 1930.

# NOTES

Page

7   "Here lies buried": These words are an abridged version of the Latin inscription on a lead cross said to be found with the bodies of Arthur and Guinevere in the twelfth century. There are two markers on the abbey grounds today, one showing where the bodies were discovered and the other where their bodies were reburied, a black marble tomb in front of the abbey's high altar.

9   Metallascope: This was one of the first portable metal detectors made available for private treasure hunters in the late 1930s. See Roy T. Roberts, "The History of Metal Detectors," *Western and Eastern Treasures* (September 1999), 24–29.

11   Collingwood: R. G. Collingwood, *Roman Britain and the English Settlements* (Oxford: Clarendon Press, 1936). Collingwood acknowledges Tolkien's help with Celtic philology and cites Tolkien in several footnotes.

23   Loose muses: See *The Oxford Book of Oxford*, ed. by Jan Morris (Oxford University Press, 1978), 269.

24   Lewis drinking cider for lunch: *Letters of Lewis 2*, 322.

25   "Polar bear": *Letters of Lewis 3*, 795.

25   Vegetable: Lewis, *Letters of Lewis 3*, 419.

26   American education like judging horses: *Letters of Lewis 3*, 1073.

27   Amalgam of Arthurian characters: *Hideous*, ch. 1, sect. 5.

27   Legends like cathedrals: *Letters of Lewis 3*, 646.

27   Civilization "on the edge of a precipice": See C. S. Lewis, "Learning in War-time: A sermon preached in the Church of St. Mary the Virgin, Oxford, Autumn, 1939." *Weight*, 44.

27   Young man with falcon: *Letters of Lewis 2*, 295.

28   Lewis's memory of Tintagel: *Letters of Lewis 1*, 581.

29   Imagining Fafnir: *Surprised*, 77.

30   Aversion to what's fashionable: *Letters of Lewis 2*, 372.

30   "Whining and Mumbling period": *Letters of Lewis 3*, 12.

31   Scratching an itch: *Letters of Lewis 3*, 346.

32   "Haunting" of English history: *Hideous*, 369.

32   Proud to call Williams his friend: *Letters of Lewis 2*, 501.

32   Holy luck: *Letters of Lewis 3*, 5.

33   Talking theology not ribaldry: *They Stand Together*, 501.

33   Lewis calls his friends a band of brothers: *Surprised by Joy*, 32.

33   "Linguistic birds": *Letters of Lewis 2*, p. 107; *Letters of Lewis 3*, 447.

35   "Most beautiful room in England": *Letters of Lewis 2*, 293.

35   Williams lectured on Milton's *Comus* in the Divinity School in January 1940, focusing on chastity as a quality of spiritual purity. This fictitious lecture, set in May 1940, is a distillation of some of Williams's characteristic ideas as set forth in ideas in *The Figure of Arthur* and *He Came Down from Heaven*.

37   Clinking coins: See Thomas Howard, "Charles Williams: The Key Inkling," *Christian History* http://www.christianitytoday /ch/2003/002/20.34.htm

38   "Faded mythology": Loomis, 4.

40   Augustine on the Eucharist: *Torso*, 14.

40   Arch-natural: A coinage by Williams for the "wholly other" world unseen by the senses. See *Letters of Lewis 3*, 995.

41   "Old self in the old way": Hadfield, 170.

41   "Limitless light": Hadfield, 29.

41   "Glory of Logres": Williams, "The Crowning of Arthur," *Taliessen through Logres*, lines 44–45.

41   "The spark of Logres": Williams, "The Crowning of Arthur," *Taliessen through Logres*, lines 71–72.

43   Williams joining listeners after a lecture at a nearby pub: Hadfield, 40, 198.

47   Duty to doubt: Heath-Stubbs, 12–13.

47 Choose what to believe: Hadfield, 35.

49 The analogy of characters vs. the playwright comes from Lewis, *Christians Reflections*, 168; *Mere Christianity*, 146. But Williams shared a similar view of God as outside of time. See *He Came Down*, 4.

58 Decoder rings: Actually, the secret decoders packaged in Cracker Jacks in the 1940s were not rings. But that is the common conception.

67 For interpretations of the figures, see Sylvia P. Beaman, *Exploring Royston Cave*. Nightingale Press, Ltd., 1998.

71 Temple Despy is loosely based on the site of Temple Dinsley, which is part of the estate owned by the Princess Helena College since 1935. My thanks to Mr. Margaret Baim, Registrar, for information about Temple Dinsley and about history of the property owned by the College. De Lott and Mirden are, of course, fictitious.

80 Throwing swords into the water: See Graham Philips & Martin Keatman, *King Arthur: The True Story* (London: Arrow Books, 1993), 40.

81 Pewter ingots: Collingwood, 231.

82 For discussion of the figures on the Gosforth Cross, see Richard N. Bailey, *Viking Age Sculpture in Northern England* (London, 1980), 125–131.

106 The pub sign hanging out front of "The Eagle and Child" today is not the same one that was there in Lewis's time. The current sign shows the baby being carried more safely and securely, as if the eagle were a stork delivering a newborn. See Poe, 63.

107 Williams acting a waiter: Howard, "Key Inkling," 1.

108 "Under the Mercy": *Letters of Lewis 2*, 219.

108 Memories haunting Lewis's dreams: *Letters of Lewis 2*, 258.

108 Lewis's memories of the front lines: *Surprised*, 196.

108 "Moving like half-crushed beetles": *Surprised*, 196.

110 Dyson on pots and kettles: Henry V. Dyson, *Augustans and Romantics* (London: Cresset, 1940), 96.

113 Doted on *The Golden Bough*: *Miracles*, 70.

113 Conversation about the dying god myth on Addison's Walk: *Letters of Lewis 1*, 974–977; *Miracles*, 139; Downing, 146–150.

115 God intervening to cancel bad choices: *Problem of Pain*, 21.

115 "When pain is to be borne": *Problem*, viii.

116 Lewis not remembering his own books: Hooper, "The Man and his Thought," 12.

116 Williams teases Lewis about *The Problem of Pain*: *Letters of Lewis 2*, 468.

116 Tolkien calls Lewis "indefatigable": *Letters of Tolkien*, 68.

116 Lewis's idea for *Screwtape Letters* came to him later in the summer, July 21, 1940. See *Letters of Lewis 2*, 426.

117 Problem of Pleasure: *Letters of Lewis 3*, 146.

117 Earthly pleasures as reminders: *Letters of Lewis 3*, 585.

117 "Whispers of a wind from beyond this world": *Letters of Lewis 2*, 12–13.

117 Fragrance of a flower: *Weight*, 5.

117 Banal dwarfs in Disney: *Letters of Lewis 2*, 242; *Letters of Tolkien*, 17.

118 "Feast of reason and a flow of soul": *Letters of Tolkien*, 102.

125 Tolkien compares himself to hobbits: Carpenter, *Tolkien*, 197.

125 "Great green dragon": Carpenter, *Tolkien*, 24.

126 Origins of *The Hobbit*: Carpenter, *Tolkien*, 181, 193.

126 Shapes and sounds of words: See Shippey, 71.

127 Strider or Trotter: Carpenter, *Tolkien*, 211.

127 Researching Middle Earth not inventing: *Letters of Tolkien*, 145.

129 Tolkien pacing when he talked, seeming to forget others are present: Carpenter, *Tolkien*, 51.

133 Northern spirit perverted by Hitler, ennobled in England: *Letters of Tolkien*, 55–56.

134 Creating a body of myths for England: *Letters of Tolkien*, 144; Carpenter, *Tolkien*, 66.

134 Tolkien still upset about the Norman Conquest: Carpenter, *Tolkien*, 45, 144.

139 Lewis on scenery from train: *Letters of Lewis 3*, 406.

139 Prefers a fire to cards: *Letters of Lewis 3*, 671.

139 Surnames are more personal: *Letters of Lewis 3*, 750.

140 Lewis doesn't know what Tolkien's initials stand for: *Letters of Lewis 3*, 855.

159 Lewis quotes "Vernal delights": *Letters of Lewis 2*, 415.

160 Less chance of dying of cancer: Carpenter, *Inklings*, 69.

161 "Eyelash of trees: See Warren Lewis, 259.

162 "Britannicus": C. C. Dobson, *Did Our Lord Visit Britain as they say in Cornwell and Somerset?* (London: Covenant Publishing, 1936; rpt. 2001.), 12.

163 Changing motivations for study: *Experiment*, 6–7.

163 Colleagues who don't want to talk about books after hours: *Experiment*, 7.

165 "A roaring cataract of nonsense": *Letters of Lewis 2*, 288; Lewis's phrase is taken from a book review by Thomas Babington Macauley.

166 Nature acts in obedience: *Letters of Lewis 2*, 177.

167 Moral universals: See *Mere Christianity*, 17–20; *Abolition*, Appendices

167 Lewis quotes Lucretius: *Surprised*, 65.

167 Basis for moral judgments: *Christian Reflections*, 66.

168 Fifth columnist in our souls: *Christian Reflections*, 41.

168 Particles or waves: *Letters of Lewis 3*, 355.

168 Science can't look behind nature: "Religion and Science" in *Dock*, 73.

169 Sweet Desire: *Surprised*, 16–18 : *Regress*, 7–10.

170 Lewis quotes Augustine: *Four Loves*, 189.

198 Lewis on "The Age of Williams": *Letters of Lewis 2*, 228.

199 Lewis describes the evacuees: *Letters of Lewis 2*, 277, 451.

199 Lewis writes one paragraph: Green and Hooper, 238.

202 "We indeed endure things": Garth, 112.

202 Williams's interpretation of Balin's Dolorous Stroke: *Torso*, 269.

203 Lewis says he's "dreamed dreams": *Letters of Lewis 3*, 348.

203 Tolkien's "Atlantis haunting": Carpenter, *Tolkien*, 25, 191.
204 Tolkien and Lewis quote *The Battle of Maldon*, Carpenter, *Inklings*, 15; Gibb, 54.
206 Seeing everything by the sun's light: A corollary of Lewis's comment on sunlight in the last line of "Is Theology Poetry?"

# ABOUT PARACLETE PRESS

*Who We Are*

As the publishing arm of the Community of Jesus, Paraclete Press presents a full expression of Christian belief and practice—from Catholic to Evangelical, from Protestant to Orthodox, reflecting the ecumenical charism of the Community and its dedication to sacred music, the fine arts, and the written word. We publish books, recordings, sheet music, and video/DVDs that nourish the vibrant life of the church and its people.

*What We Are Doing*

BOOKS | PARACLETE PRESS BOOKS show the richness and depth of what it means to be Christian. While Benedictine spirituality is at the heart of who we are and all that we do, our books reflect the Christian experience across many cultures, time periods, and houses of worship.

We have many series, including *Paraclete Essentials*; *Paraclete Fiction*; *Paraclete Poetry*; *Paraclete Giants*; and for children and adults, *All God's Creatures*, books about animals and faith; and *San Damiano Books*, focusing on Franciscan spirituality. Others include *Voices from the Monastery* (men and women monastics writing about living a spiritual life today), *Active Prayer*, and new for young readers: *The Pope's Cat*. We also specialize in gift books for children on the occasions of Baptism and First Communion, as well as other important times in a child's life, and books that bring creativity and liveliness to any adult spiritual life.

The MOUNT TABOR BOOKS series focuses on the arts and literature as well as liturgical worship and spirituality; it was created in conjunction with the Mount Tabor Ecumenical Centre for Art and Spirituality in Barga, Italy.

MUSIC | The PARACLETE RECORDINGS label represents the internationally acclaimed choir *Gloriæ Dei Cantores*, the *Gloriæ Dei Cantores Schola*, and the other instrumental artists of the *Arts Empowering Life Foundation*.

Paraclete Press is the exclusive North American distributor for the Gregorian chant recordings from St. Peter's Abbey in Solesmes, France. Paraclete also carries all of the Solesmes chant publications for Mass and the Divine Office, as well as their academic research publications.

In addition, PARACLETE PRESS SHEET MUSIC publishes the work of today's finest composers of sacred choral music, annually reviewing over 1,000 works and releasing between 40 and 60 works for both choir and organ.

VIDEO | Our video/DVDs offer spiritual help, healing, and biblical guidance for a broad range of life issues including grief and loss, marriage, forgiveness, facing death, understanding suicide, bullying, addictions, Alzheimer's, and Christian formation.

Learn more about us at our website
www.paracletepress.com
or phone us toll-free at 1.800.451.5006

SCAN
TO
READ
MORE

# YOU MAY BE INTERESTED IN THESE . . .

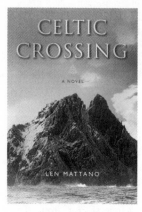

## *Celtic Crossing*
### Len Mattano
978-1-64060-305-9 | $17.99

"Mattano makes a moving debut with this story set in contemporary Ireland that weaves together ecclesiastical lessons and stories from the New Testament. . . . Featuring a passionate sleuth and God-graced relic, Mattano's scripture-heavy tale will be of interest to faith readers who enjoyed *The Da Vinci Code.*"
—*Publishers Weekly*

## *Lady at the Window*
### *The Lost Journal of Julian of Norwich*
### A NOVELLA
### Robert Waldron
978-1-64060-534-3 | $16.99

"A deeply sympathetic portrait of this medieval mystic, a wife and mother and anchoress who came to reimagine God as a merciful, nurturing and especially mothering presence. Waldron takes us through Julian's unsettling meditations during the dark hours of Holy Week, ending with an eastering vision in which we too might find comfort in what she saw: that God is there even in the darkness, and that 'All shall be well, and all manner of thing shall be well.'"
—**Paul Mariani**, professor, poet, and literary biographer